TORN IVY

A DARK PARANORMAL ACADEMT REVERSE HAREM

THORNFIELD SUPERNATURAL ACADEMY
BOOK 2

EVE NEWTON

AUTHOR'S NOTE

This is a paranormal Reverse Harem Dark Academy Romance. All main characters are 21.

The guys are essentially villains. If you are looking for a soft and cuddly read, you will not find it in these pages.

The Kings of Thornfield contains adult and graphic content, and reader discretion is advised.

A full list of TWs for this book/series can be found exclusively at my website: https://evenewton.com/kings-of-thornfield-1
Join my facebook group for real time updates on future reads: https://facebook.com/groups/evenewton

1

IVY

GLARING AT JOSH WITH UTTER SHOCK AND AN ANGER THAT quickly dissipates when I realise I'm just as big a betrayer as him, I huff out a breath. "You are a total arsehole."

"Back at you, bitch."

"What are you even doing here?"

Josh smirks, crossing his arms over his chest. "What, you thought you were the only one with a bone to pick with Death and his merry band of psychopaths?"

I narrow my eyes at him. "So what, you've been some kind of supernatural spy this whole time?"

"Not exactly," he says, "Let's just say I've got connections you couldn't even dream of."

Vex clears his throat. "As touching as this reunion is, we've got more pressing matters to discuss."

I whirl on him. "You knew about this? About Josh?"

He shrugs. "I know a lot of things. Doesn't mean I share them all."

"Fuck you both," I spit, feeling annoyed but having no leg to stand on. "I want answers. Now."

Josh sighs. "Fine. Short version? We're part of a resistance. Against Death, against The Syndicate, against the whole fucking system that's been controlling shifters and other supernatural beings for centuries."

My mind reels. "A resistance? How? Why?"

"Because the system is corrupt," Josh says, his eyes blazing with an intensity I've never seen before. "Because beings like us shouldn't be slaves to Death or anyone else. We should be free."

I look around the cavern, taking in the other creatures still working away. "And all of these beings are part of this resistance?"

"Yep."

"Why do you look like Death in your other form?" I demand.

Josh's lips curl into a sardonic smile. "Because we are Death, in a way. Or at least, we were created to be."

I blink, trying to process this. "What the fuck does that mean?"

"It means," Vex cuts in, "that Death isn't just one entity. It's a role, a chosen position, and these beings," he gestures around the cavern, "were all potential candidates."

"Candidates?" I echo, my head spinning.

Josh nods. "Yeah. Think of it like a cosmic job interview from hell. We were all created, trained, and tested to potentially become the next Death. But some of us decided we didn't want the gig."

I let out a shaky breath as this blows my mind even further than being confronted with Death in the first place. Now, there are stacks of them milling about. "So you're, what? Death's rejects?"

"We prefer to be called independently minded cosmic entities," Josh says with a smirk. "But yeah, essentially."

"And what does this have to do with me?" I ask though I'm starting to get a sinking feeling in my gut.

Vex and Josh exchange a look that makes me want to punch them both.

"You, Ivy," Vex says slowly, "are something special. Something that wasn't supposed to exist."

"A glitch in the system," Josh adds.

"You two are going to have to stop being so fucking cryptic. It's pissing me off. Just say it. I can handle it!" I snap, frustration building.

Josh's eyes bore into mine. "It means you're a wildcard, Ivy. You were meant to be Death, but you rejected the process. That has never happened before."

"Come again? Rejected the process? How? Why? What does it signify?"

He shrugs. "This is what we don't know, but we know it makes you special. It's why The Syndicate ultimately wanted you, why Death has taken a special interest in you, and why we want you on our side."

Narrowing my eyes as I attempt to process all of

that, I turn to Vex. "And you? Where do you fit into all this?"

"I'm what you might call a free agent," Vex says with a smirk. "I have my own reasons for wanting to see Death's power diminished. Let's leave it at that."

I shake my head, feeling overwhelmed. "This is insane. All of it. Apart from what you have said about me, you're telling me there's been this secret resistance right under Death's nose? How is that even possible?"

"Death isn't omniscient," Josh explains. "Powerful, yes, but not all-knowing. We've been careful and strategic. Biding our time."

"And now?" I ask, a pit forming in my stomach. "Why reveal all this to me now?"

Josh and Vex exchange a look that makes me uneasy.

"Because," Josh says slowly, "we think you might be the key to bringing Death down."

I snort, unable to help myself. "Me? The key to bringing down Death? That's fucking absurd."

"Is it?" Vex asks, raising an eyebrow. "You've already shown an ability to resist Death's power in ways no one else has. You're unpredictable, uncontrollable."

"A right pain in the arse, more like," Josh mutters, and I give him the finger. He grins. "That's what we need, though. A thorn in his side. A poison he doesn't have an antidote for."

I resist the urge to roll my eyes so hard they nearly get stuck, and shake my head instead, trying to process all this information. "So what, you want me to join your little rebellion? Fight the big bad Death?"

"It's not that simple," Josh says, his expression growing serious. "What we're proposing is dangerous. If we fail, the consequences would be severe."

"More severe than being hunted by Death and The Syndicate?" I ask sarcastically.

Vex nods grimly. "Much more. We're talking about potentially unravelling the very fabric of existence."

I blink at him. "You're joking, right?"

"I wish I were," he says.

I run a hand through my hair, feeling overwhelmed. "You're asking me to risk everything, to potentially destroy the universe, based on what? The fact that I'm some kind of cosmic glitch?"

Josh steps forward, his eyes intense. "We're asking you to take a stand against a system that's been oppressing our kind for millennia. To fight for freedom, not just for yourself, but for all supernatural beings."

I laugh bitterly. "Oh, is that all? Just topple an ancient cosmic order and liberate the supernatural world. No pressure."

"Don't you get it, Ivy? Death is manipulating the system. He is arranging for souls to be delivered before they are ready."

The blood drains from my face as I freeze. "What?"

"You heard me, and you know what I meant, so don't play dumb. He has set up The Syndicate to ensure that there is a place for his underhanded techniques to get past the cosmic balance. He is cheating the system, and we aren't standing for it anymore."

"Wow," I mutter. "What the fuck?" What does that make me? Complicit in this cosmic manipulation? By taking out these targets, bad guys or not, have I been completely screwing up the universal order?

"Look," Vex says, his tone softening slightly, "we know it's a lot to take in. But you have to understand the opportunity we have here. With your unique resistance to Death's power, we might actually have a chance."

I cross my arms, eyeing them both sceptically. "Resistance? He pulled me into a wacky dreamscape earlier and gave me a serious ultimatum. I wouldn't say that was resistant to his power."

Josh and Vex exchange another look that makes me want to smack them both.

"What was the ultimatum?" Josh asks carefully.

"That I either kill my guys or he takes my soul." I look at Vex. "That's why I was running."

"You think you can outrun Death?" he asks with narrowed eyes. "Interesting."

"Look, the plan," Josh says slowly, "is to use your connection to Death against him. To essentially hijack his power."

I blink. "Hijack his power? What the fuck does that even mean?" I seem to be asking that a lot lately.

Vex sighs. "It means we think you might be able to tap into Death's abilities, to siphon them off and use them yourself."

"What? You want *me* to become Death?" I ask incredulously.

"Pretty much, yeah," Josh says, nodding like one of those bobbleheads.

I close my eyes and breathe. *This can't be happening. It just can't.*

"Ivy."

My eyes snap open when I hear the familiar voice, and I grimace. "Aunt Cathy. I might've known you were part of this."

Her perfect eyebrows shoot up. "You knew?"

My shoulders slump. "No. I didn't know any of this. What are you even doing here? Are you one of these rejects?"

"Hey," Josh snaps. "Rude."

"Sorry," I mutter.

"I am one of these rejects," Cathy says, folding her hands primly in front of her. Her dark pants suit is smart and businesslike, much like I remember her. "Don't forget that you are, too."

"Even more so," Josh says snidely.

I shake my head at him, giving him a vicious scowl. "I can't get my head around this. How am I supposed to stave off Death taking my soul or killing my guys, or forcing me to kill my guys, or whatever? That is all I care about right now. Your end game isn't mine."

"It is, though," Cathy says. "It is your legacy."

"Huh? What legacy?" A tightening on my wrists makes me frown down at my arms. Poison Ivy has taken the place of my fingers and is creeping up my arms as dread fills my soul about what she is going to say. I beat her to the punch, "Are you saying that my parents were part of this?"

Her green eyes meet mine, and she shakes her head slowly. "No," she says quietly. "It skips certain people. It's just the way it is. My grandfather was one, not my parents, nor your father, and you."

I stare at Cathy, my mind reeling. "So you're saying this cosmic Death candidate thing runs in our family?"

She nods solemnly. "It's a rare genetic quirk, passed down through generations. Some of us are chosen, others aren't. You and I were."

"But I didn't know," I protest weakly. "How could I not know?"

"The knowledge is suppressed," Josh explains. "It's part of the process. You're not supposed to remember until you're activated."

I turn to glare at him. "Activated?"

"It means," Vex cuts in, "that something triggers your latent abilities. Something wakes up the part of you that was meant to be Death."

"But you aren't one of these Death things?" I ask him, ignoring his statement for a moment.

"Nah. But I have inside knowledge of The Syndicate, and everyone has their price."

I blink at that, wondering what his is, but push it aside. "Okay, but because I'm not really one of these Death things, I've never been activated, so I have zero idea what this even is?"

"Yep," Josh says.

"So I have to take your word for it?"

"Pretty much. Do you trust me?"

The question is fired at me, and I don't have an answer.

"You said you trusted me," Vex says. "I'm telling you everything Josh and Cathy says is true."

Well, how nicely he has boxed me into a corner.

"So what now? You want me to challenge Death for his job?"

"Not exactly," Josh says. "We want you to disrupt the system. To throw a spanner in Death's plans."

"By becoming Death myself?" I ask incredulously.

Vex shakes his head. "No. We don't want you to become Death. We want you to be the antithesis of Death."

I snort. "Life? Sorry to break it to you, but I'm not exactly nurturing a new existence over here."

Josh rolls his eyes. "Not Life. Think of it more like Chaos. A force that disrupts the natural order Death claims to maintain."

"Chaos," I repeat flatly. "Brilliant. Because my life wasn't fucked up enough already."

Cathy steps forward, her eyes pleading. "Ivy, I know this is a lot to take in. But you have to understand the importance of what we're asking. Death has become corrupt, abusing his power and manipulating the system. We need someone who can stand against him."

I laugh bitterly. "And you think that someone is me?"

"We *know* it's you. Your unpredictability is exactly

why you're perfect for this," Josh argues. "Death can't anticipate your moves because even you don't know what you're going to do next."

"Gee, thanks," I mutter, my cheeks going a bit warm.

"Look, we don't have time for you to have an existential crisis right now. Death is after you, remember? We need to act fast."

I narrow my eyes at him. "What exactly do you propose I do? Walk up to Death, slap him in the face with my glove and challenge him to a duel?"

Josh snorts. "Not quite that dramatic, but not far off, either."

"We need you to tap into your latent abilities," Vex explains. "To awaken the part of you that was meant to be Death."

"Okay, but how the fuck am I supposed to do that?"

Cathy steps forward, her expression serious. "You need to be triggered. We've been preparing for this moment for a long time. We have ways to amplify your natural resistance to Death's power."

"Amplify how?" I ask suspiciously.

Josh grins, and it's not a comforting sight. "Ever heard of chaos magick?"

"Err, no. Unless I missed that lecture option on the Thornfield Prospectus."

"Definitely not on the Prospectus. This is primal stuff, older than Death himself. It's unpredictable and dangerous, but incredibly powerful. Much like you." He beams at me.

"In fact, it *is* you," Cathy states, and now it's all just too much. I stick both middle fingers up at them and turn on my heel to take my chances with the shadow monsters.

2

TATE

I WAKE WITH A START, MY HEAD POUNDING AND MY MOUTH dry as sandpaper. Blinking against the dim light, I try to get my bearings. I'm lying on a cold stone floor in what looks like some kind of underground chamber. The walls are rough-hewn rock, slick with moisture. The only light comes from a few flickering torches mounted on the walls.

"Fuck," I groan, pushing myself up to sit. My body aches all over, like I've been hit by a truck. As my vision clears, I see Torin and Bram sprawled nearby, still unconscious.

"Welcome back to the land of the living, Mr Blackwell," a raspy voice says.

I whip my head around, wincing at the sudden movement, to see the creepy pale-faced creature from before standing in the shadows. Up close, he's even more unsettling, with skin like parchment stretched over bone, eyes sunken and ringed with darkness, mouth stretched in an unnaturally wide grin.

"Who the fuck are you?" I snarl, trying to summon my magick. Nothing happens. Panic flares in my chest.

The creature's grin widens impossibly further. "I am Death, Mr Blackwell, and you three have become quite the thorn in my side."

I stare at him, my mind reeling. Death? As in, the actual personification of death? What the fuck have we got ourselves into?

My mind races, trying to process this impossible situation. Death himself is standing before me, and he's pissed at us. What the hell have we done to attract the attention of a primordial force?

"Where's Ivy?" I demand, pushing myself to my feet despite the wave of dizziness that hits me. "What have you done with her?"

Death's skeletal face twists into something that might be amusement. "Miss Hammond is no longer your concern. She belongs to me."

White-hot rage surges through me. "Like hell she does," I snarl, taking a step forward. "Ivy doesn't belong to anyone."

"Oh, but she does," Death says calmly. "She made a deal with The Syndicate long ago. Her soul is mine to claim."

The Syndicate—the name chills my soul. I never imagined the Syndicate was connected to Death himself.

Behind me, I hear Torin and Bram starting to stir.

"What do you want from us?" I ask, trying to buy time for the others to regain consciousness. We're going to need all our strength to get out of this.

Death's grin widens impossibly further. "You are a distraction to my greatest asset. I need you out of the way until she decides to see things my way. Running was a mistake. There are very few places where I can't find her."

She ran from Death? My soul fills with relief at that comment. She didn't leave us. She was scared.

"Where is she now?"

Death's grin fades slightly. "That is none of your concern. Miss Hammond will fulfil her contract, one way or another."

Behind me, I hear Torin growl as he pushes himself to his feet. "The hell she will," he snarls. "We won't let you force her into anything."

Death turns his eerie gaze to Torin. "You have no say in the matter. The contract is binding."

"Fuck your contract," Bram spits, stumbling to stand beside us. "We'll find a way to break it."

Death's laughter echoes off the stone walls. "You foolish creatures. You have no idea what you're dealing with."

I clench my fists, desperately trying to summon even a spark of magick. Nothing. Whatever this place is, it's blocking our powers completely.

"Let us go," I demand. "Let us find Ivy."

"I think not," Death says calmly. "You'll remain here until Miss Hammond returns to complete her task."

"And what is that, then?" I ask, having a sinking feeling about it.

"To kill you three, of course."

His words hit me like a punch to the gut. That's why she ran, to protect us from herself.

"She won't do it," I growl.

Death's skeletal grin widens. "Oh, but she will. One way or another. Either she'll complete the contract willingly, or I'll claim her soul, and you will die anyway."

Rage and terror war inside me. The thought of Ivy being forced to kill us, of her soul being twisted and corrupted by this creature, is unbearable.

"We won't let that happen," Torin snarls, his fangs bared despite our lack of powers. "We'll find a way to stop you."

Death laughs, the sound like bones rattling. "You're welcome to try. But for now, you'll remain here. Perhaps Miss Hammond will come to her senses and return on her own."

With that, he vanishes, leaving us alone in the dank chamber.

"Fuck!" I roar, slamming my fist into the stone wall. Pain lances up my arm, but I barely feel it.

"We need to get out of here," Bram says, his eyes scanning the room for any weakness, any escape route. "We have to find Ivy before he does."

"How do we know he can't find her?" Torin growls.

"That bastard smile fell off his face when I asked where she was. He doesn't know."

"Not yet, anyway," Bram mutters. "Our powers are useless here. We're trapped like fucking rats."

I take a deep breath, forcing myself to think.

"We need to think," I say, pacing the small chamber. "There has to be a way out of here."

Torin runs his hands along the walls, searching for any hidden mechanisms or weak spots. "These walls are solid. No doors or windows that I can see."

Bram crouches down, examining the floor. "The stone is seamless. I don't think we're getting out that way either."

I rake my hands through my hair in frustration. "He wants to keep us trapped while he hunts down Ivy."

The thought sends a chill through me. "We can't let that happen. We have to find a way out of here."

"Our powers are useless," Bram reminds us. "We're going to have to rely on our wits."

I nod, forcing myself to think rationally despite the fear for Ivy clawing at my chest. "Okay, let's break this down. What do we know about Death?"

"He's powerful as fuck," Torin mutters.

"He's head of The Syndicate, which kind of makes sense now that I think about it. He wants Ivy to complete her contract by killing us," Bram adds.

"Right," I say. "So he needs her alive, at least for now. That gives us some time."

"But how much?" Torin asks. "We don't know how long he'll wait before deciding to claim her soul and end us."

"We need to focus on getting out of here first. Once

we're free, we can worry about finding Ivy and stopping Death."

Torin nods, his eyes scanning the chamber again. "There has to be a way out. No prison is perfect."

"Even one created by Death himself?" Bram mutters darkly.

I shoot him a glare. "Not helping, Bram. We need solutions, not doom and gloom."

He holds up his hands in surrender. "Fine. What if we try to overload whatever's blocking our powers? Hit it with everything we've got at once?"

It's not a bad idea, but I shake my head. "Too risky. We don't know what kind of backlash that might cause. We could end up killing ourselves. Besides, I'm half dead already from breaking Vex's fucking wards. When I get my hands on him, I'm going to rip his fucking head off and shove it up his arse."

"As much as I love that image, we need to focus," Torin growls. "Doing something is better than waiting here to die."

"No," I say firmly. "We need to be alive to help Ivy. Let's think this through logically."

Bram nods, his eyes scanning the chamber again. "There has to be some weakness, some flaw in this prison. Nothing is perfect, not even Death's creations."

"Maybe we're thinking about this wrong," Torin says slowly. "We can't use our *magickal* powers, but what about our other abilities? Our strength, our senses? Fuck knows I can smell that damp at an enhanced level." He scrunches his nose up.

I look at him sharply. "What are you thinking?"

Torin moves to the centre of the room, closing his eyes. "Let me try something. Everyone shut it."

We watch as he stands perfectly still, head cocked slightly, as if listening for something. After a long moment, where I don't think neither Bram nor I even breathed, his eyes snap open.

"There," he says, pointing to a spot on the wall that looks no different from any other. "I can hear something. It's like a faint humming."

Moving quickly across the room, I press my ear to the wall, but I can't hear fuck all.

"Do you hear it?" Torin asks.

"No, not a vampire," I say, stepping back. "But I trust you."

Bram joins us, his brow furrowed in concentration. "It could be the source of whatever's blocking our powers. Or maybe..."

"Maybe what?" Torin presses.

"Maybe it's not meant to keep us in," Bram says slowly. "Maybe it's meant to keep something else out."

The implications of that sends a chill down my spine. What could be so terrible that even Death wants to keep it at bay?

"So you think we aren't in the supernatural realm, but somewhere more sinister?"

"Yeah. My Fae senses are tingling."

"Hmm. Either way, this is our best lead. Let's focus on this spot. There has to be a way to use it to our advantage."

Torin nods, running his hands over the stones. "If we can disrupt whatever's causing that hum, maybe we can weaken the prison."

"Or unleash something worse," Bram mutters, but he joins us in examining the wall.

We search every inch of the humming section, looking for any crack or seam we can exploit. Just as I'm about to give up in frustration, my fingers catch on something.

"Wait," I breathe. "I think I've found something."

3

IVY

I STORM AWAY FROM JOSH, VEX, AND CATHY, MY MIND reeling from everything they've just told me. Chaos magick. Becoming the antithesis of Death. A Death rejection specialist. It's all too much…. Wait.

Death rejection. That holds way more connotations than I'm comfortable with. Am I overthinking this?

Yeah, probably.

"Ivy, wait!" Josh calls after me.

I spin around, glaring at him.

"You can't leave. Death will find you."

"You can't run from this, Ivy. Death will find you eventually," Vex says.

"Maybe," I snarl, "but you are trying to put me in the firing line when I want to do the exact opposite. I'm doing this to save my guys!"

"Are you, though?" he asks seriously. "The way I see it, if you run and don't do what Death wants, he will kill them himself. If he hasn't already."

I freeze, my blood running cold at Vex's words. "What do you mean, if he hasn't already?"

Vex's expression is grim. "Death isn't known for his patience. If you've run, he may decide to take matters into his own hands."

"No," I whisper, shaking my head. "He wouldn't…" But I know in my heart he would. Of course he fucking would.

"We don't know for sure," Josh says quickly, shooting Vex a glare. "But the longer we wait, the more danger they're in."

I clench my fists, torn between rage and fear. "So I'm just supposed to trust you and your crazy plan to become some kind of chaos entity to fight Death?"

"It's not ideal," Cathy says softly, "but it may be our only chance to save them and stop Death's corruption."

I look between the three of them, my mind racing. As insane as their plan sounds, do I really have any other choice? If Death has my guys, though. There isn't any choice, really, is there?

"Fine," I growl. "What do I need to do?"

Josh nods once. "First, we need to awaken your latent abilities, and for that, we're going to need to piss you off."

I snort. "Trust me, I'm plenty pissed off already."

"Not enough," Vex says, shaking his head. "We need to push you to your absolute limit."

"And how do you plan on doing that?" I ask, shoving my hands into my hair and tugging, the anxiety of this entire night getting to me.

"Like this."

The new voice resounds around the chamber, cutting above the hum of the computer machines and the soft murmurs of the workers.

Turning to it, I feel actual homicidal rage.

"Hey, Ives," Ramsey says, holding his hand up in a half wave. "Angry?"

My vision goes red as I lunge at Ramsey, all rational thoughts fleeing my mind. "You fucking bastard!" I scream, my fist connecting with his jaw with a satisfying crack. "I trusted you! You are my handler! My best friend!"

He staggers back but doesn't fall, a smirk playing on his lips despite the blood trickling from the corner of his mouth. "I know, but it had to be this way. You weren't ready, Ivy. You weren't ready to take on this fight. There has to be something worth it. Something you couldn't lose."

"Rah!" I swing again, but this time he's ready. He ducks under my punch and uses my momentum to flip me over his shoulder. I hit the ground hard, the wind knocked out of me, but rage and adrenaline surge through my veins, pushing me back to my feet in an instant.

"You manipulative piece of shit," I snarl, circling Ramsey. "Was any of it real? Our friendship? Or was it all just part of your grand fucking plan?"

Ramsey's smirk falters for a moment, something like regret flashing in his eyes. "It was real, Ivy. You are my friend. But this is bigger than friendship. This is about the fate of the supernatural world and, eventually, the human one, too."

"Fuck the worlds," I snap, lunging at him again. This time, I manage to tackle him to the ground, pinning him beneath me. "You lied to me. For years. You've been playing both sides. You double-crossed me!"

I punch him again, relishing the crunch of cartilage as my fist connects with his nose. Blood sprays, but I don't care. All the fear, confusion, and anger of the past few days comes pouring out of me in a torrent of violence.

"Ivy, stop!" Josh shouts, but I ignore him.

Ramsey doesn't fight back; he just takes the beating. That pisses me off even more.

"Fight back, you arsehole!" I scream, grabbing the front of his shirt and shaking him. "You wanted to piss me off? Well, congratu-fucking-lations! Mission accomplished!"

Suddenly, I feel a surge of energy coursing through my body—a raw, primal power that makes every nerve-ending tingle. The air around me crackles with electricity.

I look down at my hands and gasp. They glow with an eerie pink light, wisps of dark energy swirling around my fingers. *What the actual fuck? I don't have active magick.*

Ramsey grins up at me through bloodied teeth. "There she is," he says. "The Chaos incarnate."

The rage inside me reaches a fever pitch. With a

scream of fury, I slam my palms down onto Ramsey's chest. "You are a dick!"

He grabs my wrists. "I know, Ives. I know. But you are ready for this now. This is the right thing to do."

"No," I growl. "The right thing to do was work for The Syndicate so I could find out what happened to my parents. For real. This is some fucked up shit I want no part of." Panting heavily, I heave myself off him and move away, hands trembling.

The pink energy swirls around me, crackling and pulsing. I stare at my hands in disbelief, watching tendrils of dark mist curl between my fingers.

"What the fuck is this?" I demand, rounding on Josh and the others.

Josh stares at me in something like awe, but there is fear there, too, and it scares me. "That is your chaos magick awakening. The parts of yourself that you rejected while still in the womb."

"Eww." I glare at him with a big ick for talking about wombs. "I don't want it. Take it back."

"It doesn't work like that," Cathy says gently. "This power has always been a part of you. You've just unlocked it."

"By showing me my whole life has been one big betrayal."

"I'm sorry, Ivy. I hate that this happened the way it did. If there had been another way—"

"There was! You could have told me what was going on. Let me make my own choices with my eyes wide open. I feel like you've hoodwinked me, and that is not okay."

He looks sad, and I feel torn again. Only this time, between loving him and being so angry at him, I could smash his face in again.

"Fair enough. But I'm a lying bastard who's trying to save the world."

"Fuck that," I snarl. "What about my guys? Where are they?"

"If Death has them, they're likely in his realm. A place between life and death," Vex says.

"You," I say, pointing at him, "had better run, because you made me trust you. I should've gone on not liking you."

"Aww, she likes me," he purrs in that sexy way that really pisses me off right now.

"Never said that," I grit out. "Where is this place? How can I get there?"

"You don't even know the guys are there," Ramsey says.

I shake my head, feeling utterly defeated. "I was a fool to think I could outrun Death. Of course he has them."

"Look," Cathy says in that no-nonsense tone she is known for. "I get that this is all a big wake-up call, and you're pissed off. With every right. What Josh and Ramsey have said is true, though. You weren't ready. You had nothing to lose and everything to gain by working for The Syndicate. But here is a fun fact, Ivy.

Your parents were killed by The Syndicate. That's right. They killed your parents to get to *you*. The poor little orphan girl with so much latent power, she could blow up universes. So listen up. You have two choices. Stick your head back in the sand and be a naïve little girl or pull your big girl knickers up and face the truth as we have given it to you."

I stare at her, my mouth open at her blunt, harsh, painful words. The pink energy around me pulses and crackles, responding to the turmoil of emotions raging inside me.

"You're lying," I whisper, but deep down, I know she's not. It makes a sick kind of sense, explaining so much about my life that I've never understood.

"I'm sorry, Ivy," Cathy says, her voice softening slightly. "But it's the truth. The Syndicate has been manipulating you from the start. If I had known what you were up to, I would have tried to stop you, but it was too late when I found out. You were in too deep, and I know that nothing I could've said would have mattered… except to push you further to them."

I close my eyes, trying to process this new information. Everything I thought I knew about my life, about my purpose, has been a lie.

"I'm going to find my guys," I declare suddenly, eyes snapping open. "And then I'm going to take down Death and The Syndicate. Not because you want me to, but because they've fucked with my life for the last time. But I need to know one thing. What happens when Death, as he is now, is defeated? What then? Who takes over? Are we going to end up in a similar situation?"

"That's the thing," Josh says, shaking his head. "We don't know."

Rolling my eyes, I mutter, "Great, just great."

4

TORIN

I WATCH INTENTLY AS TATE'S FINGERS PROBE THE ROUGH stone wall, searching for whatever he's found. My enhanced hearing picks up the faint scraping of his nails against the rock.

"What is it?" Bram asks impatiently.

"I'm not sure," Tate murmurs, eyes closed to focus on his other senses. "There's some kind of seam or crack here. It's subtle, but..."

He trails off, pressing harder against the wall. Suddenly, there's a soft click and a section of stone slides back, revealing a small alcove.

"What the fuck?" I shove him out of the way to peer inside. "Is it me, or was that way too easy to find?"

"Depends on who they usually lock up in here," Bram remarks. "Vampires with enhanced hearing might not be the norm."

"True," I murmur and stoop down a bit so I can get a better look inside the hole in the wall.

Inside, there is a strange object. A sphere about the size of a cricket ball made of some kind of iridescent material that shifts and swirls as we look at it. Faint whispers are coming from it that are so subtle even my vampire hearing is struggling with it.

"What the fuck is that thing?" Bram asks, leaning in for a closer look.

"I have no idea," Tate says. "But I bet it's important."

We all stare at the shifting, whispering orb for a long moment.

"Fuck it," I finally say, making a decision. "We don't have many other options. I say we grab it and see what happens."

Tate looks uncertain. "Are you sure? This could go very badly."

I shrug. "We're already prisoners of Death. How much worse could it get?"

"Oh, you fucking had to, didn't you?" Bram mutters, but he doesn't argue further.

Taking a deep breath, I reach out and wrap my hand around the orb. The moment my skin makes contact, a jolt of energy surges through me. The whispers grow louder, becoming a swarm of voices in my head.

"Torin?" Tate mutters.

A door slides open behind us, making us spin rapidly, hands up, ready to fight, but nothing comes through.

"Did you do that?" Bram asks.

"Maybe," I reply. "Who can tell?"

"Should we go through it?" Tate asks.

"Yeah, we aren't sitting here with our dicks in our hands," I snap, moving forward.

"Wait," Bram says. "We need to talk. I've been keeping something from you guys. I've aligned myself with an organisation that reckons it wants to take out The Syndicate. I've done a couple of jobs for them. The goal was to see if I could move in the same circles as Poison. They want her. They said Ivy is special."

I stare at him as he rambles on. "Special, how?" The rest doesn't bother me. I don't give a fuck what he does in his free time, and anything that takes down The Syndicate is fine by me. It's my end game, after all. The less work I have to do in order to accomplish this task, the better.

He shrugs. "They didn't say."

"Who are they?" Tate asks carefully, less willing to let it go, it seems.

"Not really all that sure. They approached me one night in the forest. It was like they knew what I wanted. But apart from wanting The Syndicate out of the way, their motives are murky, at best."

Tate runs a hand through his hair, frustration evident in every line of his body. "We don't have time for this shit. We need to find Ivy before Death does whatever the fuck he's planning."

"Agreed," I say, shoving the orb into my pocket. The voices in my head quiet to a dull murmur. "We can deal with Bram's extracurricular activities later. Right now, we need to get the hell out of here."

Without waiting for a response, I stride through the open doorway, senses on alert. The others follow close behind, Tate muttering curses under his breath.

The passage beyond is dark and narrow, the walls slick with moisture. The air is thick with the scent of decay and something else, something ancient and powerful that sets my teeth on edge. It twists and turns, leading us deeper into whatever realm we've found ourselves in. The darkness is absolute, but my vampire vision allows me to navigate without issue. Behind me, I hear Tate and Bram stumbling occasionally.

"Can you see anything?" Tate whispers.

"Not much," I reply. "Just more tunnel. But there's something off about this place."

"No shit," Bram mutters. "We're in Death's domain. Everything's off."

I ignore him, focusing on the strange energy I can feel pulsing through the air. It reminds me of the orb in my pocket, which has started to vibrate slightly.

Suddenly, the tunnel opens up into a vast cavern. The ceiling stretches impossibly high, lost in shadow. Massive pillars of bone and stone support the weight above, carved with intricate symbols that hurt my eyes to look at directly.

"Holy shit," Bram breathes.

"The Underworld," Tate states, far more calmly than I feel right now. "The realm of the dead."

"How the fuck do you know that?" I ask, unable to tear my eyes away from the haunting beauty of the cavern.

"A fucking wild guess," he growls, and I shrug.

"Fair enough."

We stand at the edge of the vast cavern, taking in the impossible sight before us. The air is heavy and oppressive.

"So what now?" Bram whispers. "We're in the Underworld. How the hell do we find Ivy in all this?"

I pull the orb from my pocket. It's glowing faintly, the swirling colours moving more rapidly. The whispers in my head have grown louder and more insistent, though I still can't make out any distinct words.

"I think this might be able to guide us," I say, holding it up. "It seems to be reacting to something."

Tate eyes it warily. "Are you sure we can trust that thing? For all we know, it could be leading us into a trap."

I shrug. "You got a better idea?"

He scowls but doesn't argue further.

"Right then," I say, stepping forward. "Let's see where this takes us."

We make our way across the cavern floor, picking our way between the towering pillars and strange formations. The orb pulses in my hand, growing warmer as we move deeper into the Underworld.

Suddenly, a piercing shriek echoes through the cavern. We freeze, looking around wildly for the source.

"What the fuck was that?" Bram hisses, his eyes darting around.

"I don't know," I growl, "but I don't like it."

The shriek comes again, closer this time. In the

shadows between the pillars, I catch glimpses of movement. Dark shapes flit just at the edge of my vision.

"We're not alone," Tate mutters, flicking his hand out to test if he has magick.

He doesn't.

This is not good.

The orb in my hand pulses more urgently, growing almost painfully hot. I nearly drop it as a searing pain lances through my palm.

"Fuck!" I curse, juggling the orb between my hands. "This thing is going nuts."

"Maybe we should—" Bram starts, but he's cut off as a figure lunges out of the darkness at us.

It's humanoid, but only barely. Its skin is grey and withered, stretched tight over an emaciated frame. Empty eye sockets stare at us from a skull-like face, and its mouth gapes open in another piercing shriek.

"Move!" Tate yells, shoving us forward.

We run, dodging between the pillars as more of the creatures emerge from the shadows. Their shrieks echo off the cavern walls, a racket of death and hunger that chills me to my dark core.

The orb pulses frantically in my hand, guiding us through the maze-like cavern. I have no idea if we're running towards safety or deeper into danger, but we don't have much choice. The creatures are gaining on us, their bony hands reaching out to grab at our clothes.

"What the fuck are these things?" Bram pants as we run.

"Lost souls," Tate grunts. "The ones who never made it to their final rest."

"How do you know all this shit?" I demand, ducking under a grasping hand.

"I read," he snaps back. "Now shut up and run!"

We sprint through the twisting paths between the pillars, the shrieks of the lost souls growing ever louder behind us. The orb in my hand is vibrating, pulling me forward with an urgency I can't ignore.

Suddenly, we burst out of the maze of pillars into a wide-open space. In the centre stands a massive structure that looks like a cross between a temple and a fortress. Black stone walls rise impossibly high, carved with the same eye-hurting symbols as the pillars. A set of enormous doors stands open before us, darkness spilling out like a physical force.

"In there!" I shout, pointing at the open doors.

We make a mad dash for the entrance, the howls of the lost souls right on our heels. Just as we cross the threshold, there is a blinding flash, and we are tumbling out onto the Thornfield campus around the back of the car park.

For a moment, we just lay there, gasping for breath and trying to process what just happened.

"What the actual fuck?" Bram groans, pushing himself up to sit and testing to see if his magick has returned. Dark swirls surround his hands, and he breathes out with relief.

I sit up slowly, my head spinning. The orb is still

clutched tightly in my hand, but it's gone cold and dark. The voices in my head have faded to silence.

"Are we back or in some sort of parallel universe?" Tate asks, looking around in disbelief.

I nod, taking in our surroundings. It's still night. The car park is dimly lit by flickering streetlights. Everything looks normal, but after what we've just been through, I'm not sure I trust my senses anymore.

"How?" Bram demands. "How did we get from the Underworld to here?"

I hold up the now-inert orb. "I think this thing brought us back somehow. When we went through those doors..."

Tate frowns, reaching out to touch the orb. As soon as his fingers make contact, he jerks back with a hiss. "Fuck! It's ice cold."

"Yeah," I mutter. "It's like all the energy just drained out of it."

We sit in silence for a moment, trying to process everything that's happened. Finally, Bram speaks up.

"I don't like this."

"Me either."

"So what now?" Bram asks, pushing himself to his feet and brushing dirt off his clothes.

I stand as well, pocketing the now-useless orb. "We find Ivy. She's still out there somewhere, and Death is after her."

Tate nods grimly. "Agreed. But where do we even start looking? She could be anywhere."

I close my eyes, focusing on my vampire senses, but there is nothing. I shake my head.

"Could be Death's influence," Bram suggests. "If he's got her..."

"He doesn't," I growl, not wanting to even consider that possibility. "We'd know if he did."

Tate huffs out a breath. "So we're back where we started. No idea where Ivy is, Death after her, and now some mysterious organisation that wants her too." He glares at Bram.

"Something bigger is going on here," I mutter with a frown. "Everything from the last few weeks is leading up to something more."

"What do you mean?" Tate asks.

"I don't know. I haven't figured it out yet. I get the feeling that this is one giant game of Tetris that Death is playing. We just need to figure out how to start moving the pieces around ourselves."

"No sweat," Tate mutters. "Death Tetris, here we come."

5

IVY

I STAND IN THE CAVERN, PINK ENERGY STILL CRACKLING around me as I try to process everything I've just learned. My whole life has been a lie, orchestrated by forces I didn't even know existed, and now they want me to become some kind of chaotic entity to fight Death.

Part of me wants to tell them all to go fuck themselves. To run as far and fast as I can from this insanity. But another part, a growing part, feels a strange sense of rightness. Like pieces of a puzzle I didn't know I was solving are finally falling into place.

"Okay," I say finally, looking at the faces around me. Josh, Vex, Cathy, Ramsey. People I thought I knew. People who have lied to me. But also, people who might be my only chance at saving my guys and stopping Death. "What's the next step?"

Josh, his expression way too serious, says, "Now that your powers have awakened, we need to train you to use them. Chaos magick is unpredictable and dangerous. If you can't control it, it will consume you."

"Lovely," I mutter. "And how exactly does one train to use unpredictable magick?"

Vex grins, and it's not a comforting sight. "By embracing the chaos, of course."

"You sure I can't run, instead?" I ask, but it's a non-starter. If I run, my guys die. That is not happening.

"You could," Vex says, almost reluctantly, like he doesn't want to give away a big secret. "I know of maybe one place you could go where he wouldn't find you."

"And that would be?" I ask, curious despite myself.

"An Academy a few hundred miles from here called MistHallow. Much like this one, but way higher up on the food chain."

"Hmm." I ponder, but then shake my head. I'm not running. Not now. If I fail, then I can, but Poison doesn't run from fights. Ivy might on occasion, but Poison is a badass, and I need her right now.

So, I shift. Pink bobbed hair, baby blue eyes. Killer body.

And in doing so, the magickal clothes that Vex gave me disappear, leaving me naked in a roomful of creatures who want me to take on Death and win.

Fan-fucking-tastic.

It about sums up my day.

"Oh, for fuck's sake," I mutter, crossing my legs and covering up my tits in a futile attempt at modesty. "Anyone got some clothes?"

Josh snickers while Vex leers at me. Cathy rolls her eyes and snaps her fingers, conjuring a simple black outfit of leggings, a tank top, and boots.

"Thanks," I say grudgingly, quickly pulling on the clothes.

"Now then," Cathy says briskly, "let's get started with your training."

"What? Right now?" I ask incredulously. "Don't I get a moment to, I don't know, process all this bullshit you've just dumped on me?"

"Time is a luxury we don't have," Ramsey says, his face still bloody from where I punched him. *Good.* "If you go back out there, you have this ultimatum hanging over your head."

He's right, but maybe that's not the worst thing. Maybe I can buy some time.

"Actually," I say slowly, "maybe going back out there is exactly what I need to do."

Josh frowns. "What are you thinking?"

"Death gave me a choice: kill my guys, or he takes my soul, right? Well, what if I pretend to go along with it? Buy us some time while I figure out how to use these new powers?"

Vex shakes his head. "It's too risky. If Death realises you're stalling—"

"He'll what? Kill me? Take my soul? That's what he's planning anyway," I argue. "At least this way, I have a chance to save the guys and learn to control this chaos magick bullshit."

Cathy looks thoughtful. "It could work. If you're convincing enough."

"I'm a damn good liar when I need to be," I say, gesturing to my shifted persona.

Ramsey nods. "She has a point. It might be our best shot at catching Death off guard."

"Okay," Josh says after a moment. "But you can't go in blind. We need to give you at least some basic training before you face Death again."

I nod, relieved they're not fighting me on this. "Fine. Give me the basics."

"It's not as simple as that. Chaos magick is... chaotic. By its very nature, it shouldn't exist," Cathy says.

"Are you saying *I* shouldn't exist?" I growl.

"Yes," she states. "When your soul rejected Death's calling, you became something that shouldn't exist. Deal with that however you want, but do it quickly. The longer your magick is left to run wild, the more it will tear you in half."

"Do you mean that literally?"

She purses her lips but doesn't reply.

"Okay, then," I say, taking a deep breath. "Let's do this. Teach me how to control this chaos magick before it tears me apart."

Josh nods, his expression serious. "The first thing you need to understand is that chaos magick doesn't follow the rules of normal magick. It's unpredictable and wild. You can't control it so much as guide it."

"How?"

"By embracing the chaos," Vex says, stepping forward. "You need to let go of your preconceptions about how magick should work. Forget everything you think you know."

I raise an eyebrow at him. "That shouldn't be too hard, considering I didn't know I had active magick until about ten minutes ago."

"Fair point," he concedes. "But you've been around magick users. You have ideas about how it should work. Forget all of that."

"Okay," I say slowly. "So what do I do instead?"

"Feel the energy inside you," Cathy instructs. "That pink crackling power. Don't try to control it. Just let it flow through you."

I close my eyes, focusing on the strange energy I can feel buzzing beneath my skin. It's wild, unpredictable, like lightning trapped in a bottle. Every instinct screams at me to contain it, to force it into submission, but I resist the urge. Instead, I try to relax, to let the power flow freely through me.

"Good," Josh murmurs. "Now, think of something you want to happen. Don't try to make it happen, just hold the intention in your mind."

I think of my guys - Tate, Torin, and Bram. I want to find them, to know they're safe. The energy inside me surges in response to my desire, crackling along my skin.

"Open your eyes," Ramsey says softly.

I do, and gasp.

6

BRAM

"What the fuck?" I snap, staring at Ivy, or rather Poison, in disbelief. One moment we were in the Thornfield parking lot, the next we're... wherever this is. Some kind of underground cavern filled with strange creatures and Poison crackling with pink energy.

Tate and Torin look equally as baffled next to me, shaking off the very unsettling ride we just came on.

"Ivy?" Tate says cautiously. "Sorry, babe. Not calling you Poison right now. How did we get here? What's going on?"

Ivy's eyes are wide as she stares at us. "I think I did this. Somehow."

"You did what exactly?" Torin growls, his eyes darting around suspiciously at the others in the room.

"I was practising with this stupid magick, and I wanted to find you," Ivy explains, her voice shaky. "To know you were safe, and then you were here."

"Impressive," a woman I don't recognise says,

eyeing Ivy with interest. "You're more powerful than we realised."

"Who the fuck are you?" I demand, stepping protectively in front of Ivy.

"Easy, Bram," Ivy says, putting a hand on my arm. "That is my Aunt Cathy, you know the rest."

"Vex," Tate snarls. "You had better not have laid a single finger on her."

He smirks. "Only when she asked me to."

Tate's fury is like a living thing. He calls his magick to him, but Ivy stops him by slapping her hand on his wrist. "No. Don't let him wind you up. He's an idiot."

"Hey," Vex snaps. "An idiot who saved you."

"Noooo, an idiot who brought me here to this shitshow!"

"Okay, back up a fucking minute here. What is going on? Why did you run, Ivy? Was it because of Death?"

Her eyes go wide when she looks at me. Those cornflower eyes that make my dick go hard. As much as I've fallen for Ivy as herself, I can't deny the effect Poison has on me. "How did you know about Death?"

"He paid us a visit," Torin growls. "And decided to imprison us. We escaped."

Ivy's eyes widen in shock. "You escaped from Death? How?"

"Long story," I cut in. "The short version is we found some weird orb thing that transported us out of there. Now, will you please explain what the fuck is going on?"

Ivy takes a deep breath, looking around at the others in the cavern. "It's complicated. Basically, Death gave me an ultimatum to either kill you guys or he takes my soul. I ran to try to protect you, but then..." She gestures vaguely at herself and the pink energy still crackling around her. "All this happened."

"What is 'all this' exactly?" Tate asks, eyeing her warily. "Why is Vex here?"

I resist the urge to roll my eyes. Tate is so caught up in Vex and his jealousy or rivalry or whatever the fuck it is, it's like they're fucking siblings or something…

Wait. Did I just… I narrow my eyes at them. *Nah. They look like exact opposites.*

"Apparently, I have chaos magick," Ivy says, interrupting my wayward thoughts. "Because I'm some kind of cosmic glitch that rejected becoming Death while still in the womb, and now these guys want me to use it to take down Death and The Syndicate."

I blink, trying to process this information dump. "That's a lot." Frowning, I look around the room. "Are you? Do I know you?" I ask, zeroing in on the woman again.

"No, that would be me," Josh says, raising his hand. I barely know the guy, only by sight. He's Ramsey's boyfriend.

"You? You're the creature that I've been dealing with?"

"Mm-hmm."

"So you guys are really trying to take down The Syndicate?"

"Death, mostly, but The Syndicate is his brainchild, so by proxy, yes."

"So where do the kills fit into your thing… and don't give me, need to know. If you want me to get on board with whatever shit this is…" I wave my hand around, "… not to mention the fact that Ivy has something I've only ever heard of in tales of the ancient Fae, you owe me this."

"What kills?" Ivy asks, momentarily distracted.

"Bram has been doing some freelance work for us, taking out strategic allies of Death. He has several beings who deliver him souls, on the down low for extra treats."

"That fucking warlock. I knew he was a piece of shit," I spit out.

"Wait," Ivy interrupts, her eyes narrowing at me. "You've been working for them? This whole time?"

I shift uncomfortably under her intense gaze. "No. Very recently. I was trying to find a way to get closer to Poison. I didn't know who they really were. I just knew they wanted to take down The Syndicate."

"You were trying to get closer to Poison?" she asks. "Why? So you could kill me, too?" Ivy's temper has flared, dramatically increasing the pink energy around her.

"Don't be ridiculous," I snap. "I didn't want to kill Poison."

"No, just abduct her and chain her to the wall until she agreed to be with you," Tate snarls.

"What?" Eyes wide, Poison stares at me. I make the

differentiation now because I'm in seriously deep Dragon dung.

"No," I lie. "That wasn't exactly—"

"Okay, everyone, just calm down," Josh interjects, holding up his hands. "We're all on the same side here, and your personal shit can wait."

"Are we all on the same side?" Ivy asks, looking around the room with suspicion. "Because from where I'm standing, it seems like everyone's been lying to everyone else."

She's not wrong. The tension in the room is overt with all the secrets and lies bubbling to the surface.

"Look," I say, trying to defuse the situation. "We can argue about who kept what secret later. Right now, we need to focus on the bigger picture. Death is after Ivy. Are we assuming he wants her because of the chaos magick or because he knows she can kill him with it, so he wants to keep his enemies closer?"

Ivy's eyes narrow at me. "Good question. Why does Death want me so badly? Is it just because of this chaos magick, or is there more to it?"

Josh and Cathy exchange a loaded glance that sets my teeth on edge.

"There's more," Josh admits reluctantly. "We believe Death wants to use you as a weapon. Your chaos magick, if properly harnessed, could potentially destroy entire realms."

"What?" Ivy whispers, her face pale.

"Death has been accumulating power for centuries," Cathy explains. "But there are still realms beyond his reach. With you under his control, he could expand his dominion even further."

"Fuck that," Torin growls. "We're not letting that happen."

Tate nods in agreement, but I notice his eyes keep darting to Vex. There's definitely something going on there that I don't fully understand.

"So, what's the plan?" I ask, trying to focus on the immediate problem. "How do we keep Ivy safe and stop Death?"

"We train her," Josh says firmly. "Teach her to control the chaos magick so Death can't use her as a weapon."

"And then what?" Ivy demands. "I just waltz up to Death and kill him?"

Vex grins. "Something like that, yeah."

"You're insane," Tate snaps. "We can't send her against Death. It's suicide."

"We don't have much choice," Josh argues. "Death won't stop coming for her, and if he gets his hands on her, the consequences could be catastrophic."

I watch the argument unfold, my mind still trying to process that Ivy has chaos magick. That is some seriously mythical shit right there.

"Enough," Ivy says suddenly, her voice cutting through the bickering. The pink energy around her pulses ominously. "This isn't for any of you to decide. It's for me and me alone."

"Beg to differ," Torin says, his gaze boring into hers.

"You don't get to experience what we have and then dismiss us as something not worth your time."

"I never once said that—"

"Yeah, you pretty much inferred it," I interrupt. "We get a say in what goes on in your life, Ivy, whether you like it or not."

Ivy's eyes flash with anger, the pink energy crackling more intensely around her. "You don't get to dictate my choices," she snaps. "None of you do. This is my life, my power, and my decision."

"Ivy," Tate says softly, reaching out to her. "We're not trying to control you. We just want to protect you."

She jerks away from his touch. "I don't need your protection. I need you to trust me to make my own choices."

"Even if those choices get you killed?" Torin growls.

"Especially then," Ivy retorts.

I watch the standoff, feeling torn. On the one hand, I understand the guys' desire to keep Ivy safe. On the other, I know firsthand how suffocating it can be to have others try to control your destiny.

"Look," I say, trying to be the voice of reason for once. Tate is blinded when it comes to this. He can't see reason. "We're all on edge here. Why don't we take a step back and figure this out together?"

Ivy's gaze snaps to mine, her blue eyes blazing. "Really? After you've been sneaking around working for some shadowy organisation to get closer to Poison?"

I wince. "Touché. However, that isn't the issue here."

She grimaces because she knows I'm right.

"Okay, this has gone far enough," Cathy states, stepping forward. "Ivy, you are acting like a sullen child. Snap out of it. You want to be such a grown-up? Act like one. This isn't just about you, dear girl. It's about everyone. The good, the bad and the downright evil. But they all matter in the bigger scope of things. Do you understand that? Or do we need to go back to basics with you like a toddler?"

Torin and I exchange a shocked stare. Wow, this woman doesn't pull any punches.

However, it seems to have worked. Ivy is huffing, but she is losing her defensiveness.

It's not much, but it's a start.

7

IVY

I TAKE A DEEP BREATH, TRYING TO CALM THE CHAOS magick swirling inside me. Aunt Cathy's harsh words sting, but I know she has a point. I'm acting childishly when the stakes are so high.

"You're right," I say grudgingly. "I'm sorry. Tonight has been extra."

"We understand," Ramsey says gently, moving closer and looking sheepish. "But we need to work together if we're going to have any chance against Death."

I nod, looking at my guys. "I know. I'm sorry for trying to exclude you. I just don't want any of you to get hurt because of me."

Tate's expression softens. "Ivy, we would lay down our lives for you. When will you realise that?"

"He's right," Torin adds gruffly. "We would do anything you asked us to do."

Bram nods in agreement, though there is wariness in

his eyes. He knows more about this chaos magick, and he is worried about it. That doesn't fill me with great confidence.

"Okay," I say, squaring my shoulders. "So, what's our next move?"

"More training," Ramsey says. "What you did, bringing the guys here was monumental. You need to take that and hone it as a skill. Just like the gigs, you have to roll with the punches. It's what makes you so great. Why you are so good at what you do. You can think on your feet and think outside the box."

"Essentially, that is what chaos magick is," Bram says. "But there are few texts on this, from what I can remember. It's an ancient magick that has no place in this world and no bearers."

"Until now," Tate says quietly, looking at me like I fell from the moon.

"There is a place that *might* have the information we need," Vex says.

"Where?" I ask. "Because it's all very well saying I need to roll with the punches. Any help I can get, would be much appreciated."

Out of the corner of my eye, I see Cathy's nod of approval now that I've got my manners back, and I'm not acting like a spoiled brat anymore.

"Remember that place I told you about?" he mutters.

I frown and then remember he mentioned an Academy called MistHallow. "Yeah."

"There. Give me a couple of days. I know the Headmaster. He can probably help if he knows the supernatural world is in peril. He's a good sort."

"Okay, well, if you get the information, you know where to find me. Right now, I need to go home, get some sleep and try to figure out a way to stall killing my guys so Death doesn't take my soul."

Ramsey nods. "I'll walk you back."

I hold my hand up. "No. I need to be alone." His face falls, and I shoot him a weak smile. "Sorry about smashing your face in."

"Sorry for lying to you."

I shrug. "I guess we have all been hiding shit. That needs to end."

"Agreed. I have no more secrets."

"Me either," says Josh.

"Same," I mutter, and look at the guys. "I'll see you later, okay?"

I turn to leave, but then wince. "Erm, how do I get out of here?"

Vex snickers. "Allow me."

"Like hell—"

Tate's exclamation is cut off as Vex snaps his fingers, and I find myself on the front steps of his house, staring out at the full dawn in motion. Without wasting a second, I head back to the terraced house I share with Ramsey, hoping Vex can find something that will help me understand this power. I don't think anything can tell me how to wield it, but if I knew why it existed and what it is really made for; then maybe I have a shot at taking on Death and winning.

I trudge across campus and into the house. Taking the stairs, I feel utterly drained. The events of the night swirl through my mind: Death's ultimatum, discovering my chaos magick, revelations, about my past, and The Syndicate.

I head straight for the shower, hoping the hot water will help clear my head. Turning it on, I strip off and shift back to Ivy. Poison isn't going to help me with this. Climbing in, I stand under the spray, and try to sort through everything I've learned.

I'm some kind of cosmic glitch. A rejected Death candidate with unpredictable chaos magick, and now I'm expected to use that power to take down Death and dismantle The Syndicate. In theory, it's a solid plan. The Syndicate under Death's rule sounds like a pretty nasty place, and I'm adding to that by being Poison. That has to end now. Somehow. But in practice, I feel this may take more than I'm able to offer, and that thought doesn't sit well with me.

Washing methodically, I run the sponge over my body with my eyes closed, imagining it in the hands of my guys.

Gasping, I open them to see Tate with me, naked and soaking wet, as he moves in closer, his hands cupping my tits while he pinches my nipples.

"Did you bring me here?" he asks with a soft smirk.

"Must have."

"Handy magick, that."

"Isn't it just." I barely manage to get it out before he picks me up and slams me against the cold tiles, his mouth devouring mine as I drop the sponge and cling to him, wrapping my legs around him.

Tate's mouth crushes mine, hungry and demanding. I moan into the kiss, my fingers tangling in his wet hair as the hot water cascades over us. His hard body presses me against the tiles, as the marking on my lower back flares up into white hot pain.

I gasp as it drives a shot of lust straight to my pussy. There is no doubt that I'm with my fated mate. My soul knows.

"Fuck, I've missed you," he growls, his lips trailing down my neck.

"Me too," I gasp as he nips at my pulse point. "I'm sorry I ran."

He pulls back slightly, his intense gaze locking with mine. "Don't ever do that again. We don't need you to protect us, Ivy. We just need you."

I nod, unable to speak past the lump in my throat. Instead, I pull him back in for another searing kiss. His hands roam my body, leaving trails of fire in their wake. I arch into his touch, desperate for more.

Tate shifts his grip, hitching my legs higher around his waist. With one smooth thrust, his cock is inside me, filling my pussy completely. We both groan at the sensation.

"Fucking hell, Ivy," he pants against my neck. "What you do to me."

I can only whimper in response as he sets a punishing pace that drives the onslaught of pleasure.

There's nothing but this moment, nothing but Tate and the exquisite fucking between us.

My clit throbs as Tate pounds into me, his thick cock stretching me to perfection. The hot water cascades over us as he fucks me against the shower wall like there is no tomorrow, his mouth trailing hot kisses along my neck and collarbone.

"Tate," I gasp, clinging to his broad shoulders. "Oh, fuck, yes!"

He growls low in his throat, increasing his pace. One hand grips my arse while the other slides between us to rub tight circles on my clit. The dual sensations have me rocketing towards an orgasm overwhelmingly fast.

"That's it, little princess," Tate murmurs against my skin. "Let go for me. I want to feel you come on my cock."

His words, combined with the relentless pleasure, push me over the edge. I cry out as my orgasm crashes over me, my pussy clenching tightly around him. Tate grunts, shoving his dick even further into me before he unloads, pressing his forehead to mine as we are rained down on by the growing cooler water.

The intensity of our connection, both physical and emotional, leaves me feeling raw and vulnerable.

"We should probably get out before the water turns ice cold," I murmur eventually.

Tate nods, carefully setting me down on shaky legs. He reaches behind me to turn off the shower, then grabs a towel to wrap around me.

I find it hard to believe that I brought him to me, naked and ready to impale me on his rock-hard cock, but here he is.

It's slightly terrifying though. What else might this new power do without my conscious control?

8

IVY

WAKING UP ALONE AFTER POSSIBLY THE WEIRDEST NIGHT OF my life is different from how I expected it to be. There is no dread, no anxiety about what I have to do. Instead, I feel strangely at peace with my situation. Death might be a massive arsehole who wants me to kill my guys or have my soul, but there is power in knowing who your enemy is. More than that, there is power in knowing who and what you are.

Although that is debatable right about now. Really need to figure that shit out or I'll die trying. It's not exactly how I want to go out.

I stretch languidly, feeling the buzz of that chaos magick under my skin like thousands of fizzing champagne bubbles racing through my veins. It's still there, waiting to be unleashed, but it doesn't feel as volatile as it did last night. Maybe because I'm starting to accept it as part of me rather than fighting against it. Or maybe it's because I was sleeping, and once I fully wake up, all hell will break loose.

I guess we will find out shortly.

Rolling out of bed, glad of my warm pjs in the cold morning, I pad to the bathroom and yawn before setting about getting myself in order.

Once back in my bedroom, there is a knock on the door that makes me jump. The chaos magick surges in response to my startled state. Pink sparks dance across my skin before I can calm it. Frowning, I go to answer it, opening it a crack and glaring out, expecting Ramsey.

Instead, it's Cathy, looking pristine as always in another smart suit, this time a deep navy that makes her look even more intimidating than usual. "Good morning, Ivy. Ramsey let me in. I hope you don't mind the early hour. Sleep well?"

"Actually, yeah," I say, unclenching a bit, surprising myself with the truth of it. "I feel different. Like everything's sharper somehow, more real."

She nods as if this is exactly what she expected, moving into the room as I let her pass with that graceful efficiency I've always envied. "The chaos magick is settling into your system. Now that you've acknowledged it, it's becoming more integrated with your natural abilities. It's quite fascinating to watch, actually."

"So how come losing Mum and Dad didn't give this to me?" I blurt out and then chew my lip as I wait for the answer.

She sighs. "I'm not sure. I was waiting for it. But it

never came. Maybe grief isn't your trigger. Or even anger. Betrayal seems to be the ticket."

"I felt betrayed by them leaving me."

"Did you, though? I don't think you felt betrayed, Ivy. You were sad and angry, but not betrayed. Not really."

I lower my gaze, taking that in. I suppose she's right. In light of recent events, it makes sense.

She moves to the window and stares out over the campus. "Vex has left for MistHallow. He will return shortly."

"Okay. Do you think he will find anything?"

"Professor Blackthorn is a remarkable creature. If he doesn't have the answers, he will find them."

"That's nice to know. I wish we had the same here at Thornfield. Instead, we get insidious Professor Swann and a Headmaster whose name I don't even know, let alone see his face. Why is that?"

"Hmm, about Swann—"

"Oh, fuck off," I growl. "Are you telling me he is part of your organisation as well?"

"Hmm."

I roll my eyes. "What are you even called, anyway?" I huff and sit on my bed, pulling my feet up to rest on the edge and wrapping my arms around them.

"The Resistance."

"How original."

She snorts. "Like The Syndicate is so unique."

Well, okay, she has me there.

"Speaking of unique, besides a cosmic glitch, what

am I? Because right now, I feel like a walking Tesla coil."

She smiles, but it's tinged with sadness and something deeper, something that makes me think she knows more than she's telling. "You're something entirely new, Ivy. A being with the potential to become Death who rejected that destiny while still forming. The chaos magick is a result of that rejection. It's pure potential energy with no predetermined purpose. Think of it like a river that suddenly changes course. All that power has to go somewhere."

"So I can use it however I want?"

"In theory, yes. But it's dangerous. Without proper control, like I said yesterday, it could tear you apart from the inside out. Think of that river. If you try to contain it completely, it'll just find another way out, usually destructively."

I think about how easily I brought the guys to me last night, how natural it felt to tap into that power. It had been like breathing, like my body knew exactly what to do, even if my mind was still catching up. "It feels strange. I'm not sure how to explain it."

"I can imagine, but you need to act quickly, Ivy. Time is not on our side with this ultimatum. Death won't wait forever for you to make your choice. But first, let's see what you can do instinctively."

She moves to the centre of my room, gesturing for me to join her. "Close your eyes. Feel the power inside you. Don't try to direct it yet, just let it flow naturally."

I do as she says and focus inward. The chaos magick

responds immediately, surging through me like a tidal wave. Pink light fills the room, casting strange shadows on the walls.

"Good," Cathy murmurs. "Now, try to manifest something simple. A ball of light, perhaps."

I concentrate, trying to shape the wild energy into something contained. Instead, the entire room fills with floating orbs of pink light, each one pulsing with its own rhythm.

"Interesting," Cathy says. "Your power seems to want to expand rather than contract. Let's try something else. Think about protection."

The lights vanish instantly, replaced by a network of poisonous vines that crawl across the walls and ceiling, creating a natural fortress around us. The vines shimmer with that same pink energy, looking both beautiful and deadly.

"Oh!" I say, staring at them in awe. "Oh."

"What?" Cathy asks.

"The vines. I've shifted with them recently. My arms became the vines. My Professor said it was rare."

"Yes, I know. Josh told me."

"Of course," I mutter, but shake it off. "So, was that part of this magick?"

"Not necessarily. I think these," she gestures to the vines, "are an extension of your natural shifting ability, which includes what you described."

"So it takes what I have and makes it better?"

She nods. "I think so. Although, we have no case studies, so..." She shrugs. "But it appears that your natural shifter abilities are clearly influencing how the chaos magick manifests. The connection to plants, particularly defensive or poisonous ones, seems especially strong."

I wave my hand, and the vines recede, leaving no trace they were ever there. It feels natural, like breathing. "This is wild. But how do I make it do specific things? Last night, I accidentally brought Tate here when I was just thinking about the guys."

"That's actually a perfect example of how chaos magick works," Cathy says. "You had a clear intention, and the power found the most direct way to make that happen. The trick is learning to be more specific with your intentions while still allowing the magick to find its own path."

She demonstrates by holding out her hand. A small flame appears, dancing on her palm. "Normal magick is like this - contained, directed, purposeful. Chaos magick..." She waves her other hand, and the flame explodes into a swirling vortex of fire that fills the room before vanishing completely. "It's wild, unpredictable, but infinitely more powerful."

I stare at the space where the fire had been, my heart racing with excitement rather than fear. The chaos magick inside me responds to my enthusiasm, making the air crackle with electricity. "How do you know, though, when you have no reference?" I ask a question that suddenly seems important.

"It's a good question, and really, we are flying blind. That wasn't something we should admit, but you need to know. This is all guesswork based on what little we *do* know. All magick is about feeling the energy, letting it flow naturally while gently nudging it in the direction you want it to go. But think of this like riding a wave," she explains as I try to manifest the power again. "You don't control the ocean, but you can work with it, use its power to take you where you want to go."

I nod, focusing on the buzzing energy under my skin. Instead of trying to force it into shape, I let it rise naturally, feeling it swirl around me. Pink light fills the room as the chaos magick responds to my call.

"Good," Cathy murmurs. "Now, think of something you want to happen. Don't try to make it happen, just hold the intention in your mind."

I think about protection and keeping my guys safe from Death. The magick surges, stronger this time, and suddenly, the room is filled with thorny vines again, but these are different. They pulse with a toxic-looking pink glow, dripping with some kind of luminescent sap.

"Those look nasty."

Cathy nods approvingly, careful not to touch the vines. "Very. The magick appears to respond to your subconscious desires and natural affinities. Your connection to plants, particularly poisonous ones, is clearly strong. It's as if the power knows exactly what you are, both Ivy and Poison, merged into something new."

I wave my hand, and the vines recede like the last ones, leaving no trace they were ever there. But I can still feel them, like they're just beneath the surface of reality, waiting to be called forth again. "It's getting easier each time."

"That's good, but also potentially dangerous," Cathy warns. "The easier it becomes, the more tempting it will be to use it for everything. You need to learn restraint as well as control. Now, let's try something more challenging. I want you to—"

A knock at the door interrupts us. Ramsey pokes his head in, his face all healed up from my attack last night. His eyes widen at the pink energy still crackling around me. "Sorry to interrupt, but Josh thinks he's found something interesting in the old texts. Also, your hair is floating."

I quickly pat down my levitating locks and follow them down to the kitchen, where Josh has several ancient-looking books spread across the table. Josh's usually cheerful face is serious as he points to a particular passage.

"Where did you get this from?" I ask with a frown at the decidedly spooky-looking books.

"Your Dark Fae," he replies. "Seems this power may be tied to the ancient Fae somehow, as he had these in his family library."

"Which is?"

"In the Dark Fae Kingdom."

I press my lips together. "Where is he?"

"Catching some winks. Look, we can talk all you want about the hottie later, right now, this, please." He jabs the book emphatically.

"Yeah, sorry," I mutter. *Priorities.*

"It's an account of another Death candidate who rejected the position."

"Oh? Who? When? What happened to them?" *Not so unique after all, then. Boo.*

I lean in to examine the faded text, written in a language so archaic that it gives me a headache just looking at it.

"They became Death."

I blink as Cathy draws in a raspy breath.

Ramsey has his arms folded tightly as he stands beside Josh, his gaze on me.

"I see. So, there is no way out for me. I either die or become Death."

"Both," Josh says. "From what I can gather, and bear in mind the Fae talk in riddles, *when* you die, you become Death. You aren't the reject, Ivy. You are the chosen one."

My heart thumps at that. "But that makes no sense. Why would Death want to take my soul if he knows I become Death when I die?"

He shrugs. "Who knows?"

"Well, that's cheerful," I mutter, but internally, I'm filing this information away. "What if I fight it?"

"You will inevitably be torn apart by it."

"How long until that happens?"

"A few weeks-ish. It's hard to read, but what I do know is, according to this, their power grew exponentially in the days following their awakening. They became increasingly unstable until..."

"Until they went boom and became Death as we

know it? So what was Death, I mean the title, not the creature who became it, before?"

"Another good question. Current Death has been around for a while. Vex is at MistHallow looking for more information, but in the meantime, you need to step up. The texts suggest that the first week is crucial. Either you learn to work with the power, or it starts working against you."

"Are we going to assume that this creature was Fae then, if they have this information?"

"It's a solid theory."

"I have no Fae in me," I point out, hoping this matters.

"Except when you're fucking Bram," Ramsey pipes up with a grin at me, and then it fades when Cathy clears her throat and shoots him a menacing glare. I hide my smile, glad we are okay again.

Josh sidesteps neatly. "I don't think species matters. Or maybe it does. Again, who knows? We need Vex."

"Ugh, don't ever say that out loud to him. His ego is already monumental."

"What's the plan with regard to the ultimatum?" Cathy asks, watching me carefully.

"I'm going to play his game, but by my rules. He's going to learn that poison can be just as deadly to Death as it is to everyone else."

"That's all very dramatic," Josh says dryly, "but what does it actually mean in practical terms?"

"It means I need to figure out Death's weaknesses

and what his end game is, and it means I need to find a way to protect my guys while doing it."

"And how exactly do you plan to do all that?" Ramsey asks.

"By finding out what he wants. Until we do that, all of this is pointless."

"Well," Cathy says after a moment, "I think that's enough theory for now. We need to keep up with practice until we have some definitive answers."

Death might think he has me cornered, but he's about to learn what happens when you back a poisonous vine into a corner.

It grows.

It spreads.

And eventually, it kills everything in its path.

The question is, can I accept the fate I've been handed and shoved neatly under the mental mat for now?

9

IVY

"Focus on the energy, but don't try to contain it," Cathy instructs as I attempt to manifest my chaos magick in a controlled way.

We're in the back garden, which seems safer than practising indoors. The morning sun is warm on my skin, but there's a distinct chill in the air that makes me grateful for the oversized jumper I'm wearing.

"I am focusing," I mutter, trying to direct the wild energy coursing through my veins. The pink aura around me pulses erratically, responding to my frustration.

"No, you're trying to control it," Cathy sighs. "Remember what we discussed. You need to guide it, not force it."

That's all very well, but she's not the one with enough unstable power to accidentally reshape reality. Last night's accidental summoning of Tate was just the beginning - this morning, I've already turned my coffee into a swirling vortex of liquid stars and made all the plants in the garden start singing.

"Maybe we should try something simpler," Ramsey suggests from his safe position by the back door. "Like levitation?"

Taking a deep breath, I try to calm my racing thoughts. The chaos magick responds to my emotions, I've learned that much. When I'm angry, it manifests as those toxic vines. When I'm scared, it creates defensive barriers. When I think of my guys, they appear. Well, they did yesterday. Today is a different ballgame. But trying to make it do specific things when I'm not feeling strong emotions is like trying to herd wet, angry cats. Very explosive, reality-bending, wet, angry cats.

"Okay," I say, closing my eyes. "Let's try this again."

I focus on the feeling of the magick flowing through me, trying not to direct it so much as suggest what I want. Just a simple manifestation of light, that's all. Nothing complicated.

The power surges, and I hear Cathy gasp. Opening my eyes, I see why - instead of a simple ball of light, I've created a miniature aurora borealis that's dancing across the garden. Pink and green lights swirl through the air, beautiful but definitely not what I was aiming for.

"Well," Josh says brightly, "at least it's pretty."

I wave my hand, trying to dispel the lights, but instead, they intensify, spreading up into the sky. "Um, that's not good."

"Ivy," Cathy says carefully, "perhaps we should take a break."

"No, I can fix this." I concentrate harder, trying to pull the power back, but it's like trying to grab smoke with my bare hands. The more I try to control it, the more it slips away from me.

The aurora starts spinning faster, the colours deepening to a rich purple. The air crackles with energy, making my hair stand on end. This is bad. This is very bad.

"Ivy," Ramsey warns, taking a step forward. "Your eyes are glowing."

Before I can respond, the power swells again, stronger this time. A wave of magick explodes outward, and suddenly, the garden is full of people. Tate, Torin, and Bram appear first, looking confused and slightly dishevelled. Then Vex materialises, mid-conversation with someone I don't recognise. More figures pop into existence - students from Thornfield, random people from town, even a few creatures I'm pretty sure aren't from this realm.

"Fuck," I whisper as the magick continues to spiral out of control. The aurora above us has become a swirling vortex of energy, pulling at reality itself. Objects start appearing and disappearing randomly. Trees turn into fountains, the grass becomes crystal, the garden fence transforms into a wall of living shadows.

"What the hell?" Torin demands, ducking as a flock of what appear to be phoenix-like birds burst into existence above his head.

"Ivy!" Tate shouts, trying to reach me through the chaos. "You need to stop!"

"I can't!" The power is too strong, too wild. It feeds on my panic, growing stronger with each passing second. The vortex above us grows larger, threatening to tear open the sky.

Bram attempts to use his Dark Fae magick to contain the chaos, but it simply absorbs his power, adding it to the maelstrom. More people keep appearing. Professor Swann materialises briefly before vanishing again, replaced by a group of confused-looking merpeople flopping around on the crystalline grass.

"Focus, Ivy!" Cathy shouts over the growing wind. "Don't fight it. Work with it!"

Easy for her to say when reality isn't unravelling around us. I can feel the power building to a critical point, like a dam about to burst. If I don't do something soon...

A warm hand grabs mine, and I look up to see Tate beside me. Despite the chaos, he managed to reach me. His touch grounds me, the fated bond between us humming with energy, lighting up the marking on my back in a white-hot flare that makes me gasp and crashes me back to earth.

"Let me help."

I nod, grateful for his presence. He laces our fingers together, and his magick flows into me through our connection, not trying to control my chaos but working with it, supporting it. The other guys seem to understand what's happening. Torin and Bram move closer, adding their power to the mix.

My magick responds to their energy, and the wild surges begin to stabilise. Slowly, carefully, I guide the power back, not fighting it but encouraging it to settle. The vortex above us shrinks, the random manifestations slowing.

"That's it," Tate murmurs. "You've got this."

With one final push, I pull the magick back into myself. The vortex collapses, the aurora fades, and reality snaps back into place. The summoned creatures vanish, returning to wherever they came from. The garden returns to normal, though the grass remains slightly sparkly.

I slump against Tate, exhausted. "Fuck."

"Actually," Cathy says, surveying the aftermath, "that was quite impressive."

I stare at her in disbelief. "Impressive? I nearly tore a hole in reality!"

"Yes, but you also managed to fix it. With help," she adds, nodding to the guys, "but still. You're learning."

"Learning to what? Accidentally summon half of Thornfield and turn the garden into a light show?"

"Learning to work with your power rather than against it," she explains. "When you stopped trying to control it and accepted help instead, the magick responded positively."

I look around at the others. Ramsey and Josh are checking the garden for any lingering effects, while Torin, Bram and Tate haven't let go of my hands yet.

"That was terrifying," I admit quietly.

"But educational," Tate says, squeezing my hand. "We learned that your power responds well to our energy. That could be useful."

"We also learned that I can accidentally summon people across vast distances and potentially reshape reality when I lose control. That's less useful and more terrifying."

"It's all part of learning," Cathy insists. "Though perhaps we should take a break before trying anything else."

I nod weakly, still leaning on Tate for support. The magick has settled somewhat, but I can feel it buzzing under my skin, ready for action.

"Next time," Ramsey says, picking up what appears to be a crystallised flower, "maybe we should practise somewhere more remote."

"Agreed," Cathy says with a nod.

I close my eyes, feeling the lingering energy in the air. This power is more dangerous than I realised, but also more connected to the guys than I expected. Maybe that's the key - not trying to handle it alone but working together.

"Come on," Tate says softly. "Let's get you inside before you accidentally summon a Dragon or something."

"Don't even joke about that," I mutter, but allow him to lead me towards the house.

As we reach the door, I glance back at the garden. Despite returning mostly to normal, there's still a faint pink glow in the air, like an echo of what happened. A reminder that my power, while beautiful, is also potentially catastrophic.

I need to learn to control it better and fast. Because next time, we might not be so lucky.

10

TATE

Impressive isn't quite the word I'd use for what we just witnessed and what we were drawn into. Terrifying, maybe. Awe-inspiring, definitely. The raw power Ivy possesses is beyond anything I've ever encountered, and as one of the most powerful warlocks in the realm, supposedly, that's saying something.

"That was fucking intense," Torin mutters, joining us. His clothes are slightly damp from helping the merpeople. "We need to talk about this."

I shoot him a warning look. Now isn't the time for one of his lectures about control and responsibility. Ivy needs rest and support, not criticism.

"Later," I say firmly.

Once we get her settled on the sofa with a cup of tea, I join Torin and Bram in the kitchen, dried off with magick and looking around for something decidedly stronger than tea.

"This is bad," Torin says without preamble. He

looks pale from being out in direct sun and under that light show. It will have weakened him probably more than he is letting on. "That kind of power is not natural."

"Nothing about this situation is natural," I point out. "She's literally a cosmic glitch."

"A cosmic glitch who can tear holes in reality," Bram adds. "Did you feel how easily she absorbed my magick? It was like throwing a match into a bonfire."

I run a hand through my still-wet hair, frustrated. "What's your point? We can't exactly put the genie back in the bottle. The power's part of her now."

"The point is," Torin says, lowering his voice, "we need to figure out how to help her control it before she accidentally reshapes reality or summons something we can't handle."

"You saw what happened out there," I argue. "When we worked together, supported her instead of trying to contain her power, it responded to us, through her."

"Yeah, this time," Bram mutters. "But what about next time? What if we're not there to help?"

The thought sends a chill down my spine. As much as I hate to admit it, he has a point. "Then we make sure we are there. All of us."

"And Death?" Torin asks. "What happens when he finds out just how powerful she's become? You think he's going to let someone with that kind of power just walk around freely?"

"He already knows," a voice says from the doorway.

We turn to see Cathy standing there, her expression grim. "Why do you think he's so desperate to either control her or take her soul? This power is beyond anything even he could've expected."

"What do you mean?" I demand.

Cathy sighs, moving further into the kitchen. "We have learned from the texts Bram gave Josh that Death was once like Ivy. He rejected the power, but instead of making him safe from it, it chose him. The same is said for Ivy. Now, I believe that Death didn't get this far. He failed before he could. Ivy is remarkable. She is something truly unique. She's not just channelling chaos - she's becoming chaos incarnate."

"So you're saying that Ivy has been chosen to become Death?" I venture.

"Yes."

"And that she is chaos? Chaotic Death on the loose?"

"Potentially."

The implications of that statement hang heavy in the air. I think about how natural it felt when our magick combined, how right it seemed. "Is that why our power helps stabilise hers? Because we're her anchors somehow?"

"Possibly," Cathy nods. "Your connection to her seems to help her focus on the chaos rather than being consumed by it."

"So what do we do?" Bram asks.

"We can never leave her alone," I mutter.

"But what if we aren't enough?" Torin's voice is

quiet but intense. "What if she loses control again, and we can't help her?"

I meet his gaze steadily. "Then we deal with that if it happens. But I won't give up on her. I can't."

The fated mark on my chest flares hot in agreement. My connection to Ivy goes beyond logic or reason - it's soul-deep, unshakeable.

"None of us will," Bram says after a moment. "This is a lot, but it makes no difference to how we feel about her."

Torin nods slowly. "Fine. But we need a better plan than just hoping for the best. We need to understand this power better."

"Vex reckons he can help with that," I grudgingly admit. "If he finds anything useful at MistHallow, then all good."

"Speaking of Vex," Bram states, eyes narrowed. "What is your beef with him?"

"He's a dick," I snap.

"Yeah, I'm not buying that. There's more to this than you're saying."

Gritting my teeth, I glare at him, pushing aside the hatred I have for that man. "I have no idea what you are talking about."

"Yeah, sure," he mutters and sighs, irritated by my evasiveness.

"Never mind that," Torin snaps. "What about Ivy becoming Death. What the hell does that mean? She has to go around collecting souls? Does she lose her life as she knows it? What about us?"

Cathy shrugs. "All of this is unchartered territory. We don't know anything apart from what was in Bram's family's books and what we knew from our own limited research."

"Talking about me?" Ivy asks, coming into the kitchen, making me realise we've left her alone for too long.

"Just getting up to speed," I say with a smile.

She doesn't return it. She is not in the mood to be swayed by charm by the looks of it.

Ivy's eyes narrow as she looks between us. "Don't give me that. I know you're talking about what just happened and what it means. So spill it."

I exchange glances with the others, unsure how much to reveal. Cathy steps in smoothly.

"We were discussing the nature of your powers and how we might help you control them better," she says. It's not a lie, but it's not the whole truth either.

Ivy's not buying it. "That's not all of it."

"We're worried," Torin admits. "That kind of power is dangerous, Ivy. For you and everyone around you."

Her face hardens. "You think I don't know that? You think I'm not terrified of what I might do if I lose control again?"

"That's not what he meant," I say quickly, moving towards her. But she takes a step back, her eyes flashing with hurt and anger.

"Isn't it? Because it sounds like you're all scared of me. Like you think I'm some kind of monster that needs to be contained."

"No one thinks that," Bram says firmly. "We're just trying to figure out how to help you."

Tears well up in her eyes, and I gather her to me, wrapping my arms tightly around her. "Ivy, we are here to help you however you want us to. Just tell us what you need, and we will deliver."

She sniffles into my chest, and then a phone on the counter vibrates harshly, cutting through the silence.

11

IVY

RAMSEY'S PHONE RATTLES ON THE COUNTER, MAKING everyone in the room freeze.

He swoops in and snatches it up, checking it with a frown. He looks up at me with a grim stare.

"An assignment?" I ask, arching my eyebrow.

"Yeah."

"And I'm just supposed to accept it and go on my merry way to delivering a soul to Death that might be a rig of the system?"

"You don't really have a choice," he says quietly.

He's right. I know he is. Ignoring The Syndicate isn't an option. "What does it say?"

He turns it around to show me.

TARGET: David Beech

LOCATION: Thornfield Cemetery

TIME: Midnight

I frown at it. "No species or any other information? How the fuck am I supposed to know how to kill him?"

"This is unusual; I'll give you that," Ramsey mutters. "Let me call through and see if I can find out."

He dials and presses the phone to his ear as he disappears from the kitchen.

Ramsey returns a few minutes later, his expression even more troubled. "Something's not right. The Syndicate has no additional information. None. It's like this target just appeared in the system."

"What? That makes no sense. Every target has a file, a history, a reason for being marked." The magick stirs beneath my skin, responding to my unease. Pink energy crackles along my fingers. "Could someone have hacked the system?"

"Only Death has that kind of access," Ramsey says quietly.

We all let that sink in. The implications are clear - this isn't just an assignment, it's a deliberate move in whatever game Death is playing.

"This could be a test," Tate says.

"That's exactly what it is. He's testing how I'll handle an impossible assignment."

"The question is," Bram says from his position by the window, "what's he really looking for?"

I look down at my hands. Since the incident this morning, my power has felt different. It is more integrated, less likely to explode, but also more profound somehow, like it's waiting for something.

"There's only one way to find out," I say finally. "I have to go."

"Not alone," Tate says immediately.

"He wants to see what we'll do," I murmur. "All of us."

"Then let's give him exactly what he wants," Torin says. "I'm done being this arsehole's puppet."

"Agreed," I growl and march off upstairs to my bedroom, slamming the door behind me while I try to figure out what this shit is all about. I open the box of weapons and stare at them, deciding what the hell I'm supposed to take with me on this assignment.

As midnight approaches, I'm no closer to trying to figure out what Death wants from this charade. I stand in front of my mirror, having shifted to Poison to play this game.

"Ready?" Tate asks from the doorway.

I turn to face him, noting how his eyes track the pink energy that flows around me. "As I'll ever be."

We set off on foot, as it's not too far away that we need to drive. The moon hangs full in the sky, which makes the creepy vibes I'm getting so much worse. The cemetery at midnight is exactly as ominous as you'd expect. Moonlight casts long shadows between the headstones, and a light mist curls around my ankles as I walk the familiar paths. Alone, but not. The guys are watching me from strategic points. Tate in the old church tower, Torin among the ancient oak trees, and Bram in the shadows of the mausoleum. Their presence is a comfort, even if I can't see them.

The cemetery appears empty, but my senses tell me differently. There's a disturbance in the air, a ripple in reality that sends skitters across my skin.

"Miss Hammond," Death's voice echoes from everywhere, making me jump. The mist thickens ominously.

He materialises in front of me, his skeletal face grinning wider than usual. "Ah, chaos incarnate. You've exceeded all expectations."

"Hello, David Beech," I say.

He chuckles and moves closer, unaffected by the toxic vines that instinctively spring up around me. "He was rather like you, Miss Hammond. Someone who defied their intended path. It didn't end well for him."

"Is that supposed to be a warning?"

His laugh is like bones rattling. "More like a preview. Unless..."

The air shifts, and suddenly, the cemetery is full of shadow creatures, more solid than the ones I encountered in Death's realm. They move among the graves, not attacking but definitely threatening.

"Unless what?" I demand, calling more power to me. The pink energy swirls faster, mixing with the mist to create a storm of chaos and magick around us.

"Unless you learn to truly embrace what you are." Death waves a hand, and reality ripples. "Show me, little chaos bearer. Show me what you can really do."

The shadow creatures surge forward, not to attack me directly, but to cut off any escape route. I feel the guys tensing in their positions, ready to intervene, but something tells me that's exactly what Death wants.

"I already know what I can do," I say, letting the chaos magick flow freely. Pink energy fills the cemetery, and reality begins to bend around us. "The question is, can you stop me?"

The ground beneath us transforms, toxic vines weaving patterns that pulse with chaotic energy. The shadows try to cross them but recoil, hissing. Interesting.

"Fascinating," Death murmurs, watching as my power continues to spread. "You're learning to shape reality quickly. But can you maintain control when everything falls apart?"

He raises his skeletal hand, and the shadow creatures suddenly multiply, hundreds of them filling the cemetery. They start tearing at the fabric of reality, creating rips in the air through which I glimpse other realms, other possibilities.

Pink energy explodes outward in a wave that freezes everything - the shadows, the tears in reality, even the mist. Time seems to stop, caught in my power.

The guys materialise beside me, drawn by the magick. Their own power adds to mine, supporting it and letting their energy merge with the chaos.

The pink energy pulses, and the shadow creatures dissolve into nothing. The tears in reality seal themselves, leaving only a faint pink aurora dancing in the air.

Death stands perfectly still, watching this display with what looks like satisfaction. "Very good. You've learned the most important lesson already - chaos isn't meant to be controlled, only guided."

"Why this test?" I demand, maintaining my hold on the magick. It hums through me, ready to unleash at a moment's notice. "Why create a fake assignment?"

"To see what you would do, of course. To understand how your power has evolved." He moves closer, unaffected by the toxic vines that snap at him. "You were meant to be my successor, but instead, you've become something else entirely. Something new."

"Sorry to mess up your plans," I say, not sorry at all.

He laughs again. "Oh, but you haven't. Not really. You've just complicated them. In the most delightful way." His empty eye sockets fix on the guys. "Your connection to these three is most fascinating. The way your magick interacts with their power is informative."

"What do you really want?" Tate demands, black sparks flying from his fingertips.

"Want? I want to see how this plays out." Death spreads his skeletal hands. "Chaos is change, and change is coming. The question is, will you be its harbinger or its victim?"

Before any of us can react, he vanishes, taking the oppressive atmosphere with him. The cemetery returns to normal, though my toxic vines remain, glowing softly in the moonlight.

"Well," Bram says after a moment, "that was anticlimactic."

"He's playing a longer game than we thought,"

Torin observes. "This wasn't just about testing your powers."

"No," I agree, watching the pink energy still dancing through the air. "He wanted to see how we work together. How the chaos magick responds to your presence."

"And?" Tate prompts.

I look at my hands, where pink energy still flows like liquid starlight. "And I think he got exactly what he wanted. He knows now that I'm stronger with you, that the chaos magick responds differently when we're together."

"Is that a bad thing?" Bram asks.

"I don't know." I meet their gazes one by one. "But I think we just showed our hand, and Death is definitely playing cards I can't see yet."

I'm pretty sure he has changed his mind about me killing the guys now. He can see it would be disadvantageous to whatever end game he has.

But the question is, what does Death plan to do with this knowledge?

What are we going to do about it?

This is just the beginning of something much bigger than any of us realise, but we need to get up to speed and fucking fast before Death comes for us all.

12

TORIN

The cemetery's sacred ground still crackles with residual magick. Pink energy dances through the mist like the aurora borealis. Watching Ivy wield such power, I'm beginning to understand why I'm instinctively drawn to her. I grew up with law and order. It flew in the face of my vampire nature, which just wanted to rebel every chance it could. But for that, there were severe punishments from dear old Mum. Dad was more 'don't give a fuck' than she was. Now that I'm out from under their thumbs, almost, and free to do whatever the fuck I want, *that* side of me which wants to kick up chaos and see where the cards fall, has sought out this creature that can bring on the destruction. It's not that I haven't fallen for Ivy. I have. In a big way. But before I knew who she was, what she was, when I knew her only as Poison, it was instinct.

"Yeah, anticlimactic," I murmur, but I'm not convinced. Something went down here; we just aren't privy to it. Yet. We will be once we can figure out what the fuck is actually going on here. I feel like I'm missing something I should know, but trying to put my finger on it is like trying to pin down a single beam in a laser light show.

My phone buzzes in my pocket. With a frown, I pull it out and glare at it. The screen displays my mother's name. Of course she'd call now. The timing is too perfect to be coincidental.

"I need to handle something," I tell the others, moving away from them. Ivy watches me go, still in the guise of Poison. I can't deny the pull. I want to slam her to the ground, rip her clothes off and impale her on my cock until there is nothing left inside me to dump in her pussy.

I answer once I'm out of earshot. "What?"

"Well, that's rude."

"Who cares? What do you want?"

I get a sick satisfaction in talking to her this way and hearing her huff and flounder. She isn't used to it, but there is nothing she can do to me anymore. I'm done.

"I trust the entertainment at the cemetery has concluded?" Her voice is arctic, carrying that edge of superiority that always sets my teeth on edge.

"You knew about this."

"I know everything about where you are and what you do," she says.

Narrowing my eyes, I pull the phone away from my ear. That bitch.

Her tone sharpens. "But forget about that. It's time

you remembered where you came from. The Coven is meeting in a few days. I expect you to be there, ready to take your place as your father's heir."

I grip the phone tighter. "No."

"I beg your pardon?"

"I said no." The words feel like breaking chains. "I'm done being your pawn, Mother. Find someone else to manipulate."

"Don't be ridiculous. You are my son. Everything I've done has been to secure your future."

"No," I correct her, "everything you've done has been to secure your power. But I'm done with you, the Coven, and this family name."

"You ungrateful little—" Her voice cuts off abruptly. When she speaks again, her tone is dangerously calm, which I've come to learn is never a good sign. "You will regret this, Torin. The Coven doesn't take kindly to deserters."

"Threaten me all you want," I say, feeling strangely liberated. "I'm not coming back."

"This is about that chaos witch, isn't it?" she hisses. "You think I don't know what's going on? She'll destroy you, Torin. She'll destroy everything."

I glance back at Ivy, still glowing with pink energy. "Maybe. But at least it'll be my choice."

I hang up before she can respond, knowing full well this isn't the end of it. But I don't care. Things have shifted, and it's about time my mother realised that.

Chaos witch.

The words echo in my mind. Witch. Not bitch.

Witch. My mother doesn't usually mince words, so did she mean witch in the sense of species and not as a slur? I look over at Ivy again. It makes sense. Witches are naturals at magick. It's who they are; it's their raison d'être. The rest of us learn. It's something we have, but it doesn't define us. Witches and warlocks, though? That's different. My gaze shifts between Ivy and Tate, and the Death Tetris starts to slot pieces together with my hand. I knew I wasn't seeing anything, but this isn't everything.

It's something, though.

And that bitch mother of mine is the cause. Of course she is. She made sure she would be. She knows how my brain works. "Fucking cunt," I mutter and return to the others.

They are deep in discussion about Death's motives. Ivy looks up as I approach, her eyes narrowing slightly.

"Everything okay?" she asks.

I nod, not quite ready to share the details of this yet. I need more facts. "The usual of my mother being a total and utter bitch. What did I miss?" I throw the phone on the floor and stamp on it, smashing it with my vampire strength.

Ivy stares at it and licks her lips. "Sure you're okay?" she asks, taking my hand and lacing our fingers together.

The simple act makes me feel like a god. I can't explain it, and I'm not even sure I want to. I nod once, and she accepts that I don't want to talk about it.

"We were just discussing our next move," Tate says.

"Death clearly has a plan, but we're still in the dark about what it is."

"We need more information," Bram says, running a hand through his dark hair. "About Death, about chaos magick, about everything."

"Vex might have found something useful at Mist-Hallow," Tate grudgingly admits. "He should be back soon."

Ivy nods. "Let's head off and regroup. To be honest, I think flying blind into situations right now is a bad idea. We need to hold fire and wait for Vex to see if he has anything useful. If not, then we—"

"Are screwed?" I ask with a smirk.

She giggles. "Yeah, but I was going to say, then we go in all guns blazing and figure shit out later."

"A woman after my own heart," I murmur, pulling her closer.

She brushes her lips over mine with a slow smile before she turns and stalks off, leaving us to follow.

13

TATE

After Ivy wanted to be alone to think, me and the other guys returned to our house across campus. Torin and Bram have disappeared, leaving me to mope in the kitchen with a glass of whiskey, strong enough to knock your head off. But it's needed. Something isn't adding up here. We are missing something vital about who Ivy is. I just can't figure it out because I can't clear my head enough to do it. Not that the booze will help. If anything, it will make it worse.

A sharp rap on the back door has me looking up from the swirl of amber liquid sloshing around the glass as I rotate it.

Crossing over to it, I glare at the arsehole on the other side. "You."

Vex smirks and holds up a book that has seen better centuries and crackles with dark magick.

"You're going to bring that into my house?" I ask, gesturing to it with the glass.

"Only if you want to know what I know."

That makes me step aside with a grimace. No way am I letting him have information about Ivy that I don't. "I'll get everyone."

"No. Just you."

Frowning, I sit at one end of the kitchen table, and he takes the other side.

The grimoire he retrieved from MistHallow sits between us, its ancient pages humming with dark energy. It sets my teeth on edge.

Storm clouds gather outside, matching my mood. The soft patter of rain against windows fills the heavy silence between us.

"You need to read it," Vex says eventually, his usual smug expression absent. "Found something interesting while researching the chaos magick."

"And you had to show me alone? Could've just sent a text." I swirl the amber liquid in my glass again, watching the light catch it.

He shifts uncomfortably in his chair, a warning sign that whatever this book holds, I'm not going to like it. "Not about this."

Lightning flashes outside, illuminating the kitchen. The grimoire shifts in response, dark energy rippling across its surface.

"Your mother's name was Sarah Well," Vex states, sitting back. His words drop into the quiet kitchen like stones into still water. "Before she married your father."

I freeze, glass halfway to my lips. The whiskey

catches the lamplight, gleaming like amber. "I'm aware. What of it?"

"Because my mother's maiden name was Well too." He opens the grimoire to a family tree, aged parchment crackling beneath his fingers. Pointing to two branches that split decades ago, he continues, "They were sisters."

The whiskey burns as I knock it back. Rain drums steadily against the windows, nature's percussion to this twisted family reunion. "We're cousins?"

He shakes his head. "No. Worse."

"Worse?" I feel a dread spike in my blood. What could be worse than being his cousin? *Oh, you just had to ask, didn't you?*

Vex chuckles. "Your dad fucked my mum."

"Oh, for the love of all things unholy," I mutter, resisting the urge to throw up. "Are you fucking kidding me?"

"Wish I was. Explains why we hated each other on sight at university, *bro*." His laugh is bitter, echoing in the small space between us.

"Fuck, right off," I growl. "I'm not buying that for a second."

Thunder rolls outside as I think back to that first day at Thornfield three years ago, the instant clash of power between us. How it had felt familiar somehow, even as we tried to blast each other across the courtyard.

"Why tell me now?" I ask, studying the family tree's intricate lines, despite my unwillingness to accept this travesty. Names and dates spread across the parchment like a web, connecting people long dead to the two of us sitting in my rain-dark kitchen.

"Because I'm leaving." He closes the grimoire carefully, ancient leather creaking. "Got a job offer at Mist-Hallow. I can't refuse it, and to be quite honest, when Death finds out I've betrayed him, my nuts will be on the chopping block. I don't exactly trust you all to save my arse when the time comes, yeah?"

I study him - my rival, my half-brother, this person I've spent three years hating for reasons I never fully understood. The resemblance is there, now that I know to look for it. Something in the set of his jaw, the angle of his cheekbones. "This doesn't change fuck all."

"No. We are not suddenly going to be best friends just because we are family."

"Too fucking right." I think of Torin, who became more family to me than any blood relation ever could. Of that rainy night in an alley that changed everything. "Family's what you make of it anyway."

Vex nods, understanding passing between us like lightning. "That's not all this book has. You'll find it an interesting read. It has information about chaos magick that might help with everything." He stands.

"Try not to be such a dick at MistHallow," I say, but there's no real heat in it. It's strange how one revelation can drain away years of antagonism.

He chuckles, and then he's gone, leaving me with a grimoire full of secrets and a family connection I never expected. Rain continues to fall outside, washing away the old as something new takes its place.

I pour another whiskey and pull the grimoire closer, thinking of Ivy, of chaos magick and bloodlines and the family you choose versus the family you're born to, of power that recognises power, and connections that run deeper than blood.

Lightning flashes again, illuminating the family tree's intricate branches. Sometimes, the past surprises you. Sometimes, it explains things you never understood about yourself, and sometimes, knowing where you came from helps you figure out where you're going.

Time to see what other secrets this book holds.

The grimoire's pages are brittle beneath my fingers as I read. The first few pages detail the Well family history and about how our bloodline traces back to the first convergence of magick in Britain.

It's interesting, and I will definitely read more, but this isn't about me. It's about Ivy and what we can learn to help her. So, I search for the chapter on chaos magick. Detailed diagrams show how natural energy flows through ley lines and how certain bloodlines act as conduits for different types of power. The Wells, it seems, were known for their ability to channel and direct raw magick - exactly what Ivy's struggling with now.

A hastily scrawled note in the margin catches my attention: "Chaos requires anchor. Blood calls to blood. Balance must be maintained."

I turn another page, and a sketch makes me pause. It shows a warlock standing between two forces - Chaos and order - acting as a channel between them. The pieces are starting to fit together in ways I never expected.

The text swims on the page, ancient ink shifting as if alive. A whole section details how chaos magick seeks out natural conduits - bloodlines that can withstand its raw power without burning up.

"The Well line serves as the foundation stone," one passage reads. "Where Chaos flows unchecked, our blood remembers. We do not control; we channel. We do not command; we guide. This is our gift and our burden."

My hands tingle as I read, my Blackwell magick responding to the words.

Another page shows detailed notes about what happens when chaos magick meets an anchoring blood-line. The diagram is like a sketch of what happens between Ivy and me - her wild power meeting my more structured magick, the way they sync instead of clash.

"The anchor must be willing," I read aloud. "The connection cannot be forced. Trust flows both ways, or the channel breaks."

Lightning crashes outside as I turn to a chapter titled 'The Price of Power.' The words are darker here, written in what looks suspiciously like blood:

'The Price of Power' bleeds across the page in dark crimson ink. The storm outside seems to pause as if holding its breath.

"To channel Chaos is to court destruction. The anchor bears not only the weight of power but also its consequences. Each time chaos flows through willing blood, it leaves its mark. These marks accumulate like scars upon the soul. Few bloodlines can withstand repeated exposure. Those that do emerge changed. The Well line carries this burden through generations, but even we are not immune to its effects." *That doesn't sound good.*

The grimoire's pages rustle on their own and stop at a diagram that shows how repeated exposure to Chaos magick can alter a person's essence over time. It's not just about power - it's about fundamental change on a cellular level.

"The anchor becomes both conduit and container," I read aloud. "In times of great need, they may call upon the stored chaos, but at great personal cost."

My mind races, thinking of how Ivy's power stabilises when we're together. Am I unknowingly acting as her anchor?

If this is true, then every time I help Ivy control her power, I'm taking on part of that chaotic energy and changing myself in ways I don't fully understand.

Lightning flashes again, and for a moment, I swear I see pink energy crackling along my fingertips. But when I blink, it's gone. *Must be the booze.*

The final pages of the chapter are ominous:

"As Chaos grows, so too must the anchor. But beware - there is a tipping point. A moment when the scales tip irrevocably towards destruction. When that time comes, only sacrifice can restore balance."

As I close the grimoire, the words hang heavy in the

air, my mind reeling. Lightning flashes again before thunder crashes overhead.

Sacrifice. The word echoes in my head, filling me with dread. What kind of sacrifice? Who would have to make it? Ivy? Me? Someone else?

I think of the raw power that flows through Ivy and how natural it feels when our magick intertwines.

I pour another glass of whiskey, needing something to steady my nerves. The alcohol burns going down, but it does little to calm the storm of thoughts in my head.

How do I explain this to Ivy, and to everyone, that our connection might be more than just attraction or fate, but a cosmic balancing act with dire consequences?

I don't have any answers. Not yet, anyway.

14

BRAM

SOMETHING'S SHIFTED IN THE MAGICKAL ATMOSPHERE tonight.

But it's not that which draws me to pause in the rain. It's the echo of Ivy's chaos magick, still lingering in the air from earlier. There's something about her energy that calls to my true nature, something I've been trying to understand ever since I first tasted it. Wild raspberries.

I move down the rain-slicked street as the shadows bend around me. The Court would be appalled at the carelessness which I have shown lately, but then, they've always been appalled by my choices.

Ivy's house is just ahead, lights still on despite the late hour. I can feel this new magick in the air, but beneath it, there's something else. Something older. Something wild that responds to my presence in a way that magick from this realm never does. My steps slow as I near her home. I can see her staring out of her bedroom window at the top of the house, a soft glow of light behind her. She is still in Poison's guise. I stop to look at her, knowing she doesn't know I'm here.

The rain around me starts falling upward, just slightly, responding to my distracted state. I quickly restore my control, but not before Ivy glances down as if her gaze was drawn to me. Our eyes meet through the darkness, and for a moment, her chaos magick reaches out, tangling with the ancient power in my blood like it's found something familiar.

What does this mean? That she is part Fae? Or is it the magick that is Fae? That would make more sense. I seem to have been the only one to hear about this kind of magick and have text on it. The Ancient Fae were a strange bunch. They weren't divided as we are now, but one group that went their separate ways several centuries ago.

Lightning flashes and thunder rumbles but still we stare at each other, neither of us moving.

My power feels unsettled tonight, responding to her proximity.

Drawing my attention away from her, I see Tate appear at the end of the street, a book tucked under his arm. He spots me immediately.

"Lurking?" he asks.

"Always. What's that?"

"Vex's offerings."

I raise an eyebrow. "Oh? Care to share?"

He gestures with his head towards Ivy's house. "Do you know where Torin is?"

I shake my head and follow him up Ivy's garden path. She opens the door before he can knock, Torin is standing behind her.

"Hey guys," she says. "Come in."

We enter, dripping wet, but a bit of magick sorts that out quickly.

"Come upstairs," she murmurs and takes them two at a time as we follow.

Once inside her room, I feel the atmosphere shift to something more seductive.

"I need to not think for a while. Can you help me?" she murmurs, stripping off her clothes and standing naked before us. She shifts back to Ivy, and it sends a pang of longing straight to my cock. In a flash, I'm in front of her, slamming her up against the wall. "Shift back," I murmur. "I want this to be rough, hard, painful. I want to fuck you until you beg me to stop. I want to see tears in those blue eyes, Poison."

She gasps, but the scent of her arousal hits my nose, and she does as I ask.

My hand closes around her throat, and I lean in to whisper, "You want to forget? You won't even remember your name after I'm done with you, little whore."

I tighten my grip on Poison's throat, feeling her pulse race beneath my fingers. Her eyes are wide, pupils dilated with her arousal. Good. That's exactly what I want to see.

"On your knees," I growl, releasing her and shoving

her down. She goes willingly, her pink hair falling across her face as she looks up at me.

I glance at Tate and Torin. "You two can join or watch. Your choice."

Torin moves forward first, his fangs already extended. "I think I'll take her mouth," he says, unzipping his pants.

Tate hesitates for a moment before setting the book aside and moving closer.

I grab a fistful of Poison's hair, yanking her head back. "You wanted to forget? Then let's see how well you can focus when you're being used like the little slut you are."

She moans as Torin shoves his cock into her mouth, not giving her time to adjust.

I reach down to grab one of her wrists and then behind her to reach for the other. Pulling her arms right behind her, I give up her control for her as Torin fucks her face roughly.

I twist her arms behind her back, pinning them there with one hand while I undo my belt with the other. Poison gags as Torin thrusts deeper.

"What's the matter, little whore? Can't take it?" I taunt, running the leather of my belt across her exposed back. She shivers but doesn't pull away.

Releasing her wrists, I wrap the belt around her neck and pull it tight, hearing her gag again. I hold on tight as Torin pulls out of her mouth, his cock bouncing and wet. Pulling on the belt, I get Poison to her feet and lead her to the bed. I bend her over, watching her hands clench tightly in the covers. She knows she is going to be destroyed. Unzipping my pants, I grip my cock with my free hand as Tate crawls onto the bed, naked and cock ready for her mouth.

With one brutal thrust, I bury myself inside her tight, wet cunt. She cries out, the sound muffled as Tate shoves his cock down her throat.

"That's it," I growl, setting a punishing pace. "Take it like the greedy slut you are."

Poison's body shakes with each thrust, her muffled moans vibrating around Tate's cock. I yank on the belt, tightening it around her neck. Her pussy clenches around me in response.

"Fuck, she's loving this," Torin says, stroking himself as he watches.

I smirk, bringing my hand down hard on Poison's ass. The sharp crack echoes through the room, followed by her choked whimper.

"Of course she is," I say, spanking her again. "Dirty little whores like her crave being used."

Tate groans, his hips jerking as he fucks Poison's face. "Shit, I'm close."

I increase my pace, pounding into Poison mercilessly. Her legs tremble, threatening to give out.

"Don't you dare come," I snarl at her.

Poison whimpers, her body tensing. I can feel her struggling to hold back her orgasm as I ravage her. Good. I want her desperate and aching.

Tate grunts, gripping Poison's hair tightly as he

comes down her throat. She swallows obediently, gasping for air when he pulls out.

I yank on the belt, pulling her upright against my chest. My free hand snakes around, and my fingers clamp down on her clit, twisting it until she chokes back a sob.

"You want to come, don't you?" I growl in her ear. "Filthy little slut, getting off on being used like this."

She nods frantically, unable to speak from the pressure of the belt.

"Too bad," I laugh cruelly. I let go of her clit and hand the leash to Torin. He grips it firmly as I push on Poison's back, before gripping her hips tight enough to bruise her. She whimpers again as I shove my dick as far into her as her body will let me. "Fuck," I grunt. "Fuck, you are such a good little slut for me. Drenching my cock so I can fuck you harder."

I slam into her relentlessly, her body jerking with each brutal thrust. Torin yanks on the belt, choking her as I pound her. Her pussy clenches around me, desperate for release.

"Please," she gasps out between thrusts.

I laugh darkly. "Begging already? Pathetic."

I pull out suddenly, leaving her empty and moaning. With a rough shove, I grab the leash from Torin and flip Poison onto her back. Torin takes the belt from me again and keeps it tight around her neck as I spread her legs wide.

"Look at you," I sneer, swiping a finger over her

gushing cunt. "Dripping wet and aching to be filled. Such a needy little whore."

I shove my finger inside her, then another. Then, a third. She writhes on the bed as I add a fourth. Pulling out, I make a fist and ram it back inside her, hearing her scream.

Poison's scream cuts off abruptly as Torin yanks the belt tighter. Her eyes roll back, face flushing as she struggles for air. I keep my fist buried inside her, feeling her cunt spasm around me.

"Fuck, look at her," Tate says, stroking himself. "She loves it. She's fucking gorgeous."

I smirk, twisting my fist inside Poison. Her body jerks, trapped between pleasure and pain. "Of course she is. It's what filthy sluts like her are made for."

I pull my fist out slowly, watching her cunt gape open. She whimpers, hips lifting off the bed.

"Does the little whore want more?" I taunt. I shove my fist back into Poison's cunt, feeling her pussy clench around me as she cries out. Tears streak down her face, just like I wanted. But her hips are still rocking, desperate for more.

"Fucking insatiable," I growl, pumping my fist in and out of her. "Is this what you needed? To be stretched and used like the dirty slut you are?"

I pull my fist out and thrust my cock back inside her in one brutal motion. She arches off the bed.

"You want to come?" I snarl. "Then fucking come. Come on my cock like the whore you are."

Poison's body convulses as her orgasm hits her

hard. I don't slow down, fucking her through it as she writhes and moans.

"That's it," I growl. "Take it. Take every fucking inch."

She practically breaks my cock with her pussy, and it's heaven. With a roar, I bury myself deep inside her and come hard, filling her with my hot cum.

For a moment, we're all still, the only sound our heavy breathing. Then I pull out roughly, admiring the sight of my cum dripping from Poison's abused pussy. She lies there, trembling and gasping for air as Torin loosens the belt around her neck.

"What's your name, slut?"

"P-Poison," she rasps.

The smile that curves my lips is wicked as she gives us the green light to keep going.

15

TORIN

Gripping the belt like a lifeline of control, my fangs drop when Bram pulls out of Poison's little cunt. She is giving us a creampie that sends my arousal into outer space. With a low growl, I let go of the belt and drag her over to me. I lie down with her on top of me, trembling and weak as I shove my cock into her. "Ride me, bitch," I snarl.

Poison's eyes flutter open as I impale her on my cock. She's still shaking from her intense orgasm, but she obeys, starting to move her hips.

"Faster," I growl, gripping her waist hard enough to bruise.

She whimpers but picks up the pace, bouncing on my cock. Her tits jiggle enticingly with each movement. I reach up and grab them roughly, pinching and twisting her nipples until she cries out.

"That's it, scream for me. Let everyone hear what a dirty little slut you are."

I grab the belt and pull it tighter. She gags, and her eyes roll back. She slumps forward, and I smile. Rolling us over, I impale her. I've cut off her oxygen supply, and she has passed out. I have seconds to enjoy this moment of completely disgusting abuse before I have to bring her around. My cock is like iron in her pliant pussy, and I groan as I slam into her unconscious body with savage intensity, my fangs fully extended. The primal part of me revels in her complete vulnerability, her limp form at my mercy.

But I know I can't let this last.

With a frustrated growl, I loosen the belt. "Wake up, slut. I'm not done with you yet."

Her eyelids flutter, and she gasps for air as her innate shifter healing kicks in. As soon as I see awareness return to her gaze, I pound into her brutally.

"That's it," I snarl. "Stay with me. I want you to feel every. Fucking. Thrust."

Poison's body jerks beneath me, her pussy clenching around my cock as she struggles for air. Tears leak from the corners of her eyes, but I can smell her arousal spiking.

"Filthy little whore," I growl. "Getting off on being fucked while you're unconscious."

"Ahh!" she rasps, her voice so hoarse it's barely a whisper. "Yes," she moans. "More."

Fucking hell. Could she be more perfect?

I feel my orgasm building, my thrusts becoming erratic. With a roar, I bury myself deep inside her and climax like I never have before, filling her already cum-soaked cunt enough for it to gush back out.

My cock is still twitching when I pull out, I loosen the belt again, allowing Poison to gulp in desperate breaths.

I look over at Tate, who's been stroking himself as he watches. "Your turn. I want to watch you punish her pussy."

Tate's eyes darken as he moves towards Poison's trembling form on the bed. He grabs her roughly by the hair, yanking her head back. But as he looks into her eyes, I see him smile softly, and I sigh. Rough and tumble time is over.

"I love you," he murmurs. "Shift back."

With a smile that speaks volumes, Poison shifts back to Ivy and rewards him by slamming him back to the bed and straddling him.

"You soft arse," I grumble. "We were having fun."

"And now I'm having fun," he says with a bright smile as Ivy starts to bounce up and down on him with great abandon, her blonde hair whipping around as she bounces on his cock. I can't deny the appeal of seeing her take charge.

"Fuck, Ivy," Tate groans, gripping her hips. "You feel so good."

She leans down, capturing his lips in a passionate kiss. I roll my eyes at the tender display, but my cock twitches with renewed interest.

Bram moves closer, his hand trailing down Ivy's

spine. She shivers at his touch but doesn't break her rhythm.

"Don't forget about us, little one," Bram purrs. "We're not done with you yet." Ivy moans into Tate's mouth as Bram's fingers dip between her ass cheeks. "Fuck, all that cum is slippery over your hole. Do you want me to fuck you there?" I watch with interest as he slowly works a finger into her tight hole.

"Mm," Ivy moans, wiggling her backside for him.

Ivy gasps, her movements faltering slightly as Bram adds another finger. Tate takes advantage, gripping her hips tightly and thrusting up into her.

"Fuck," Ivy whimpers. "More. I need more."

Bram is happy to oblige. With a wicked smile, he positions himself behind her and shoves his cock into her arsehole slowly.

"Fuck!" Ivy cries out as Bram's cock stretches her. Her body shakes, caught between the two men impaling her.

"That's it, take it all," Bram growls, gripping her hips as he pushes deeper.

"So fucking tight," Tate grunts.

I move closer, my erection bobbing. "Lick me clean," I purr, grabbing a fistful of Ivy's hair and yanking her head back.

Her lips part in a silent gasp, and I shove my cock into her mouth. She gags slightly but quickly adjusts, her tongue swirling around my length.

"That's it," I groan. "Use that talented mouth of yours."

Ivy moans around my cock as Bram and Tate set a brutal pace, fucking her from both ends. Her body jerks between us, entirely at our mercy.

"Fucking hell," Bram grunts. "You're squeezing me so tight."

I tighten my grip on Ivy's hair, fucking her face roughly.

"Such a good little princess," I praise, switching tactics now that she is Ivy again. "Taking all our cocks like you were made for it."

Tate groans, his hips working up faster. "Fuck, Ivy, I'm coming."

Ivy whimpers around my cock, her body trembling as she's pounded from all sides.

"Come for us, little killer," I growl.

With a muffled cry, Ivy's orgasm hits her hard. Her body convulses wildly, shaking uncontrollably.

"Fuck!" Tate shouts, burying himself deep as he comes.

Bram follows soon after with a guttural groan, filling Ivy's ass with his cum. The sight of her taking all of us at once pushes me over the edge, and I spill down her throat with a roar.

For a moment, we're all still, panting heavily. Then I slowly pull out of Ivy's mouth, watching as she gasps for air. Her body slumps between Bram and Tate, thoroughly used and dripping with our cum.

Running a hand over her sweat-drenched hair, I grip it lightly and tilt her head back. "What's your name, little killer?"

16

IVY

I BLINK UP AT TORIN, MY MIND HAZY WITH PLEASURE AND exhaustion.

"I can't remember," I murmur.

Torin smiles with satisfaction and something softer in his eyes. "Good girl."

I whimper as Bram and Tate slowly pull out of me. My body aches in the most delicious way, thoroughly used and marked by the three of them. I collapse onto the bed, cum leaking from my abused holes.

"Fuck," I mumble into the sheets.

Bram chuckles darkly. "You took it beautifully. Such a good girl for us."

I shiver at his praise, a spark of arousal igniting despite my exhaustion. These men will be the death of me.

"Come on," Torin says, scooping me up in his arms. "Let's get you cleaned up."

As he carries me to the bathroom, I catch sight of the

book Tate brought. It sits forgotten on my desk, a reminder of the chaos that awaits us outside of this moment. But for now, I let myself sink into the afterglow, surrounded by the men who captivate me.

Torin sets me down gently in the shower, his touch surprisingly tender after the brutal fucking I just endured. The hot water cascades over us as the guys join us, their hands roaming my body and cleaning me with reverent care.

"Fuck, you're incredible," Tate murmurs, pressing a kiss to my shoulder.

I lean back against his chest, letting the water sluice away the evidence of our debauchery.

"Did we help you forget?" Bram asks, his dark eyes searching mine. "Truly?"

For a moment, I'd actually managed to push aside the looming threats and mysteries. But reality comes crashing back as I remember why I needed the distraction in the first place.

"For a while," I admit. "But we can't ignore what's happening forever."

Torin's jaw clenches. "We'll figure it out. Let's just take this night, yeah?"

I want to agree, but I'm impatient at the best of times. "The book. What did Vex find?"

Tate's arms tighten around me. "Let's get dried off first. Then we'll go through it together."

I nod, allowing myself a few more minutes of peace before facing whatever new revelations await us. As we step out of the shower, I catch sight of myself in the steamy mirror. My hair is wild, skin flushed and marked with bruises and bites. I look thoroughly fucked and claimed.

"Fuck, you're gorgeous," Bram murmurs, coming up behind me and meeting my eyes in the mirror. His hands slide possessively over my hips.

I lean back against him, a small smile playing on my lips. "You guys certainly know how to make a girl feel wanted."

Torin snorts as he towels off. "Wanted? Try fucking irresistible."

We dry off and head back to my bedroom. I pull on an oversized t-shirt, not bothering with anything else. The guys get comfortable as Tate retrieves the book from my desk.

"Let's see what Vex dug up," I say, settling on the bed between Bram and Torin.

Tate opens the book, flipping through pages of ancient text. "There is a lot of my family history in here," he starts carefully. "Apparently, my bloodline, the Well and Black bloodline, is an anchor for chaos magick. It's why you feel more stable around me."

"What?" I ask, eyebrows raised. "Really?"

He nods, almost shyly. Torin is staring at him with something wary, and a little bit annoyed.

"Is that why we are fated?" I murmur, shifting my gaze back to Tate.

"We are more than that," he says. "We are two pieces of the same whole."

"Oh, fuck off," Torin snaps. "You don't get to swoop in here and take her away from us with this crap."

Tate growls. "Who's taking her away, you arsehole? I'm stating facts." He jabs the book harshly.

"Never mind that," I snap, eager to learn more about this magick that is threatening to tear me in half. "What does it say about the magick?"

"That's where it becomes a bit blurry," he says with a huff at Torin and refocusing.

"Well, I think it's Ancient Fae magick," Bram blurts out. "Somehow, you, being not Fae, are able to wield it. It chose you, obviously, but the basis of it is from my heritage."

"Oh?" I ask interestedly. "How do you figure?"

"Like recognises like," he says and holds his hand up. Dark shadows filter out of his palm and wrap themselves around me, drawing out my pink energy and combining with it.

"Fuck," I mutter. "Okay, Fae, it is."

"I think you're a witch," Torin adds, almost triumphantly, with a glare at Tate.

"What?" I ask, scrunching up my nose. "How so?"

He rolls his eyes. "Something my mother said. She doesn't just say things. Every word is measured. She called you a chaos witch. I thought at first it was a slur, like bitch, but it's not. It's fact."

"And how does she know this?"

He shrugs, and then glowers at me. "You're going to get me to ask her, aren't you?"

"Only if you want to. I get family drama, and I

won't ask you to do anything you don't want to. But it might help."

"She won't tell us anything she doesn't want us to know."

I sigh, running a hand through my damp hair. "So, if we cut her out of the equation, what we know is that I'm some sort of chaos witch with Ancient Fae magick, anchored by Tate's bloodline."

Bram nods solemnly. "That about sums it up."

"Great," I mutter. "The witch thing is interesting. I've never had active magick before now. I wonder where the witch side has come in and why it's never manifested before."

Torin's hand slides up my thigh, his touch is both possessive and comforting. "We'll figure it out without my mother's hindrance."

I snicker. "Yeah, if we can't trust her, we don't need her."

"Thank you," he says with a rush.

I cup his face and give him a soft smile.

Tate flips through more pages of the book, his brow furrowed in concentration. "There's something here about balancing the chaos. It says the anchor - that would be me - needs to...oh."

"What?" I ask, sitting up straighter. "What does it say?"

Tate's cheeks flush slightly. "It says we need to, uh, merge our energies. Frequently and deeply."

Torin snorts. "So, you need to fuck. A lot. How convenient."

I roll my eyes at Torin's barb. "Is that all it says? Just 'merge energies'?"

"Yeah. It's sharing magick. Letting mine touch yours. Just like you did with Bram a minute ago."

"Okay, well, that doesn't sound terrible—" But I stop when I see the look on his face. "What?"

"I'm supposed to take the burden from you. Absorb some of that power and filter it."

"Is that dangerous?"

He shrugs.

"Okay, maybe we don't do that then until we know."

We sit in silence, each lost in our own thoughts. This is getting way more complicated than I could've imagined. I didn't want any of this. I was happy being a shifter, and now I'm all sorts of other things that I don't understand or even know where they came from.

"Maybe we need to start with my own family tree," I murmur. "Try to find out where the witch came from."

Before the guys can answer, reality bends. I feel nauseous as Death materialises in the room with an ominous rumble. "That would come from me."

17

IVY

The nausea fades as Death's presence settles in my bedroom. His eye sockets seem to hold galaxies as he studies me.

"What do you mean, it comes from you?" I demand, pulling my oversized t-shirt down self-consciously. "And before you even try it, lay one gross finger on them and I will end you even if it means ending myself in the process."

Death's laugh echoes like bones rattling in a tomb. "My dear girl, do you think I care about killing them? No, this is all for your benefit. With regard to your power, did you think your remarkable abilities came from nowhere? The chaos magick that flows through your veins is no accident. It's evolution."

I narrow my eyes at him. "Evolution of what?"

"Of the most powerful witch bloodline to ever exist." He waves a skeletal hand, and reality ripples. Suddenly, we're no longer in my bedroom but in an ancient library, having left the guys back in my bedroom. Books line the walls from floor to ceiling, their spines crackling with ancient power. "You come from my line." Death moves to one of the shelves, pulling out a massive tome that looks older than time itself. "Many, many generations ago, before I became Death, I was the patriarch of the most powerful witch family in existence."

The book floats between us, its pages turning on their own until they stop at a family tree. Names and dates spread across the parchment, some so old they're barely legible.

"Your chaos magick is old power evolved. When you rejected becoming Death while still in the womb, you didn't just create a cosmic glitch, you transformed our family's inherent witch magick into something entirely new."

I stare at the family tree, watching as lines of power pulse through it like veins. My name sits at the bottom, glowing with that familiar pink energy. Above it, through countless generations, the line traces back to… "David Beech."

"Indeed," Death says, sounding almost proud. "Our bloodline has always been different. We don't just use magick; we are magick. But you, my dear descendant, you've taken it further than any of us could have imagined."

"The Ancient Fae magick? Does that have something to do with this evolution?" Despite my anger and fear of this arsehole, he is actually being forthcoming and telling me shit I need to know to kill him. It's like everyone is always telling me that I roll with the punches, think on my feet, think outside the box. Well, right now, I'm doing all three plus playing along with him, so he will tell me everything and think I'm being amenable—the old double cross.

"The witch magick in our bloodline has always had an affinity for Fae power. Something about the way we perceive and channel energy. But your transformation has merged them completely."

My head spins as I try to process this. "So I'm not just some cosmic accident? This was all predetermined? Is that what you're saying?"

"Not predetermined," Death corrects. "Potential. Our bloodline has always carried the potential for transformation. You're simply the first to achieve it."

"But why?" I demand. "Why did it happen to me?"

Death moves closer, and I resist the urge to step back. The stench of darkness and death surrounds him, and it's truly terrifying. "Because you were strong enough to reject what was meant to be. Strong enough to create something new from something ancient." He reaches out as if to touch my face, but stops just short. "The chaos magick isn't fighting your witch nature - it is your witch nature, evolved into something more powerful than either has any right to be. This..." he gestures to the pink energy crackling around me, "this is beyond anything we've seen before."

"So what happens now? What do you want from me?" I ask, watching as my magick reaches out instinctively towards Death's power. Where they touch, reality shivers. "What does this mean for me?"

"It means, dear girl, that you have choices to make. The power you possess could reshape everything. The natural order, the balance between realms, even death itself."

"Is that why you want my soul?" I demand. "Because I could potentially fuck up your whole operation?"

Death's laugh echoes through the library. "Oh no. I want your soul because it's the key to something far greater than mere death and souls." He waves his hand again, and we're back in my bedroom. "But that's a revelation for another time."

"Wait!" I call as he starts to fade. "I have more questions!"

"Of course you do," his voice echoes as he disappears. "But some answers must be earned, not given."

"Well, that was fucking helpful."

"Actually," Bram says thoughtfully, "it was. We know more now than we did before."

"You heard?"

"We saw. Like it was on TV."

"That information is valuable," Torin says. "It explains why you can do things no other supernatural can. Why your power feels both ancient and new."

I look down at my hands, watching the pink energy dance between my fingers. "It doesn't explain everything, though. Why now? Why did the power wait until now to manifest?"

"Maybe it didn't," Tate suggests. "Maybe it's been there all along, just dormant. Your shifting ability when it evolved to include the vines could be part of it, an expression of the power before it fully awakened."

"So, what do we do with this information?" I ask, looking between the three men who have become so essential to my existence.

"We use it," Bram says simply. "Knowledge is power, and now we know your magick isn't just random chaos - it's inherited power that's evolved. That means it can be understood and controlled. It's not what everyone seems to think it is. It is chaos, yes, but it's not complete entropy."

"And what about Death?" Torin asks the question we're all thinking. "What's his real game here?"

I shake my head, remembering the way our power had resonated when it touched. "I don't know. But I get the feeling we've only scratched the surface of what he's planning."

Tate pulls me closer, his magick wrapping around mine soothingly. "Whatever it is, we will figure it out. This revelation is surprising but, truthfully, not that unexpected."

I lean into his embrace, feeling the other guys move closer, too. Their presence grounds me and helps me focus through the whirlwind of revelations.

"He said some answers must be earned," I murmur. "I think it's time we started earning them."

"How?" Torin asks.

A slow smile spreads across my face as an idea

forms. "By doing what I do best - causing chaos. But this time, with purpose."

The pink energy surges around me, stronger than ever now that I understand its origin. I'm not just some cosmic glitch or random accident. I'm the evolution of an ancient power.

"Death wants to play games?" I say, watching as my power responds to my intent, creating patterns in the air that look like constellations being born. "Then let's show him how chaos really works."

They know as well as I do that this changes everything, not just what we know about my power but also how we approach using it.

I'm done being reactive. Done letting others dictate the rules of engagement. I might be Death's descendant, but I'm also something entirely new.

And it's time to show everyone exactly what that means.

After I crash and sleep until I can't sleep anymore.

18

IVY

THE MORNING AFTER DEATH'S REVELATION BRINGS MORE than just a hangover from information overload. I wake to find my entire body crackling with uncomfortable energy, like I've got lightning trapped under my skin.

"Fuck," I mutter, rolling out of bed. The guys had gone home late last night after we'd discussed Death's bombshell until we were talked out. Now, standing in front of my mirror, I can see something's definitely wrong.

Pink energy pulses through my veins, visible beneath my skin like a roadmap of chaos. It's beautiful in a terrifying sort of way, but the burning sensation that accompanies it is less than pleasant.

"Shit, shit, shit." I press my hands against my stomach as a wave of nausea hits me. The magick surges, and suddenly, my reflection shows both Ivy and Poison overlaid, like a double exposure photograph.

My phone buzzes on the nightstand. Grimacing, I grab it, seeing Tate's name flash up.

"Hey," I rasp.

"You need to come over," he says without preamble. "Something's happening."

"Yeah, no kidding." I watch as my hair shifts between blonde and pink without me actively trying to shift. "I'll be there in ten."

I throw on clothes, not bothering with anything fancy since my body seems to be having an identity crisis all on its own. The walk across campus to the guys' house is interesting, to say the least. My power keeps fluctuating, making reality ripple around me. Trees briefly turn crystalline before shifting back, and I swear I can hear colours.

By the time I reach their door, I'm sweating despite the cold morning air. Tate opens it before I can knock, looking as rough as I feel.

"Inside," he says quickly, pulling me in. "Before someone sees you."

"What's wrong with me?" I demand as soon as we're in the kitchen. Torin and Bram are already there, eyebrows raised at the state of me.

"Fuck," Bram breathes, his Fae sight obviously picking up something we can't see. "Your aura is fragmenting."

"My, what is doing what now?"

"He's right," Torin says, moving closer. "It's like your power is trying to split apart. It's visible to the naked eye," he says, shooting Bram with a sidelong glare.

Another wave of nausea hits me, and I grab the kitchen counter for support. The pink energy crackles more intensely, and suddenly, every metal object in the kitchen starts floating.

"Ivy," Tate says carefully, "I think your—shall we call them identities?—are fighting each other."

"But Death said they were the same thing," I protest, watching as the floating cutlery starts spinning in complex patterns. "Just evolved."

"Maybe that's the problem," Bram suggests. "Evolution isn't always smooth. Sometimes there's a conflict between the old and the new."

A sharp pain shoots through my chest, and I gasp. Looking down, I see that a fork has flown across the room and buried itself deep in my chest.

"Ah," I gag as I pull it out and see it coated with pink, not red, blood.

The rest of the floating objects crash back down as my knees buckle. Tate catches me before I hit the floor.

"This is bad," Torin mutters, helping Tate get me to a chair. "Her temperature's all over the place."

He's right. One minute, I'm burning up; the next, I'm freezing. My skin keeps shifting between Ivy and Poison without my control, and the pink energy is becoming more erratic.

"What do we do?" I ask through gritted teeth as another wave of pain hits. "Because this fucking hurts."

"We need to stabilise her," Bram says, his Dark Fae

magick reaching out tentatively toward mine. Where they touch, there's a brief moment of relief before the pain returns worse than before.

"Stop," I gasp. "That makes it worse. It wants to devour it. I can't—"

Tate kneels in front of me, taking my hands in his. "Let me try. I'm supposed to be your anchor, right?"

I nod, unable to speak, as another tide of power rips through me. His magick wraps around mine, trying to contain the chaos, but something's different this time. Instead of helping, it again feels like his power is being consumed by mine.

"Fuck!" Tate yanks his hands away, his skin smoking slightly where we touched. "That's not working either."

"No shit," I manage to say before doubling over as my insides feel like they're rearranging themselves. "Oh, god, what's happening to me? Is this the tearing me apart stage? I thought I had more time."

"No, I don't think so. Your power is trying to settle," Bram says, watching me carefully. "The witch side of you and the Fae-type chaos magick aren't just merging, they're creating something entirely new. Again."

"Again?" I grit out. The windows rattle ominously.

He nods. "Evolving, like Death said, but I'm starting to think this was the fine print. It's continuous."

"We need help," Torin says firmly. "This is beyond us."

"Who?" Tate demands. "Death? The Resistance? We don't know who to trust."

Another wave of pain hits, and this time, I scream. Pink energy explodes outward, shattering every window in the house. Reality bends around us, and suddenly, the kitchen is filled with various versions of me. Some Ivy, some Poison, some strange combinations of both.

"Oh, that's new," one of my duplicates says before flickering out of existence.

"Focus," Bram commands, his voice cutting through the chaos. "Ivy, look at me."

I force my eyes to meet his, trying to ignore the way my duplicates are starting to affect the physical world around us. One of them has turned the refrigerator into a fountain of starlight, and then Aspen shows up, startling the guys into inaction for a second.

"The power isn't fighting itself," Bram says intently, the first to come back to his senses. "It's fighting you. You're still trying to keep Ivy and Poison, and Aspen separate, still trying to maintain the division between the shifts. Badass assassin…s and normal shifter trying to go to classes and live a normal life. But they're not separate, Ivy. They're you. All of you."

"How very fucking philosophical, *Bram,*" I snarl as another duplicate appears, this one crackling with pure chaos energy. "But how does that help me right now?"

"Stop fighting it," he insists. "Stop trying to be either Ivy or Poison. Be both. Be neither. Be whatever this power is making you become."

"He's right," Tate says, his burned hands now healed. "You've been trying to control it, to keep it contained in neat little boxes. But that's not how evolution works."

A particularly violent stream of power sends me into the foetal position. The duplicates flicker and multiply, each one showing a different aspect of who I am and who I could be.

"I don't know how," I admit through tears of pain. "I don't know how to be both."

"Yes, you do," Torin says quietly. "You do it every time you're with us. Every time you let yourself just be, without labels or expectations."

The pain reaches a crescendo, and I feel something inside me start to break. But maybe it needs to break. Maybe that's the point.

Taking a shuddering breath, I close my eyes and stop fighting. Stop trying to be Ivy or Poison, witch or chaos wielder. I just... am.

The power whirls one final time, but this time, it doesn't hurt. It feels like something clicking into place, like puzzle pieces finally finding their proper alignment.

When I open my eyes, the duplicates are gone. The kitchen is a disaster zone, but the pain has subsided. Looking down at my hands, I see the pink energy still flowing through my veins, but it's different now - more integrated, less like it's trying to escape.

"Your aura is whole again," Bram says. "But a vibrant purple. You have combined your personas."

"For how long?" I ask weakly.

He presses his lips together before answering, "That's what we will have to figure out."

I stand carefully, testing this new equilibrium. My power still snaps beneath my skin, but it no longer feels like it's trying to tear me apart. Instead, it feels right. For now.

"Well," I say, looking around at the destruction my transformation has caused and rubbing my chest, which has healed of the three-pronged attack, "that was fun."

Tate snorts, examining his healing hands. "That's one word for it."

"Are you okay?" Torin asks, moving closer but still maintaining a safe distance.

I consider the question seriously. "I think so. It feels different, like everything's settled into a new configuration."

"And the shifting?" Bram asks. "Can you still control it?"

I focus briefly, and my appearance changes smoothly between Ivy and Poison before settling back. "Yeah, but it feels different too. Less like putting on a mask and more like expressing different aspects of the same whole."

"That's what Death meant," Tate says suddenly. "About evolution. This isn't just about power growing stronger, it's about it becoming something new entirely."

I nod, watching as pinky-purple energy dances between my fingers, responding to my thoughts without trying to overwhelm them. "I think you're right. But something tells me this is just the beginning."

"Of what?" Torin asks.

Looking around at my guys—my anchors, my lovers, my partners in whatever this chaos is becoming—I smile. "Of finding out exactly what I'm capable of now that I'm not subconsciously fighting myself anymore."

The power purrs beneath my skin, no longer trying to tear me apart, but eager to show me what it can do. What we can do, now that we're truly integrated.

"Should we be worried?" Tate asks, but he's grinning.

"Probably," I admit. "But when has that ever stopped us?"

He chuckles, but I can see the worry underneath. I'm scared too, but I won't show it. Whatever this evolution is, I have to learn how to identify it and control it before I'm torn apart by it. If that happens, I'm not sure what will be left of *me*.

19

TATE

WATCHING IVY INTEGRATE HER POWER IS CONCERNING, BUT also a relief. But there's a cost to all this power, and I'm starting to feel it. She's gone back to her place to shower and change, leaving us to deal with the aftermath of her transformation. What I had to tell her can wait in light of this development. I know she knows it isn't going to last, and that thought is what is worrying me.

When she pulled on her power to accept her personas, she drew on mine as well. My hands still tingle from where her magick burned me earlier, but that's not what concerns me. It's the deeper ache, the way my own magick feels different since I started anchoring her power.

"You look like shit," Torin says bluntly as we clean up the kitchen.

"Thanks," I mutter, wincing as another wave of discomfort rolls through me. My magick flickers erratically, causing the broken glass I'm sweeping to briefly turn into butterflies before returning to normal.

"He's right," Bram says, watching me with those too-perceptive Fae eyes. "Something's wrong."

I straighten up, fighting back a wave of dizziness. "I'm fine."

"Bullshit," Torin snaps. "Your aura is almost as fucked up as Ivy's was, and just as visible," he adds, shooting a look at Bram, who rolls his eyes.

Running a hand through my hair, I try to focus my magick on fixing a broken window. Instead, reality warps around it, creating a portal that shows glimpses of other dimensions before I quickly shut it down.

"Fuck," I breathe, stumbling back. That's definitely new.

"Sit down before you fall down," Bram orders, guiding me to a chair. "What's happening?"

I shake my head, trying to clear the strange double vision that has developed. "I don't know. Ever since I started anchoring Ivy's power, things have been weird."

"Weird, how?" Torin demands.

"Like my magick isn't entirely mine anymore." I hold up my hands, watching as black sparks mix with traces of pink and purple energy. "It's changing, adapting to handle her chaos."

"The grimoire mentioned this," Bram says suddenly. "About anchors bearing consequences. We didn't read far enough to see what those consequences were."

Another surge of foreign power races through me,

and I grip the arm of the chair as reality threatens to bend again. "Well, I think we're finding out."

"We need to tell Ivy," Torin says, but I shake my head vigorously.

"No. She's just gotten control of her power. She doesn't need to worry about this, too."

"She'll notice eventually," Bram points out. "Especially if you keep warping reality every time you try to use magick."

He's right, of course. Ivy's too observant not to notice something's wrong, especially now that her power has settled. But the thought of adding to her burden makes me sick.

"Look," I say, forcing myself to stand despite the room's tendency to tilt sideways, "I just need to adjust. Figure out how to handle this new, whatever this is."

As if to prove my point, my magick flares again. This time, instead of creating portals or transforming objects, it reaches out and connects with the traces of Ivy's power still lingering in the air. The resulting feedback loop sends me to my knees.

"Tate!" Torin catches me before I faceplant. "That's it. We're calling Ivy."

"No," I gasp, fighting through the kaleidoscope of sensations flooding my system. "Just... give me a minute."

Bram crouches beside me, his Fae magick probing gently at whatever's happening to mine. "This isn't just adaptation," he says grimly. "Your magick is being fundamentally altered by exposure to her chaos."

"Is that bad?" I manage to ask as another wave hits.

"No idea. Your bloodline may be meant to anchor chaos magick, but this level of power is changing you on a cellular level."

"Fucking hell," Torin mutters. "Can we stop it?"

"Only by stopping the anchoring entirely," Bram says. "But that would leave Ivy without stability again."

"Not an option," I growl, finally getting my feet under me. The room has mostly stopped spinning, but my magick feels like it's trying to rewrite itself from the inside out.

"Then we need to find a way to manage it," Torin says practically. "Because you can't go on like this."

He's right. Every time I anchor Ivy's power, every time our magick mingles, the changes become more pronounced. I can feel it now in the way my naturally structured magick is being infected with chaos, creating something hybrid and unpredictable.

"The Well bloodline," I say suddenly, remembering something from the grimoire. "It's supposed to be able to handle this. My ancestors did it."

"Your ancestors didn't deal with power like Ivy's," Bram points out. "This is evolution, remember? New territory."

Another bolt hits, but this time, I'm ready for it. Instead of fighting the chaos and trying to integrate it with my magick, I let it flow, just like we told Ivy to do. The sensation is bizarre, like having a second heartbeat, a rhythm of power that doesn't quite match my own frequency.

“Oh,” I breathe as something shifts inside me. “That’s different.”

“What?” Torin demands. “What’s happening?”

I hold up my hands, watching as my black magick now streams with permanent threads of pink. “I think I’m adapting.”

Bram moves closer, studying the change. “It’s not just affecting your magick anymore,” he says. “It’s becoming part of it.”

“Is that supposed to happen?” Torin asks, genuine fear tinging his tone. That is not good.

“Who knows?” I let out a slightly hysterical laugh. “None of this is supposed to happen. We’re literally making this up as we go.”

The front door opens, and Ivy’s voice calls out, “You guys will not believe what I just did!”

Panic flashes across Torin’s face, but I shake my head sharply. We need more time to understand what’s happening before we tell her.

Ivy bounces into the kitchen, practically glowing with controlled power. She stops short when she sees us all clustered together. “What’s wrong?”

“Nothing,” I say quickly, forcing a smile. “Just discussing the clean-up.”

Her eyes narrow suspiciously, tracking over each of us before settling on me. “You’re lying.”

“Ivy—”

“Don’t.” She moves closer, her power reaching out toward mine. I try to pull back, but it’s too late. The moment our magick touches, she gasps. "What the fuck?"

The connection between us flares, stronger than ever now that her power has settled and mine has started to change. Pink and purple energy swirls with black, creating patterns that twist reality around us.

"Tate," she breathes, staring at where our power mingles, "what's happening to you?"

"It's fine," I insist, even as another wave of transformation rolls through me. "Just some side effects from anchoring."

"Side effects?" Her voice rises. "Your magick is literally changing colour!"

"It's not just the colour," Bram says, ignoring my glare. "The chaos magick is altering him fundamentally. Every time he anchors your power, it changes him a little more."

Ivy takes a step back, horror dawning on her face. "I'm hurting you?"

"No," I say firmly, reaching for her despite the way it makes my magick surge. "You're not hurting me. I'm adapting. Evolution, remember?"

"Evolution that could kill you," Torin mutters.

"Not helping," I snarl at him.

Ivy's power pulls back sharply, leaving me feeling strangely bereft. "We have to stop this."

"No." I grab her hands, ignoring the way our combined power makes reality ripple. "We knew there would be consequences. The grimoire warned us. But this is necessary."

"Nothing is worth risking you," she says fiercely.

"You are," I tell her, meaning it completely. "Besides, it's too late now. The change has already started, and honestly?" I look down at our joined hands, where pink, purple and black energy dance together in perfect harmony. "I don't think I want to go back."

20

IVY

It's been three hours since my power settled into its new configuration, three hours of learning to control this evolved form of witch-fae-chaos magick. Three hours of watching this energy dance beneath my skin like lightning trapped in crystal. The afternoon light streams through our kitchen window as I nurse my third coffee, trying to ignore how reality occasionally ripples when my concentration slips.

The evolution of my power might be stabilising, but 'stable' is a relative term when you're basically chaos incarnate.

"Stop moping," Ramsey says, dropping into the seat across from me. "Your power is fine, and the world hasn't ended yet."

I glare at him over my coffee. "Yet being the operative word, and when is *fine* ever good?"

"Well, you have me there," he grins, but the expression freezes as his phone buzzes with that familiar

Syndicate tone.

The sound makes my stomach clench. But Ramsey's face goes pale as he reads the message, and something cold settles in my gut.

"What?" I demand. "Who's the target?"

He swallows hard, looking up at me with genuine fear in his eyes. "Cathy Hammond."

The mug in my hand shatters as my power destabilises and fires through my body at a rate of knots. Coffee transforms into shimmering butterflies that dissolve into deep pink mist. "My aunt? The Syndicate wants me to kill my aunt?"

"It's worse," Ramsey says quietly. "You have twelve hours to complete the assignment, or they'll despatch other agents to do it, and they won't be quick about it."

Magick crackles around me as rage builds. The sunlight flickers outside, and storm clouds gather unnaturally fast. "They know?"

"Or they're testing your loyalty. The Resistance isn't exactly flaunting their activities. I doubt The Syndicate knows about them, and I also doubt they know what you are now."

"Well, forgive me if I doubt your doubt." Reality warps slightly around me as I stand up. The tiles beneath my feet transform into a living crystal that spreads up the walls. "That's not loyalty, that's torture."

"It's a message," Ramsey says grimly. "This is their way of showing they control you."

My power lashes out, turning the kitchen table into

a mass of writhing vines before I get it under control. "They don't control me."

"No?" He holds up his phone. "Then why is there already a team of elite assassins being assembled to handle this if you refuse?"

That stops me cold. "What team?"

"The Wraiths."

The name hits me harder than I'd have liked. Memories flood back to my first year as Poison, watching from the shadows as they worked. The Thompson case. The stench of decay and madness. The way they'd kept him conscious through everything, how they'd made him watch as they systematically destroyed everything he loved before finally ending him.

"Fuck," I whisper, and the crystal walls crack with my fear.

"You have twelve hours," Ramsey repeats softly. "After that, they move in. And Ivy? They won't just go after Cathy. Anyone who tries to protect her will be considered a target."

"They're really not fucking around," I mutter.

"No, they're not." Ramsey stands, moving to the window where storm clouds now press against the glass like living things. "This is a power play, pure and simple. They want to prove they own you."

"But why now if they don't know about The Resistance or about my new powers?"

He shrugs. "I don't know."

"Tell me about Wraith Team Alpha," I say, forcing

myself to think tactically even as my power threatens to tear reality apart around us.

Ramsey's expression grows grave. "They're the worst of the worst. Five members, each specialising in a different form of torture. Their leader, Echo, she's something else. Rumour has it she can make a single moment of pain last for what feels like eternity."

"And the others?" I need to know what I'm up against, need to understand exactly what threat they pose to my aunt.

"Shade works with shadows. He turns them solid, uses them to flay skin from bone. I saw their work once, early in my handler career. The victim... they looked like they'd been carved by living darkness."

My power pulses with each revelation, turning the crystal walls into mirrors that reflect infinite versions of us, each slightly different. In one, I'm fully Poison. In another, pure chaos energy given form.

"Whisper specialises in psychological torture," Ramsey continues. "Gets inside your head, makes you experience your worst fears on loop. They drove an older vampire mad in less than an hour. He's still in an asylum, screaming about shadows that speak."

The storm outside intensifies, rain beginning to fall upward as my control slips slightly.

"Grave can control decay; makes you feel your body rotting while you're still alive. Keeps you conscious through the whole process." Ramsey shudders. "And then there's Silence..."

"What does Silence do?"

"No one knows exactly. Those who've encountered them never speak again. Literally can't. Something about their power steals your voice, not just physically but deeper. Like it takes your ability to express yourself at all."

Ramsey's phone buzzes again, and I gulp as he looks at it. "What does it say?"

"This is the final test. Do this, and they tell you what happened to your parents."

"What? Are you for real?"

He turns his phone around to show me. "Very for real."

"Fuck. Well, I already know what happened to my parents, so I don't need to do this, right?" I let out a weak laugh that is devoid of all humour.

"Wrong. If you don't do it, they take your soul as per your contract, and Cathy dies anyway. Painfully and slowly."

"So what?" I snap. "I'm supposed to make it quick and painless?"

He shakes his head. "I don't know, Ives. I'm here as your handler, giving you facts when you can't see them."

"Shit." I sit back down and drop my head into my hands. "I don't know what to do. Can they still take my soul with me like this? Won't Death stop them?"

"Unless Death is in on it, which, let's face it, he more than likely is."

"Fuck." The crystal spreads across the ceiling, creating a kaleidoscope of reflections that show different versions of possible futures. In most of them, there's blood.

"They want you emotional, off-balance. Easier to manipulate. The Wraiths aren't just killers - they're a psychological weapon. The threat of them is often enough to ensure compliance."

Pinky purple magick fritzes around me as I process this information. The Syndicate isn't just sending assassins - they're sending their most sadistic team, knowing exactly what they'll do to my aunt.

But they've made a crucial mistake.

"You can't save everyone," Ramsey says softly, watching as my power begins to stabilise, focusing into something deadly rather than chaotic.

"Watch me. Neither of us dies tonight." I head for the door, my power humming with lethal plans. Reality bends slightly around me, responding to my clarity of purpose.

Stepping out into the storm, I let my power flow freely. Pink and purple energy dances around me, responding to my rage and determination. Let them watch. Let them think they know what I'm planning.

The thing about poisons is that they work best when you don't see them coming. The Syndicate wants to play games? Wants to test my loyalty. Fine.

But they don't know something crucial: I'm not just Poison anymore. I'm not just a shifter assassin. I'm a witch and a chaos wielder related to Death. I'm something new, something evolved, and they're about to learn exactly what that means.

The game is on, and this time, I'm not playing by anyone's rules but my own.

Time to show them why you don't back a poisonous vine into a corner.

It tends to grow in unexpected directions, and everything it touches dies.

The storm clouds begin to rain purple fire.

It's deeper and darker than what I started out with.

It's evolving.

Let them watch.

Let them worry.

The hunt is on.

21

IVY

The streets shimmer with untapped potential as I walk, each step leaving diamond-like footprints that fade to stardust. My power hasn't just evolved in the last few minutes, it's become something entirely new, something that doesn't play by the old rules. But that's exactly what I need right now.

First things first: intelligence gathering.

"Show me," I whisper to the Thornfield campus, which is covered in a hazy mist that has nothing to do with the weather. My power responds. The magick spreads through the concrete beneath my feet, creating a web of awareness. I can feel five distinct signatures of wrongness moving through the shadows. The Wraiths are already here, positioning themselves.

They're good, I'll give them that. But I'm better. Because while they're watching me, waiting for me to make a move toward Cathy, they don't realise that I know exactly where *they* are.

My power isn't just chaos anymore, and evolution, by definition, adapts.

I find a quiet spot on the campus, around the back of the main building, and lean against the wall, closing my eyes. Magick spirals out from me in all directions, carrying my consciousness with it. I can feel every rat in every sewer, every spider spinning its web, every cockroach scuttling through the walls. Life, in all its forms, ready to be adjusted.

The Syndicate thinks they know what I can do, but they haven't seen anything yet. Yes, this will out me in a big way, but who cares? If I'm being honest with myself, I think Ramsey is wrong, and they know everything already.

They're trying to scare me with their countdown, their threats, their elite kill squad. But they've forgotten something about me, or maybe it's something they never knew in the first place. I'm not just fighting for myself anymore. This isn't about loyalty to The Syndicate versus love for my aunt, which, let's face it, is thin on the ground. But family is family and all that bullshit.

This is about advancement versus stagnation. Change versus control. The future versus the past.

And I know which side I'm on.

My power ripples again, but this time, I direct it with a single thought. Every insect, every rodent, every tiny life form on the campus becomes an extension of my awareness. I can feel the Wraiths moving and can track their progress through the gaps in reality they think no one else can see.

Come on, you fuckers. You are blind, and you don't even know it.

Lightning crawls across the sky as I push away from the wall, my power humming with deadly purpose. Time to show them that they picked a fight with the wrong girl.

In nature, it's not the strongest that survive, it's those most responsive to change, and change has never been a problem for me. Only this time, it's not just my face or my name… it's everything.

I move through campus like a ghost, my power rippling reality around me. The Wraiths think they're hunting me, but they have no idea they've just become the prey.

I spot Echo first, her energy signature a discordant note in the symphony of life around us. She's perched on a rooftop, eyes scanning the grounds below. *Time to make my first move.*

With a thought, I send a swarm of moths spiralling towards her, infusing them with chaos. As they near Echo, their wings glow with eerie purple light.

Echo notices too late. The moths explode in a burst of chaotic energy, momentarily blinding her. In that instant of distraction, I'm there, moving myself through time and space with something that sings *witch power* to me.

She whirls, hands already weaving some dark spell, but I'm faster. My power lashes out, wrapping around her like living vines. They sink into her skin, injecting havoc directly into her system.

Echo's eyes go wide as she feels my magick invading her. "What are you?" she gasps.

I smile, letting a bit of Poison show through. "Something you wouldn't understand even if I explained it with crayons. You are now obsolete."

With a twist of my will, I shatter Echo's connection to her own power. She screams as it tears away from her, leaving her drained and powerless.

Echo collapses, her body convulsing as my frenzied energy ravages her system.

One down, four to go.

I grin. This is the most fun I've had on the job in a while. But I don't have time to revel in this small victory. Already, I can sense the other Wraiths converging on my location, drawn by Echo's scream. Good. Let them come.

Shade materialises from the shadows first, his form rippling like sentient darkness. "What have you done?" he snarls, seeing Echo's prone form.

"Eradication of the weakest," I reply, letting my power flare around me. The air shimmers with the stench of ozone.

Shade doesn't waste time with words. Tendrils of shadow lash out, aiming to flay the skin from my bones. But my magick is faster, transmuting the darkness into butterflies that dissolve into mist.

His eyes widen in shock. "Impossible."

I smile, feeling the chaos sing through my veins. "You have no idea what you're fighting."

With a thought, I send a wave of mutated insects

swarming towards him. Each one carries a spark of my magick, ready to explode on contact. Shade tries to disperse into shadow, but my power is already there, infecting the darkness itself.

He screams as the madness invades him, twisting his essence. I watch dispassionately as his form unravels, scattering into wisps of tainted shadow that dissipates on the wind.

Two down.

A whisper of sound is my only warning before Silence appears behind me, their hands already reaching for my throat. But I'm not there anymore. My power surges, shifting me through space in a burst of purple energy.

I reappear behind Silence, lightning flickering between my fingers. "Nice try," I taunt. "But you'll have to be faster than that."

Silence whirls, their eyes widening as they take in my transformed state. They open their mouth, but no sound comes out. Instead, I feel a pressure building in the air around us, like reality is being compressed.

With a thought, I shatter the silence they're trying to impose. The pressure explodes outward in a wave of sound that shatters windows and sends Silence stumbling back.

Before they can recover, I'm on them. My hands clamp down on either side of their head, and I pour anarchy directly into their mind. Silence screams, a grating noise like nails down a chalkboard, as my power overloads their senses.

They collapse, their power broken, and their mind shattered.

The air grows thick with the stench of decay as Grave approaches. Rotting vegetation sprouts from the ground with each step he takes.

"Impressive," he rasps. "But can you take two of us at once?"

I step back as Whisper moves into view, and I smile coldly as they approach. "Two against one? Hardly seems fair." My power crackles around me, reality warping in its wake. "For you."

Grave's eyes narrow. "Arrogant little bitch. Let's see how cocky you are when your flesh is rotting off your bones."

He raises his hands, dark energy swirling around them. The greenery around campus withers and decays. But before the effect can reach me, I twist reality around myself, creating a bubble where his power can't touch me.

"Impossible," Grave snarls.

"If by that you mean *possible*, then yes."

Whisper doesn't waste time with words. I feel the pressure of his power trying to invade my mind, to trap me in a loop of my worst fears. But my evolved magick shrugs it off like water off a duck's back.

I lash out with twin tendrils of power, one for each of them. Grave tries to counter with a wave of decay, but my magick simply absorbs it, growing stronger. Whisper attempts to retreat into the shadows, but I'm there waiting for him. I flood his system with pure chaos, overloading his ability to manipulate fears.

Grave roars in frustration as his power fails to affect me. He charges forward, hands outstretched to touch me directly. But I'm no longer there. I blink behind him, my power coalescing into a physical form.

"You want decay?" I snarl. "I'll show you decay."

With a single slash, I sever Grave's connection to his power. He screams as his own abilities turn inward, his body beginning to rot from the inside out.

Whisper, realising he's outmatched, turns to flee. But my power is everywhere now, infused into the fabric of reality around us. There's nowhere for him to run.

I reach out with my mind, grasping the threads of his consciousness. With a vicious twist, I shred his psyche, leaving him a drooling husk.

The campus below carries on as if nothing has happened while I stand on the rooftop in the centre of destruction. My power hums contentedly, having feasted on their abilities. I can feel their stolen magick integrating with my own, making me stronger.

"Still want to ask me to kill my aunt?" I call out. "If the answer is 'yes', then you're next in line. Choose wisely."

I run and leap off the top of the building. Holding my arms out as I plummet to the ground, for a moment, lost in the beauty of flight, my feet hit the ground, knees bent, and the earth cracks under the pressure. I straighten up with a wicked smile.

In the moment that follows, I know I've lost myself. I've been torn apart, and I don't know if I can ever be put back together again.

But maybe I don't want to be.

22

BRAM

THE DARK FAE MAGICK IN MY BLOOD SCREAMS A WARNING seconds before the attack comes. I drop and roll as a blade of pure shadow slices through the space where my head had been.

"Getting sloppy, Prince Bram," Draxon's voice whispers from behind me. "Or is she making you weak?"

I pull darkness around me like a cloak, my shadow magick responding to the threat. The university courtyard is packed at this hour, and that's probably why my family's political enforcer has come to pay me a visit.

"Jealous?" I ask the shadows. "That she's beyond your reach?"

A laugh like breaking glass cracks the concrete under my feet. "Beyond our reach? Look around you. Everything's within our reach."

He's not wrong. Every dark corner holds potential threats. Every whispered conversation carries hidden meanings.

Draxon materialises from the darkness; his form is more suggestion than substance. "The Dark Court sends its regards," he says, wielding shadow-blades like extensions of himself. "They're very interested in your association with Death's Heir and wonder why you haven't informed them."

Of course they are.

"Tell them to get in line," I growl, meeting his attack with my own shadow constructs. "Everyone seems to have an opinion lately."

"You've aligned yourself with chaos incarnate," Draxon says, our shadow weapons clashing in displays of impossible darkness. "Did you think there wouldn't be consequences?"

The fight moves across the courtyard in bursts of speed too fast for mortal eyes to track. Draxon is good, one of the best. But I was trained by the Dark Court itself, and some lessons you never forget.

"You're not here for me," I murmur, catching glimpses of his true purpose in the patterns of his attacks. "This is about her. About showing her what's at stake."

His laugh confirms it.

"Smart boy," Draxon purrs, his form rippling like oil on water. "So many pieces in play. So many ways this could end."

I switch tactics, pulling on the Fae magick that marks me as royal blood. The shadows respond differently now, taking on aspects of starlight and frost.

The starlight-infused shadows swirl around me,

responding to my blood. Draxon's eyes widen slightly as he recognises the true power of the royal bloodline.

"Ah, there it is," he says, a hint of respect colouring his tone. "I was wondering when you'd stop holding back."

"You want a show?" I snarl, feeling the magick surge through me. "I'll give you a fucking show."

I lash out with tendrils of shadow and starlight, each one carrying the deadly chill of the Dark realm. Draxon counters with his own shadow constructs, but I can see the strain on his face as he struggles against the royal magick.

"The Court underestimates her," I say, pressing my advantage. "They think she's just another pawn in their games."

Draxon laughs, a sound like cracking ice. "Oh, we know exactly what she is. The question is, do you?"

His words give me pause, and in that moment of distraction, he strikes. A blade of pure shadow slices across my chest, drawing a line of silvery blood.

I stumble back, more shocked than hurt. It's been a while since anyone has managed to wound me.

"You're compromised," Draxon says, circling me like a predator. "Your feelings for her have made you weak."

"You're wrong," I growl, letting my royal blood flow freely now. The shadows around us twist and writhe, responding to my unleashed power. "She doesn't make me weak. She makes me stronger."

The students around us have formed a massive

circle, unable to look away even though they should run as far as they can. There will be collateral damage.

Draxon's eyes narrow as he senses the shift in the air. The veil bends around us as I tap into the full potential of my heritage.

"You've forgotten who I am," I say, my voice echoing with ethereal power. "What I am."

The shadows coalesce into solid forms, nightmarish creatures born of darkness and starlight. They circle us, snarling and snapping.

Draxon takes a step back, real fear flickering in his eyes for the first time. "This is beyond your station, Prince Bram. The Court will not tolerate such a display of power on this realm."

I laugh, and the sound sends cracks, spiderwebbing across the concrete. "And yet they sent you here to test me, to see if I was still their obedient little prince." I bare my teeth in a feral grin. "Consider this my resignation."

With a thought, I send my shadow beasts lunging for Draxon. He fights back valiantly, his shadows clashing with mine in a dizzying display of dark magick. But he's outmatched, and he knows it.

"You can't protect her forever," Draxon gasps as my minions tear into him. "The Court will come for her and for you."

"Let them come," I snarl, tightening my grip on reality. The veil between worlds grows thin, and I can feel the pull of the Dark realm. "I'll show them exactly what happens when you threaten what's mine."

With a final burst of power, I rip open a portal to the Dark Fae realm. Draxon's eyes widen in panic as he realises what I'm about to do.

"You can't," he pleads. "They'll kill you for this."

I smile coldly. "They can try."

With a thought, I send Draxon hurtling through the portal, his screams echoing across realities. The gateway snaps shut behind him, leaving only a lingering chill in the air.

The shadow creatures dissolve as I release my hold on them, reality settling back into place. The students who witnessed the fight stand frozen, their minds struggling to process what they've just seen.

I turn to address them, letting a hint of my true nature show through. "This never happened," I say, my voice layered with Fae glamour. "You saw nothing unusual here today."

Their eyes glaze over as the suggestion takes hold. Within moments, they disperse, returning to their normal routines as if nothing had occurred.

"Neat trick. Doesn't work on this bitch, though."

Ivy's voice makes me whirl around. "How much of that did you see?"

"How about all of it." She moves closer, a seductive sway to her movements. It perks me up immediately.

I reach for her and slam her against the nearest tree, my hand going between her legs to squeeze her pussy.

She bites her bottom lip and wiggles closer to me. I work the button and the zip on her jeans undone, sliding my hand inside to find her dripping wet for me.

Ivy moans softly as my fingers slide through her slick folds. "Fuck, Bram. Right here?"

"Right here," I growl, nipping at her neck. The adrenaline from the fight still courses through me, making me reckless. "I need you. Now."

She grins wickedly, her eyes flashing with that new power. "Then take me."

Pushing her jeans down over her thighs, she keeps her legs pressed together as I undo my pants. Moving in closer, I thrust up into her tight pussy, wedged between her thighs and causing friction that is irresistible.

"Yes," she hisses as I thrust into her, burying myself to the hilt.

I set a punishing pace, fucking her hard against the rough bark

"Harder," she demands, her voice thick with lust as, once again, students stop to stare. But neither of us cares. "Make me feel it, Bram."

As I pound into her mercilessly, she writhes against the tree, which creaks ominously behind her, but I'm beyond caring. All that matters is the tight heat of her cunt around my cock, the way she gasps and moans with each thrust.

"Fuck, Ivy," I groan, feeling my release building. "You drive me fucking crazy."

Her pussy clenches around me as she comes with a cry, her power flaring out in waves of vibrant energy.

Ivy's orgasm triggers mine, and I come with a guttural roar, spilling deep inside her. As we both shudder through the aftershocks, I become acutely aware of our surroundings and chuckle.

"Well," Ivy says breathlessly, "that's one way to make a statement."

Slowly pulling out of her and stashing my dick, I help her straighten her clothes. "Subtlety was never my strong suit."

She grins, her eyes sparkling with mischief and lingering arousal. "Clearly. Not that I'm complaining."

As we make ourselves presentable, I notice the crowd of students starting to disperse, probably turned on by this live sex show.

"We should probably get out of here," I mutter. "I'm surprised the staff haven't already appeared."

"Please. They wouldn't know what to do with themselves."

Ivy's casual dismissal of potential consequences makes me chuckle, but there's an edge to my laughter. The fight with Draxon and its implications still weigh heavily on my mind.

"We need to talk," I say, taking her hand and leading her away from the scene of our very public tryst. "Somewhere private."

She nods, her expression growing serious as she picks up on my mood. We make our way across campus, eventually ending up in a secluded corner of the library.

"Spill," Ivy says once we're alone. "What's got you so worked up? Besides the obvious," she adds with a smirk.

I run a hand through my hair, trying to organise my thoughts. "That fight wasn't just about me. The Dark Court is making moves, Ivy. They're interested in you."

Her eyes narrow. "Because of this Fae power?"

"Yeah, they probably think it belongs to them, and therefore, you belong to them. Draxon was here to take you."

"So, what do we do about it?"

I sigh, staring out over the library without the first idea what to tell her. "We make sure that doesn't happen."

23

TORIN

"THE BLOODLINES ARE MORE COMPLICATED THAN ANYONE realises," Mum says, her hair pulled back severely. She looks more like a university professor than one of Britain's most powerful vampires, but there's something in her eyes that betrays the facade. Something ancient. "Especially when it comes to Death's lineage."

She spreads out what appears to be a family tree, but unlike any I've seen before. The lines between names shine with faint light, and some branches seem to exist in multiple dimensions at once, overlapping in ways that hurt my eyes to look at directly.

I glare at her in annoyance. She showed up here moments ago, unannounced and is forcing me to listen to her because she says it's about Ivy. One word that is even a slight insult, and I will stake this woman myself and get her out of my life, once and for all.

"These connections," she traces one glowing line, "aren't just genealogy. They're magical bindings, carefully orchestrated over centuries. Look here - the Smith line merging with the Thornes in 1742. Not a natural union. They were drawn together by forces they never understood."

I lean closer, trying to focus on the intricate patterns, giving her exactly five minutes to make her point before I start throwing stakes around.

"The Hammond line appears here," she continues, pointing to a section where multiple lines converge like a spiderweb. "And here. And here. Always at critical junctions. Always when Death's power needs to be adjusted."

"Adjusted how?"

She pulls out another document, this one bound in what looks suspiciously like human skin. "Death chooses vessels from specific bloodlines - ones with a natural affinity for chaos magick. But it's more than simple compatibility. The Hammond line isn't just attuned to Death's power. It's engineered. Has been for centuries."

"Engineered?" I study the complex web of marriages and magical bindings. Certain names keep appearing - old families, powerful witches, mysterious figures marked with symbols I've never seen before.

"Watch," she says, laying out three more documents in a triangle formation. They glow, creating a projection in the air between them. A three-dimensional map of magical bloodlines stretching back through time. "In 1503, the first deliberate binding. The Hammonds were nothing then but a minor family of hedge witches. But they had potential."

The projection shows two lines merging, accompanied by a surge of power that makes the air taste like lightning.

"Then here - 1648. The Midnight Convergence. Seven families, seven ritual bindings, all designed to concentrate certain abilities in the bloodline."

I watch as the magical lines twist and merge, creating patterns that seem to follow some grand design. "Who orchestrated this? Death?"

Mum's laugh holds no humour. "This goes back further. Much further."

She reveals another document, this one written in a language that seems to change every time I try to read it. "There are patterns, if you know where to look. Certain families orchestrating specific unions, guiding the bloodlines toward a singular purpose."

"What purpose?"

"Evolution," she says softly. "Controlled, directed evolution of magickal ability. The ability to not just channel Death's power but to change it. To make it more."

The projection shifts, showing more recent convergences. I recognise some names now - families still active in supernatural politics.

"Every marriage arranged, every child born, every death carefully timed, are all part of a greater design. The Hammond line wasn't chosen by Death. It was created for Death."

That's new and interesting. She gets five more minutes. "Created by who?"

"That's the interesting part." She pulls out another document, this one bearing symbols that make my eyes water. "There are older powers than Death. Older magicks than chaos, and they've been waiting. Planning. Preparing."

There is a knock at the door, and Bram pushes it open with Ivy by his side. "Hey. We need to talk—"

He cuts off as he takes in my mother and her documents.

Ivy's reaction is interesting, though. She stops dead as she stares at my mother. The floating projection of bloodlines warps, responding to her presence like iron to a magnet.

"You," Ivy states. "You were there. At the cabin."

Mum's expression doesn't change, but her eyes narrow. "Miss Hammond. Good to see you again."

"Again?"

"When I killed your father," Ivy says, not taking her eyes off my mother, "there was a woman there. Watching before she disappeared in a cloud of purple power."

"The advanced mage Tate reckoned was there," I grit out. "It was you."

"The pieces were already in motion," Mum says calmly, brushing it off as if discussing the weather rather than her presence at my father's murder. "Certain things had to happen in a specific order. Your father's death was a necessary catalyst."

"The question is why? Why did you want him dead? Why reveal these bloodline secrets now?"

Mum straightens, and for a moment, I glimpse something ancient and terrible in her eyes. "Because Death is not the only one playing a long game. The Syndicate thinks they're the puppet masters, but there are older powers at work."

She gestures at the scattered documents, each one shining with centuries of carefully woven magick. "Look at the pattern. The Hammond line crossing with chaos practitioners in 1742. The dark magick infusion through the Smith marriage in 1823. The binding of elemental power through the Thorne alliance in 1901. Every generation, every union, carefully orchestrated to create the perfect vessel."

"The bloodlines," I say, pieces clicking into horrible place. "You're not just sharing information. You're part of whatever's been engineering them. Part of the organisation that's been manipulating supernatural bloodlines for centuries."

"Smart boy." Mum's smile holds secrets within secrets. "Though perhaps not smart enough, if you haven't figured out why your father really had to die."

"Explain."

"Death's vessels aren't chosen," she says, tapping the ancient family trees. The magickal lines respond to her touch, creating new patterns in the air. "They're created. Through centuries of careful breeding, magickal bindings, and..." she glances at Ivy, "precisely timed removals of certain obstacles."

"My father was an obstacle?" I ask, feeling the irony. He was definitely an obstacle to me.

"He discovered too much. Started asking dangerous questions about old families and older magicks." She traces a particularly complex binding in the floating pattern. "He was going to expose everything. All the careful work of centuries, undone by one man's greed for power. We couldn't allow that."

"We?" Ivy demands. "Who exactly is we?"

Mum's smile grows sharper. "Now that's the real question, isn't it? The one The Syndicate should be asking, instead of playing their little games with ultimatums and power plays."

She waves a hand, and the magickal projections reform, showing new patterns, deeper connections I hadn't noticed before. "Every major supernatural event in history, every rise of power, every fall of an old family, every seemingly random tragedy are all part of the pattern. All moving us toward this moment."

"What moment?" I demand, but I see it now in the bloodlines. The way they all seem to converge on this point in time. On Ivy.

"Evolution," Mother says again, but this time, the word holds weight. Power. Promise. "True evolution of magickal ability. The Hammond line was crafted to be more than just Death's vessel. It was designed to change Death itself."

"You know what?" Ivy snaps. "I'm getting really sick of that fucking word. No one uses it again, or I start kicking arses."

Mum looks at Ivy with something like hunger. "You're feeling it already, aren't you? The way your power is growing, changing, becoming something new. Something more than Death ever intended. We orchestrated your entire existence. Centuries of careful breeding and magickal manipulation, all leading to you. The perfect vessel for what's coming."

"What's coming?" I ask.

Mum gathers the ancient documents with a sweep of her hand, and they vanish, her smile holding centuries of secrets. "The old powers are stirring. The barriers between worlds are thinning. And you, my dear children, are standing at the crossroads of history."

She looks between us, and for a moment, I see something vast and dark behind her eyes. Something that makes Death's power seem young in comparison.

"The question isn't who I am or what I've done," she says. "The question is: when you finally understand what's coming, which side of history will you choose to be on?"

We glare at her, speechless.

"Choose wisely, children," Mum says, turning to leave. "The dance is only beginning."

She disappears in a cloud of power, leaving us with nothing but questions and the crushing weight of revelation.

The truth settles around us like falling ash:

Nothing is what we thought.

No one is who we believe.

And the real game?

It hasn't even started yet.

"What the fucking fuck is older than Death?" Bram snaps, frustrated and annoyed as I am.

"The only thing that comes before it," Ivy mutters. "Life."

24

IVY

THE REALISATION HITS ME LIKE A TON OF BRICKS, MAKING my crazy-arse power burst to life in response. Life. Of course. The word echoes through my mind, carrying weight beyond its simple syllable. What else could be powerful enough to orchestrate centuries of bloodline manipulation? What else would have the patience, the foresight, to craft the perfect vessel across generations?

My power ripples beneath my skin, no longer a light-coloured chaos but something deeper and more primal. It's like my cells are awakening to a truth they've always known.

"The veils are thinning," I murmur, watching as reality ripples around us. My power responds differently now, more attuned to the subtle shifts between realms. "Can't you feel it?"

The air grows thick with possibility, taking on a strange quality that makes breathing feel like drawing in liquid light. Suddenly, the room fills with a brilliant radiance that blinds me momentarily. Lifting my hand up to cover my eyes, every cell in my body sings with recognition.

Before any of us can move, reality splits. There's no other word for it. The fabric of existence parts like a curtain, creating a wound in the world that bleeds pure, unfiltered life force. Through that tear steps a figure that makes my breath catch and my limbs turn to jelly.

She's beautiful in a way that defies description. Her form constantly shifts and grows. Flowers bloom in her footsteps, bursting into vibrant life only to wither and be replaced by new growth in endless cycles. Her skin glows with an inner light that hurts to look at directly, like trying to stare at the sun. Her hair moves like vines, each strand a separate organism reaching for the light.

The marking on my lower back burns suddenly, a searing pain that makes me gasp. The fated mate bond is reacting to something, trying to tell me something crucial.

"Tate," I whisper, and as if summoned by my need, the door bursts open.

He staggers in, his face pale with strain. Where our magick usually connects smoothly, there's now a disturbing resonance, like two discordant frequencies trying to align.

"What the fuck is happening?" he demands, his power reaching for mine instinctively. But when our magick touches, something strange occurs. Instead of the usual stabilising effect, reality warps more violently around us.

"Hello, anchor," this creature says, her voice containing multitudes of life - the crack of seeds sprouting, the rustle of leaves, the eternal cycle of growth and renewal. "How fascinating. You've begun to adapt as well."

Tate's eyes widen as he takes in her impossible form. "Who—"

"Life," I breathe, understanding flooding through me. My power responds to her presence, creating strange patterns in the air where our energies meet. "She's Life."

She smiles, and it's like watching a flower unfold in fast motion, beautiful but nauseating. "You've grown beautifully, better than we could have hoped. And your anchor..." she studies Tate with unnerving intensity, "he's reconfiguring perfectly to contain your chaos."

"We?" Torin demands, moving protectively closer to me. His vampire nature recoils from Life's overwhelming presence. Her pure vitality is anathema to his undead state.

Life waves a hand dismissively, and where it passes, reality blooms with impossible vegetation that grows and dies in seconds. The walls sprout fungal growths that shimmer with bioluminescence, while the floor becomes a living carpet of moss that breathes beneath our feet.

"Death and I have been playing this game for aeons," she says, her attention fixing back on me. "But the rules are about to change."

"Because of me?" I ask, watching as my chaos

magick reacts to her presence, creating swirling patterns of dark purple and gold where our powers touch. The colours blend and separate like oil on water, neither fully mixing nor fully repelling.

Tate moves closer to me, but I can feel his struggle. His role as my anchor is to help stabilise my power, but Life's presence affects our connection, making it volatile and unpredictable.

"Because of what you represent," she corrects, her form shifting subtly with each word. "The perfect balance between life and death, chaos and order. A bridge between what is and what could be."

The room continues to transform around us, walls becoming living tissue that burst with magickal energy. Bram's shadows writhe uncomfortably, and Torin looks physically ill from the overwhelming presence of pure life force. Even Tate's usually steady magick fluctuates erratically.

"You want to destroy Death," I say, the truth forming in my mind as pieces click into place. "That's what all this has been about. The bloodline manipulation, the engineered evolution of my power. You want to use me to end Death."

Her smile turns predatory, and I feel sick as my blood pounds in my ears. This isn't just about Death; it's about death.

Flowers burst from her skin, blooming and dying in rapid succession as I stare at her in horror. "Imagine it, little catalyst. A world without end. Pure, eternal life. No more loss, no more grief, no more endings."

"That's not life," I argue, feeling the wrongness of it in my bones. "That's stagnation. Without death, nothing truly lives. It just exists."

"Indeed." Life moves closer, and reality warps around her. The air vibrates, thick with spores and microscopic life that shouldn't be visible to the naked eye. "But you're thinking too small. This isn't about preserving individual lives. It's about transforming existence itself. Making it more."

As if to demonstrate, she touches a nearby plant. It grows rapidly, becoming something impossible - a hybrid of flesh and flower that writhes with unnatural vitality. Veins pound beneath translucent petals, and what might be eyes blink wetly from within its core.

"This is what you want?" I ask, horrified. "To turn everything into these abominations?"

Tate grips my fingers tightly, his touch grounding me even as our combined magick makes reality fluctuate more violently. I can feel him trying to anchor me, but Life's presence corrupts the connection, turning our usual harmony into something wild and unstable.

"I want to fulfil the potential of all living things," she says, her voice taking on the edge of madness. Flowers burst from her mouth with each word, blooming and withering between syllables. It's horrific to watch, but I can't look away. "To free them from the arbitrary constraints of mortality. And you, my perfectly crafted vessel, are going to help me do it."

"She's not helping anyone," Tate growls, his magick wrapping itself protectively around me. But the moment it touches Life's power, it transforms, black energy sprouting tiny buds of chaotic growth.

Life laughs, and the sound makes reality shiver as Tate stumbles back. "Oh, sweet anchor. You're already helping. Every time you try to stabilise her power, you create new pathways for expansion. New possibilities for growth."

My power surges in response to her words, but not in agreement. The chaos magick that flows through me recoils from her touch, recognising the fundamental wrongness of her vision. Where our energies meet, reality itself seems to buckle.

"That's why Death chose me," I mutter, pieces clicking into place as Tate's grip on my hand tightens. "Not because he wanted a successor, but because he needed someone who could stand against this."

Life's laugh this time is like breaking glass, and the flowers burst around us, their petals falling like rain. But they are wrong somehow. They are too symmetrical, too perfect, and lack the beautiful flaws that make natural things real.

"Death didn't choose you, child. I did. Millennia ago, when I began crafting what would become the Hammond line. Death merely played his part, thinking he was grooming his own successor."

The room continues to transform, with walls becoming living tissue that hums with sickening vitality. Vines burst through the floor, growing, dying, and regrowing in endless cycles. Each iteration becomes more twisted and wrong. Life's corporeal presence corrupts the natural order.

"You're insane," Bram hisses, his Fae magick recoiling from the twisted life force filling the room. His shadows try to provide cover, but wherever they touch Life's power, they sprout grotesque luminescent fungi.

"Natural." Life's beauty twists into something terrible. Her perfect features become too perfect, too alive, cells visibly multiplying and dying across her skin. "I am nature. I am life itself, and I am tired of sharing power with Death. Tired of watching my creations wither and die when they could flourish eternally." Life's smile turns enigmatic as reality shudders around us. "You'll understand soon enough," she says, her form beginning to blur at the edges. "After all, that's what evolution is really about."

25

IVY

Before any of us can respond, she simply... unmakes herself. That's the only word to describe it. There's no flash of light, no dramatic exit - she just stops being, leaving behind an absence that feels more substantial than her presence. The twisted vegetation remains, though, with an unsettling vitality that gives me the heebies.

"Well, that was unexpected," Torin mutters, but his voice sounds strained. The overwhelming life force has taken its toll on his vampire nature.

"Are you okay, vamp-boy?" I ask, still staring at the space where Life had been. My advanced power still crackles beneath my skin. But something's different now. The chaos feels purposeful, somehow, like it's trying to tell me something I should have realised ages ago.

"Yeah," he croaks, looking paler than usual.

"Ivy?" Tate's hand is still wrapped around mine, his

touch steadying despite the way our combined magick makes reality ripple. "What are you thinking?"

"Death," I say slowly, pieces clicking into place like a puzzle solving itself. "We've been looking at this all wrong. He's not the villain in this story."

Bram frowns, his shadows finally settling now that Life's presence has faded. "What do you mean?"

"Think about it," I say, as understanding floods through me. "Why would Death choose a vessel that could potentially destroy him? Why orchestrate my adaptation if it meant giving Life the perfect weapon against him?"

"Unless," Tate says, "that wasn't the plan at all."

"Exactly. He wasn't grooming me to destroy or replace him. He was preparing me to maintain balance. To fight against Life taking over. All this time, everyone's been talking about—insert groan at his blasted word—*evolution* like it's about becoming more powerful. But what if it's about becoming more balanced?"

The chaos inside me responds to my realisation, creating a display that looks like a double helix in the air - one strand dark as Death, one bright as Life, with my dark purple energy weaving between them erratically.

"The Hammond line wasn't engineered to destroy Death," Tate says thoughtfully, his magick reaching out to stabilise the pattern I've created. "It was designed to stand between Life and Death. To maintain the natural order."

Bram moves closer, studying the floating design

with his Fae sight. "That's why the Ancient Fae magick responded to you. The Fae understand balance better than most - we exist in the spaces between realms."

"And why I'm your anchor," Tate adds, his black energy now threaded with hints of my chaos. "The Well bloodline isn't just about containing chaos - it's about helping channel it productively."

I nod, feeling the truth in my bones. "Death knew Life was planning something. He knew she'd been manipulating bloodlines for centuries, trying to create the perfect vessel for her power. So, he adapted. Used her own plan against her."

"By making sure her perfect vessel would be equally attuned to his power," Torin says, catching on. "Fucking brilliant, actually."

"More than that. He made sure I'd be capable of understanding both sides. Life and Death. Creation and destruction. Growth and decay. They're not opposing forces—they're parts of the same whole. Or they're supposed to be."

The twisted vegetation Life left behind responds to my presence differently now. Instead of growing wildly, it settles into a more natural pattern, finding equilibrium between growth and decay.

"That's why you rejected becoming Death while still in the womb," Tate realises. "Not because you were fighting against Death's power, but because you were meant to be something else entirely. Something new."

"Not new," I correct, as I see the bigger picture. "Ancient. As old as Life and Death themselves. There has to have been a balance keeper. Someone or something that maintains equilibrium between realms. Life's been trying to eliminate that role, to tip everything toward endless growth."

Reality ripples around us again, but this time, I don't fight it. Instead, I let my magick flow naturally, watching as it stabilises the fluctuations rather than exacerbates them.

"It's not about becoming powerful enough to destroy Death. It's about becoming balanced enough to stand between Life and Death. To prevent either force from dominating the other."

"That's why Death gave you those choices," Bram says. "Kill us or lose your soul - he was testing whether you could understand the necessity of balance. That sometimes sacrifice is needed to maintain the natural order."

"I'd be willing to bet that's why he imprisoned us as well. To see if we could escape and get back to Ivy or give up and face our fate," Torin murmurs.

Nodding, I find this all makes sense on a level that is so whacked out, it probably takes a mad bitch to understand it. "I found another way."

"Because that's what balance is really about," Tate says softly. "Finding the path between extremes. Not just accepting the options you're given but creating new possibilities."

The marking on my lower back flares warmly, and I understand something else, too. "The fated mate bond - it's not just about romance or destiny. It's about creating connections that help maintain balance. Each of you brings something essential to this equation."

"Tate anchors your chaos," Torin says, counting off on his fingers. "Bram brings the Fae understanding of between-spaces, and I..." he pauses, frowning.

"You bring the perspective of someone who exists between life and death," I tell him. "Vampires aren't fully alive or fully dead. You understand liminality in a way few others can."

The room falls quiet as we all process these revelations.

"So, what now?" Bram finally asks. "How do we stop Life from unmaking everything?"

"We don't fight her directly," I say slowly. "That's what she wants. Conflict, disruption, a chance to prove that her way is better. Instead, we restore balance. Every time she tries to tip the scales toward endless life, we find ways to maintain equilibrium."

"And Death?" Torin asks. "Where does he fit into all this?"

"He's been playing the long game as well. Working against Life's plans while appearing to oppose us. Everything he's done, the ultimatums, the tests, even setting The Syndicate against me - it's all been about preparing me for this role."

"The perfect vessel," Tate murmurs, "not for Death's power or Life's, but for balance itself."

"Well," I say after a moment of quiet reflection. "At least now we know what we're really fighting for."

The others nod, and I feel our bond strengthen - not

just through fate or circumstance, but through shared purpose. Life might have spent centuries crafting the perfect vessel, but she never understood what that vessel was really meant to become.

Not a weapon of destruction.

Not an agent of eternal life.

But a keeper of balance.

A force for equilibrium in a universe that desperately needs it.

The real evolution isn't about power at all.

It's about understanding.

About balance.

About finding the path between extremes.

And for the first time since my power awakened, I feel truly ready to walk that path.

No matter where it leads.

No matter if it tears me apart.

26

IVY

The peaceful moment of understanding shatters as reality ripples again - but this time, it's not from my chaos magick. Three figures materialise in the room, their bodies reforming from shadow in a way that puts me on the defensive until I see who it is.

"Oh good, more drama," Torin mutters, but I notice he moves protectively closer to me anyway.

Josh waves, but his usual smile is absent. "We have a problem."

"When don't we?" I reply. "What's happened?"

"The Syndicate," a female says, her silver eyes gleaming with urgency. "They're going after Cathy tonight."

"And you are?" I ask with a raised eyebrow.

"This is Eva," Josh says hastily.

"How did you know about Cathy?"

"You pissed them off in a big way, Ivy. It threw them

to know what you can do now, and they have targeted your aunt."

"They had before," I murmur. "I thought it was over."

He shakes his head.

Reality ripples around us in response to my anger. Tate grabs my hand, his anchor power struggling to stabilise the chaos that threatens to explode outward.

"When?" I demand.

Josh shrugs. "We don't know for sure. It's rumbles."

"Fuck."

"Actually, there's more," the third Resistance member—another woman I don't recognise—says. "That's why we're here. The Syndicate's not acting on their own anymore. They're being influenced."

"By who?"

"Good question."

But I think I already know. Death is losing his grip on his little band of sideshow assassins, and Life is stepping up her game. This is not good. Life isn't just trying to unmake death, she's systematically eliminating anything that might help maintain balance.

"This had nothing to do with Death. The Wraiths. It was Life. She went after my aunt to get to me."

"Huh?" Josh asks, scrunching up his nose. "Who the fuck is Life?"

I shake my head, and Torin goes into an explanation as my mind whirls with all that is going on.

Suddenly, I've reached a point where I'm tired. Really fucking tired. I've been going on all cylinders for what feels like days now and I just want to close my eyes and wake up in last week where everything made sense.

Slamming my hands to my head to cut out the noise, the chatter of the creatures around me, I close my eyes with a moan, and crouch down.

"Ivy!" Tate's voice cuts through the fog in my mind.

The world spins as I crouch there, hands pressed to my head. Everything's too much - the revelations about Life and Death, the threat to Cathy, the weight of this new role I'm meant to play.

My power ebbs and flows in unpredictable patterns, causing the world around me to twist and distort in nauseating waves.

"Ivy, breathe," Tate says. His hands are on my shoulders, trying to steady me. "Focus on my voice. Find your centre."

I try, but it's like grasping at smoke. Whatever burgeoning of understanding I had about balance feels distant, theoretical. In this moment, all I can feel is the overwhelming tide of chaos tearing me apart.

"I can't," I gasp. "It's too much. I don't know how to—"

"Yes, you do," Bram says firmly. He kneels beside me, his shadow magick wrapping around us like a cocoon. "You've been doing it all along. Every time you've found a third option, every time you've rejected false choices. That's balance in action when you didn't even realise it. You are stronger than this. Stronger than all of them. You are fucking Poison, a badass bitch who takes what we give her and begs for more. You are nobody's puppet, Ivy. You are better than all of them."

Torin joins us, his cold hand on my back under my tee sends chills over me. "Remember what you said about vampires existing between life and death? That's you right now. You're the bridge, the in-between. Embrace it."

Their words penetrate the fog of overwhelm. I focus on their touch, on the way our energies intermingle. Tate's steady anchor, Bram's shadowy protection, Torin's liminal nature.

Gradually, the chaos inside me begins to settle. Not disappearing but finding a state of equilibrium. I take a deep breath and open my eyes.

"There she is," Torin says with a smirk. "Our badass bitch."

I manage a weak smile. "Thanks, guys. I needed that."

"Anytime," Bram murmurs.

Standing slowly, I face the others. Josh and the Resistance members look concerned, but there's no time for explanations.

"Right," I say, my voice stronger now. "We need a plan. The Syndicate's going after Cathy, and we can't let that happen."

"Agreed," Tate says. "But we can't just rush in blindly. If Life is influencing them now, we don't know what we're up against. We need a plan. Something that satisfies The Syndicate without actually harming Cathy."

"Can we fake her death?" I ask slowly.

"It won't be easy," Eva warns. "They aren't fools."

Josh studies us thoughtfully. "It might work. But you'll need inside help. Someone who knows exactly what The Syndicate will look for in a death confirmation."

"Can The Resistance help with that?" I ask.

The unknown woman steps forward again. "That's why I'm here. I'm Katie, a former Syndicate death validator. I know every protocol they use to confirm a kill."

"A death validator?" Torin's lip curls. "They really do bureaucratise everything, don't they?"

"You have no idea," Katie says dryly. "There are seventeen distinct protocols for confirming different types of supernatural deaths. They'll expect specific markers."

"What exactly do they need to see?" I force myself to ask. "I've never had this checklist before, and the vamps turn to dust, so how do they even check?" I never even thought about it before, but assumed they must know somehow. Maybe I didn't want to know.

Katie begins listing requirements clinically, but I tune out. I don't care. All I care about is fixing whatever mess I've been dumped into as fast as possible so I can finish at Thornfield and just go and live my life with my guys. The sooner that happens, the better.

That wave of exhaustion washes over me again, but I push it aside. There will be time to sleep later.

I tune back in as Bram says, "We need to be clever

about this. The Syndicate expects chaos and destruction from Ivy. They'll be watching for big, messy displays of power."

"So, we give them subtle instead," I say, an idea forming. "They're so focused on protocols and procedures... what if we use that against them?"

Josh raises an eyebrow. "What are you thinking?"

"A perfect death," I say slowly. "I have an idea about that. But first, we need to get to Cathy before The Syndicate does. Where is she?"

Josh nods. "At home. She said she had something to take care of."

"Then we need to move fast." I turn to my guys. "Ready?"

Katie nods grimly. "Be careful. The tides have turned with this shift in the hierarchy. You need to be—"

"Better?" I say bitterly.

She nods.

"Wonderful," I mutter.

"We're not losing her," Tate says firmly, his hand finding mine. "We can do this."

"The Resistance will help," Josh adds. "We've been watching some of The Syndicate's other operatives for a while now, wondering what was going on with them. We've been learning their patterns. They're strong, but they're predictable. Everything has to be just so with them."

"Life's influence," I murmur. "They're like those

twisted plants, too perfect to be natural. No variation, no chaos, no..."

"Balance," Katie finishes. "Exactly. They follow protocols because they can't conceive of alternatives. It's all black and white to them. No grey areas."

"Then we use that rigidity against them," I say. "They don't live long enough to hurt anyone else."

27

IVY

Travelling through Bram's shadows feels natural. The Fae part of this power, which I still don't understand, recognises the space between realms, understanding it not as darkness but as another form of balance. The natural counterpoint to light.

We emerge in Cathy's back garden, materialising behind her prized rose bushes.

Stepping toward the back door, I test the handle. It's open, and I shake my head, my mouth in a grim line. She never was all that concerned about security. I can see why now, knowing that she works for The Resistance. But still. That should make her more security conscious.

"Cathy? You here?" I call out.

She enters the kitchen holding out something that looks like a laser gun. She lowers it when she sees me. "Ivy? What are you doing here?"

"We came for you—"

"You need to leave. There are creatures coming—"

"You know?"

She huffs at me as I cut her off, much like she did to me and her eyes narrow as she takes in our group. "Of course I know. I'm not some helpless civilian, Ivy. I've been preparing for this."

I blink, taken aback, but then shake my head at myself. I should've known. The Resistance *should have* known… Something doesn't add up here. "Preparing how?" I ask suspiciously.

She gestures to the strange weapon in her hand. "Prototype. It is designed to disrupt supernatural energy signatures. Should incapacitate most threats, at least temporarily."

"Impressive," Torin murmurs, eyeing the device with interest.

"We don't have time for show and tell," I say, forcing us back on track. "The Syndicate is coming for you, Cathy. We need to get you out of here."

She shakes her head firmly. "No. I'm not running. They want to come for me? They are more than fucking welcome."

I press my lips together at my aunt's brash attitude. I suddenly see her for what she is. A badass bitch. It's not that she didn't care or love me. She works for a supernatural agency tasked to take down The Syndicate. Simple, really, now that I know. I can see everything a lot clearer.

"It's not just the Syndicate anymore," Tate explains quickly. "There are larger forces at play. Cosmic-level entities that make the Syndicate look like schoolyard bullies."

"Life," Cathy states. "I know."

"Okay, so what are we even doing here?" I ask in exasperation, "If you are all in the know."

"Beats the shit out of me," she says with a shrug. "Why are you here?"

"Josh," I mutter and then shake my head. "No. He isn't a traitor."

"I did not like that Katie," Bram states emphatically. "She gave me the heebies."

"Same," Torin says. "My vampire senses went haywire around her."

"What are you saying? Josh is in danger?" I ask, panicked. Ramsey would never forgive me if I left his boyfriend to die.

"Look," Tate snaps, all of this getting the better of him. "We are about to be surrounded by these perfect being shitheads, and we are standing around here chatting. More moving, less talk."

Too late.

Reality warps as two of those perfect beings phase through Cathy's kitchen wall. Their movements are unnaturally smooth, and their features are too symmetrical. Where they step, the tile sprouts tiny, identical flowers. Life's signature written in their every action.

"Down!" Bram shouts, his shadows surging forward to create a barrier between us and them. But where his darkness touches their perfection, it begins to transform, sprouting the same mathematical flowers in precise patterns.

My power reacts instinctively, recognising the fundamental wrongness of their existence. They're living weapons of pure order, created to eliminate chaos.

"The shadows won't hold them," Tate warns, his anchor power struggling to stabilise the wild burst of my magick. "We need another way out."

"Ivy Hammond," they speak in unison, their voices carrying harmonics that make reality shiver. "The natural order must be preserved. All chaos must be contained."

"Oh, piss off," Cathy snaps. "Natural order, my arse. You're about as natural as plastic roses."

I hold back my snort as she levels her weapon at them and fires. Bram's shadows explode, causing a backlash that knocks us all off our feet. My ears ring as I struggle to my feet, blinking away spots from my vision.

"Fuck," Torin groans, already moving to put himself between me and the intruders. "That packed a punch."

But when the dust settles, I see that Cathy's prototype did more than just disrupt. Where the beings once stood, reality wavers, like looking through the heat haze. Their perfect forms flicker and distort, struggling to maintain cohesion.

"Ha!" Cathy crows triumphantly. "Take that, you symmetrical bastards!"

Her victory is short-lived. Even as we watch, the

distortion begins to stabilise. Impossibly perfect flowers bloom from the cracks in reality, knitting it back together with sickening precision.

"Okay, new plan," I say, grabbing Cathy's arm. "We're leaving. Now."

She starts to protest, but Bram's already moving. His shadows, still reeling from the weapon's blast, manage to merge just enough to form a swirling portal.

"Go!" he shouts, strain evident in his voice. "I can't hold it long!"

We don't need to be told twice. Tate grabs my other hand, and we plunge into the darkness. Torin and Cathy are right behind us. Bram follows last, sealing the portal just as the beings lunge forward.

The shadow realm swirls around us, a dizzying vortex of darkness and half-formed shapes. Tate's grip on my hand is an anchor in the chaos. Cathy's presence is a bright spark of defiance, her energy pulsing with adrenaline and anger.

We emerge in a forest clearing, and the sudden shift from darkness to moonlight momentarily blinds us. As my eyes adjust, I take stock of our surroundings. Ancient trees loom overhead, their branches creating intricate patterns against the night sky. The air is thick with magick, old and wild.

"Where are we?" I ask, recognising nothing about our location.

Bram steadies himself against a tree, looking drained from the portal creation after Cathy blew up his magick. "One of the in-between places. A marginal space where the barriers between realms are thin. We should be safe here, at least for now."

Cathy whistles, low and appreciative. "Impressive. I've heard rumours about places like this, but I've never actually seen one."

"Yeah, well, enjoy the scenery while you can," Torin grumbles, his vampire senses clearly on high alert. "Those things will find us eventually. We need a plan."

"Find us?" Cathy sneers. "Oh no, dear boy. We are not going to hide out here while they hunt us. We are going to annihilate them. Ivy?" she says, hoisting her laser gun higher. "Are you with me?"

28

TATE

I WATCH IVY CAREFULLY AS SHE CONSIDERS HER AUNT'S words. There's a fire in her eyes, but there's something else, too, a flicker of uncertainty.

"Cathy," Ivy says slowly, "I get that you want to fight. But we can't just charge in guns blazing. These aren't normal enemies."

"They seemed pretty vulnerable to my prototype," Cathy argues, patting her weapon.

"For about five seconds," I grit out, feeling a bit sweaty and unstable. "Then they started regenerating. We need a better plan."

Ivy nods, her brow furrowed in thought. I can practically see the wheels turning in her mind, weighing options and possibilities. This is what makes her so unique in the ring. She truly does think outside the box.

"What if..." she starts, then pauses, chewing her lip. "What if we fall back on the original plan and use their own perfection against them?"

Bram raises an eyebrow. "That was all well and good in theory, but you got anything concrete?"

"They're creatures of pure order, right? No chaos, no variation. Everything has to be just right." Ivy's eyes light up as the idea takes shape. "So what happens if we introduce a little disorder into their perfect system? Like Cathy's weapon, but on a more severe scale."

I catch on to where she's going. "Overload them with chaos?"

"Exactly," Ivy says, her eyes gleaming with that slightly unhinged look I've come to love and fear. "We don't just introduce a little chaos. We flood their system with it."

"And how exactly do we do that?" Torin asks sceptically.

Ivy's grin widens. "We use me. Or, more specifically, my magick. Those beings are pure order. The antithesis of everything I represent. So, what if we turn that up to eleven?"

I feel a chill run down to my soul. "Ivy, your power is already incredibly volatile. Pushing it further could be dangerous."

"For them or for me?" she challenges.

"Both," I say firmly.

Bram nods in agreement. "He's right, Ivy. We don't know what channelling that much chaos could do to you."

"I do," Cathy interjects, her expression grim. "Or at least, I have an idea. The Resistance has been studying what we could of chaos magick for years. Trying to understand its potential and its limits."

Ivy turns to her aunt, curiosity evident. "And?"

Cathy sighs. "We've been through this, Ivy, already. You will be torn apart. It will literally unmake you at a molecular level."

I feel my heart clench at the thought. "Absolutely not," I growl. "We're not risking Ivy like that. There has to be another way."

Ivy's eyes flash with determination. "What if we combine approaches? Use Cathy's weapon to destabilise them, then hit them with a *controlled* burst of chaos magick?"

"Define 'controlled,'" Torin asks, eyes narrowed.

"That's where you guys come in," Ivy explains. "Tate, you anchor me. Bram, your shadows can help contain the blast radius. Torin, your vampire nature gives you a unique perspective on the balance between life and death. You can help me fine-tune the chaos."

I want to argue, to insist it's too dangerous. But I see the resolve in Ivy's eyes and know this is a battle I won't win. Instead, I nod grimly. "Fine. But at the first sign of trouble, we pull the plug. Your life isn't worth sacrificing."

"Agreed," Bram says firmly.

Cathy looks between us, her expression unreadable. Finally, she sighs. "It's risky as fuck, but it might just work. Those beings rely on perfect order. A targeted burst of chaos could shatter their cohesion."

"So, we have a plan," Ivy says, a fierce grin

spreading across her face. "Now we just need to draw them out."

"How do you propose we do that?" Torin asks.

"We give them what they are after," Cathy replies. "Me."

"No," Ivy says, shaking her head. "We give them me."

"No," Cathy echoes. "We give them me. This part isn't about you. They want me out of the picture."

I narrow my eyes as I take in this exchange. There is something Cathy isn't saying. "Why?" I ask.

Cathy shrugs. "Because I'm Ivy's aunt, because I work for the resistance? Who knows? Take your pick?"

Bram nods slowly. "It could work. We lure them in, thinking they've got you cornered, then spring the trap."

"I don't like it," I growl.

"Me either," Ivy protests.

Cathy checks her weapon, a grim smile on her face. "Well, tough shit. Decision made. Bram? Take us back?"

He looks at Ivy for confirmation.

She nods slowly, and I groan. This is going to end in disaster. We aren't ready for this.

Bram creates a shadow portal, and we jump through, landing in Cathy's back garden again, hidden behind some big bushes.

I watch uneasily as Cathy strides confidently into the middle of the grass, her weapon held at the ready. The rest of us are hidden, poised to spring our trap.

"Here I am, you symmetrical freaks!" Cathy shouts. "Come and get me!"

For a long moment, nothing happens. The garden is eerily silent, not even a breeze rustling the leaves. Then reality ripples and two of those perfect beings step through, their movements unnaturally fluid.

"Catherine Hammond," they intone in unison. "You will be eliminated to preserve the natural order."

Cathy snorts. "Natural order my arse. You lot wouldn't know natural if it bit you on your perfectly sculpted backsides."

She raises her weapon and fires. The blast hits the beings square in the chest, causing them to flicker and distort. But just like before, they begin to reorganise almost immediately, impossible flowers blooming from the cracks in their forms.

"Now!" Ivy shouts.

We burst from our hiding places. Bram's shadows lunge forward, creating a barrier to contain the chaos that's about to be unleashed. I grab Ivy's hand, channelling my magick to help anchor her to the here and now. Torin moves in next to Ivy and places his hand on the back of her neck. I feel her shiver at his touch.

Ivy's eyes blaze with purple fire as she coils the magick deep inside her. Static forms around us, sending our hair standing on end.

I watch with a bad feeling in my soul as Ivy gathers her power, purple energy crackling around her. She takes a deep breath and unleashes her magick. Raw chaos erupts from her in a swirling vortex of purple and black energy. It slams into the perfect beings with devastating force.

For a moment, nothing seems to happen. The beings stand motionless, absorbing the chaotic energy. Then cracks form in their perfect symmetry. Tiny fissures that spread and multiply.

"It's working," Cathy murmurs.

But something's wrong. I can feel it through our connection. Ivy's power isn't just affecting the beings, it's tearing at the fabric of reality.

"Ivy!" I yell. "Pull it back! It's too much!"

She doesn't seem to hear me. Her eyes are distant, lost in the flow of pure chaos.

The perfect beings are coming apart now, their forms dissolving into swirling patterns of impossibly ordered chaos. But reality is fracturing around us. I see glimpses of other realms through the cracks - places that shouldn't exist in our world.

"Bram!" I shout. "We need to contain this!"

His shadows strain against the onslaught of chaos, barely holding it back. "I'm trying!" Bram grits out. "But it's too much!"

Torin's eyes are wide with panic. "We need to stop her!"

I try to reach Ivy through our connection, but it's like trying to grasp smoke. Her consciousness is lost in the swirling vortex of chaos magick.

"Ivy!" I yell again, desperation clawing at my throat. "Come back to us!"

For a heartbeat, I see recognition flicker in her eyes.

Then she screams. A sound of pure agony that chills me to my core. Purple energy explodes outward, shattering Bram's shadow barrier.

The perfect beings dissolve completely, their ordered perfection torn apart by raw chaos. But the vortex doesn't stop. It keeps growing, reality fracturing further with each passing second.

"No!" Cathy shouts. She aims her weapon at Ivy, her finger on the trigger.

I move without thinking, tackling her to the ground. "Are you insane?" I snarl. "You could kill her!"

"She is dead anyway if we don't do something!"

She's right. The chaos is spreading, consuming everything in its path. Trees warp and twist into impossible shapes. The ground beneath our feet ruptures, sending clumps of dirt high into the air, but Ivy is my main focus. Ivy is suspended in the heart of the chaos vortex, her body arching in agony as reality fractures around her. Purple energy courses through her veins, visible beneath her skin like lightning. She's being torn apart at a molecular level, just as Cathy warned.

"Hold on!" I scream, fighting against the turbulence to reach her. My anchor magick strains against the pure havoc, trying to ground her, to give her something to hold onto.

Bram's shadows dance wildly, attempting to contain the destruction even as they're shredded by the raw power. "We're losing her!" he shouts over the roar of reality coming apart.

Torin grips her by her shoulders roughly, shaking her. "Her life force is fragmenting!" he calls out. "The chaos is unmaking her!"

I watch in horror as Ivy's form blurs at the edges, coming apart like a photograph dissolving in acid. Purple light blazes from her eyes and mouth as she screams again. It's a sound that tears at the fabric of existence itself.

"Ivy!" I push forward, fighting against the maelstrom with everything I have. My magick wraps around her like dark chains of pure order, trying to hold her together. But it's not enough. The chaos is too strong, too primal.

Through our connection, I feel her consciousness fragmenting.

"Fight it!" I bellow, pouring more power into our link. "Remember who you are! Remember us!"

But the chaos is winning. I watch in despair as pieces of Ivy literally tear away. Fragments of her being scatter across dimensions we were never meant to see. Her body flickers like a bad transmission, existing in multiple states at once.

Cathy's voice cuts through the mayhem as she steps up next to me and holds out the laser gun. "Here."

"No! I can't!" I shove my hands into my hair as I stare between the gun and Ivy. "I can't!"

"Do it!" Torin roars. "She is as good as dead if you don't!"

With a shaking hand, I take the laser gun and aim it

at Ivy, panic and fear ripping through me with an overdose of guilt.

"I'm sorry. I love you." I pull the trigger and watch, feeling sick to my stomach as the laser hits her and disrupts her aura, shattering it completely. "No!" Grief bears down on me, forcing me to my knees as she falls. Torin is holding her up like a macabre puppet, a sickened shock on his face.

The chaos vortex contracts, drawing back into Ivy like water down a drain. Reality knits itself back together, though everything feels slightly askew - as if the world has been broken and put back together imperfectly.

Finally, the last of the purple energy fades.

She's barely recognisable. Parts of her keep shifting between states of existence, never quite settling into one reality. Her skin is translucent in places, showing the chaos still coursing through her veins.

"We were too late. She's been torn apart at the quantum level. This is exactly what I was afraid of."

"Can we fix her?" I demand, my voice cracking.

Bram moves closer, almost robotically. "She exists in multiple dimensions now. Parts of her scattered across realities we can't even comprehend."

I take Ivy's limp hand and press it to my lips. "We'll fix this. I promise. We'll find a way to bring you back."

But looking at what's left of the woman I love, I wonder if some things can't be fixed. If sometimes the price of power is too high to ever truly come back from.

The perfect beings may be destroyed, but they've taken Ivy with them. Torn her apart in ways that might be impossible to repair.

29

IVY

I AM EVERYWHERE AND NOWHERE.

Torn apart like confetti scattered across infinite dimensions. Each fragment of my consciousness experiences a different reality, a different version of existence that my simple shifter mind cannot comprehend.

In one dimension, I am pure energy, dancing through crystalline structures of impossible geometry. In another, I am liquid thought, flowing through spaces between moments. Somewhere else, I am nothing but a collection of quantum possibilities, existing in all states simultaneously.

Tate?

I try to call out, but my voice splinters across realities. In one dimension, it emerges as a burst of purple light. In another, it becomes a cascade of mathematical equations.

Anyone?

But I am alone here, in these spaces between spaces. My memories scatter like autumn leaves, each one drifting into a different dimension. I catch glimpses of them as they pass:

First day at university, excitement and fear mingling.

Tate's eyes, filled with concern as my chaos magick surges.

Torin's cold touch, anchoring me to reality.

Bram's shadows, dancing with my chaos.

Each memory feels both intimately mine and impossibly distant, like trying to recall a dream while still dreaming. I reach for them, but my consciousness is too fragmented, too scattered across dimensions I was never meant to experience.

In one reality, I am versions of myself that collapse into quantum uncertainty. In another, I see my body through Tate's eyes, broken and shifting between states of existence, before it switches back to me. The grief on his face tears at what's left of my heart, but I can't reach him. Can't tell him I'm still here, somewhere in this multidimensional maze.

Focus, Ivy. The word echoes strangely through realities. *Remember who you are.*

But who am I now? The chaos magick has torn me apart at levels deeper than physical, scattered my essence across dimensions that defy comprehension.

The thoughts fragment, each piece drifting into a different dimension. I am losing myself, losing the very concept of self. My consciousness spreads thinner across infinite realities, each fragment experiencing a different version of existence.

Reality cracks and reforms around my scattered essence but somewhere else, I experience time flowing backwards, forwards, sideways through dimensions I can't name.

Please. I'm no longer sure who I'm calling to. *Help me.*

But help seems impossible when I exist in so many places at once, when my being has been torn apart at the quantum level. Each fragment of my consciousness experiences its own reality, its own version of existence, with no way to pull them back together.

The chaos magick has become my undoing, scattering me across dimensions like stars across the night sky. Each piece of me shines in its own reality, but none of them can find their way home.

I am purple light dancing through quantum foam.

I am mathematical uncertainty given form.

I am chaos scattered across ordered dimensions.

I am everything and nothing, everywhere and nowhere.

Time has no meaning here.

A world where I never discovered my chaos magick.

A reality where Tate and I never met.

A dimension where the perfect beings won.

Timelines branching endlessly, each one carrying a fragment of who I was.

My consciousness stretches thinner across the multiverse. I try to hold onto memories, onto the core of who I am, but they slip away like starlight through glass.

The taste of Tate's kiss dissolves into mathematical equations.

The sound of Torin's laugh becomes a burst of red energy.

The feeling of Bram's touch transforms into geometric patterns.

My mother's face fragments into infinite possibilities.

In some dimensions, I am aware of my body lying broken in Cathy's garden. I see through fractured perception as Tate holds my hand, as Torin's eyes fill with grief, as Bram's shadows dance uselessly around my shifting form. But these images feel increasingly distant, like memories of memories of dreams.

I should be scared. But fear requires a coherent self to experience it, and I am anything but coherent now. I am uncertainty given consciousness, chaos magick torn apart at levels deeper than physical.

I am Ivy Hammond.

But am I when my very essence has been scattered across dimensions I was never meant to know?

Life wanted order? Well, they've achieved its opposite - chaos so complete it transcends physical reality. I am their antithesis taken to its logical extreme, order's nightmare made manifest across dimensions.

Each heartbeat occurs in a different dimension.

Each thought spans multiple realities.

Each emotion resonates across quantum states.

Each moment of existence fragments further.

I am scattered.

I am undone.

I am lost.

I am torn apart.

30

BRAM

WE STAND IN STUNNED SILENCE, STARING AT THE BROKEN form that was once Ivy, now resting on Cathy's couch inside the too-quiet house. Reality still feels wrong, like it's been stretched too thin and has snapped back into place but is saggy. My insides twitch and writhe, sensing the lingering chaos in the air.

"We need to do something," Tate says, his voice cracking. He hasn't let go of Ivy's hand, even though parts of her keep phasing in and out of existence. "There has to be a way to bring her back."

"Back from where?" Torin asks bitterly. "She's been torn apart. Scattered across dimensions. We have no idea where she is or how many pieces she's in."

Tate growls at Torin's blunt words, but the vampire is right. I feel a chill run through me at his words. As a Fae, I understand liminality better than most, except maybe vampires. The spaces between realms, the thin places where worlds overlap. But this is beyond anything I've ever encountered.

"We start by stabilising what's left of her physical form," Cathy says, all business despite the horror of the situation. "My prototype might be able to disrupt the decoherence fluctuations, at least temporarily."

She aims her weapon at Ivy's shifting body.

Tate backhands the laser gun out of Cathy's hand. "No."

"Easy," I say, placing a hand on his shoulder. "We need to try something."

"It can't get any worse," Torin mutters.

I glare at him. "Will you fucking shut up?"

"What? There is no point sugarcoating this. It's fucked. Everything is fucked!" He turns away and moves to the window to stare out of it into the night sky.

As I stare at Ivy, ignoring Tate and Cathy arguing, I see a flicker of very recognisable magick under Ivy's skin.

"Fae," I murmur. "What do you want?"

Narrowing my eyes, I stare at it. It slithers out and aims for me, wrapping itself around me.

With a grunt of surprise, I'm yanked out of this realm and thrust directly in front of the King and Queen of the Dark Fae in their throne room back at home, toppling over and hitting my knees painfully on the floor at their feet.

"Welcome home, son," Dad says brightly, a big

beam of what can only be described as amusement on his face.

I stagger to my feet, disoriented by the sudden shift in reality. The familiar opulence of the Dark Fae throne room surrounds me, a stark contrast to the chaos I just left behind.

"What the fuck?" I growl, glaring at my parents. "You couldn't have sent an invitation?"

Mum raises an eyebrow, her expression full of amusement and disapproval. "Language, darling. And we did try more conventional methods. You've been ignoring our summons."

"I've been a little busy," I snap. "In case you hadn't noticed, there's a cosmic war brewing in the supernatural realm."

Dad waves his hand dismissively. "Supe problems. We have more pressing matters to discuss."

I feel my temper rising. "More pressing than veils being torn apart?" I nearly add, *Than Ivy being scattered across dimensions?* But think better of it.

"The Hammond witch," Mum says, waving her hand dismissively. "That's why we've brought you here."

I narrow my eyes. "What do you know about her?"

Dad stands, his imposing figure radiating power. "We know that she represents a convergence point of ancient magicks. A nexus of chaos and order that could reshape existence itself."

"Yeah, well, she's currently reshaping existence by being torn apart molecule by molecule," I growl. "So, unless you have something that can help me save her, I'm going."

"This magick of hers is Ancient Fae. You know that, right?"

"What of it? It's not helping her."

"Not helping her?" Dad laughs, the sound echoing unnaturally through the throne room. "My dear boy, it's the only thing keeping her from being completely unmade, right now."

I freeze, hope and suspicion warring within me. "What do you mean?"

Mum stands, her gown shimmering like a starry night as she descends the dais. "It is clinging to her. A lifeline for her, of sorts."

"But Ivy's not Fae."

"No," Dad agrees. "But her bloodline was engineered to channel Fae magick. To harness chaos in ways even we cannot fully comprehend."

My mind reels with the implications. "So, you're saying..."

"That the very thing tearing her apart is also what's keeping her together," Mum finishes. "The Ancient Fae magick is both poison and antidote."

"How do we fix her?" I demand. "How do we bring her back?"

Dad's expression grows serious. "It won't be easy. She's been scattered across dimensions, her essence fragmented. But there might be a way."

"Tell me," I growl.

Mum produces an ancient tome, its cover writhing

with living shadows. "There's a ritual. One that can call back fragments of a shattered soul. But it requires sacrifice."

"What kind of sacrifice?" I ask instantly, knowing I will lay down my own life to save her.

My parents exchange a loaded glance before Mum answers, "The ritual requires three sacrifices: one of blood, one of power, and one of spirit."

"Explain."

Dad sighs heavily. "The Ancient Fae were dark. Really pitch black. Bear that in mind. The blood sacrifice is straightforward, a willing offering of life force to anchor the scattered fragments. The power sacrifice involves channelling and burning out a significant portion of one's magical essence. The spirit sacrifice..." he trails off, looking grim.

"What?" I growl impatiently.

"The spirit sacrifice requires surrendering a core piece of one's identity," Mum finishes. "A fundamental aspect of self, given up willingly and permanently."

I feel the weight of their words settle over me. These aren't just sacrifices. They're mutilations of self on the deepest levels.

"But this will bring Ivy back?" I ask, needing to be certain.

"It should reconstitute her essence," Dad says carefully. "But she won't be the same. The ritual will leave scars, both on those who perform it and on Ivy herself."

I nod grimly. "Better scarred than scattered across dimensions."

"You understand that you alone cannot complete this ritual," Mum says. "It requires three willing participants. One for each sacrifice."

My mind immediately goes to Tate and Torin. I know, without a doubt, they'd be willing to pay any price to save Ivy. The question is, who will take on which sacrifice?

"I'll do it," I say firmly. "I'll gather the others, and we'll perform the ritual."

Dad nods solemnly. "Be warned, son. This magick is ancient and dark. It will exact a terrible price."

"On top of what it will take from us?" I ask steadily.

Mum nods and hands me the ancient tome. Its cover shrinks away from my touch. "The instructions are within. Choose your sacrifices wisely."

"How do we perform the ritual?" I ask, pushing aside my doubts for the moment.

"The ritual must be performed at a nexus point between realms. A place where the veils are naturally thin."

"Thornfield," I mutter. "Ivy ripped the place apart earlier."

Dad nods approvingly. "That would work. You'll need to create a ritual circle using blood from all three participants. The sacrifices must be made in a specific order - blood, then power, then spirit."

"The blood sacrifice anchors her scattered essence," Mum explains. "The power sacrifice provides the energy to pull her back together. And the spirit sacrifice..." she pauses, looking grim, "it gives her something to come back to. A beacon in the chaos."

I absorb this information, my mind already racing with plans. "How long do we have?"

"Not long," Dad says gravely. "The longer she remains scattered, the harder it will be to bring her back. And there's a risk..."

"What risk?" I demand.

Mum's expression grows solemn. "The longer Ivy remains scattered, the more her essence will fragment. Eventually, there may not be enough left of her original self to reconstitute."

I feel a chill run through me at her words. "How long?"

"It's hard to say," Dad replies. "Time moves differently across dimensions. But I wouldn't wait more than a day in your realm."

I nod grimly, clutching the ancient tome. "I understand. Thank you for this."

Mum steps forward, placing a hand on my cheek. For a moment, her regal facade cracks, showing the concern beneath. "Be careful, my son."

"I will."

Dad nods approvingly. "You've chosen well, Bram. She's a worthy mate for a prince of the Dark Fae."

I start to protest that it's not just about me, that Tate and Torin are equally important to Ivy. But I realise now isn't the time for that conversation. Instead, I simply nod.

"I need to go," I say. "We don't have much time."

Mum waves her hand, and I feel reality shift around me. "We'll send you back to the moment we pulled you from." But then she leans to whisper in my ear. "Good luck, Bram. Tap into the Ancient Fae running through your veins. It is the only way."

The throne room dissolves, and I find myself back in Cathy's living room, the ancient book wriggling in my grip. Tate and Cathy are still arguing, frozen in the exact positions they were in when I was pulled away. Torin remains by the window, his back to the room.

"Enough," I growl, my voice cutting through their bickering. "I know how to save Ivy."

They all turn to stare at me, expressions ranging from hope to suspicion.

"How?" Tate demands, his eyes fixed on the writhing book in my grasp. "Where did you get that?"

I take a deep breath, steeling myself for their reactions. "I've been back home. Long story short, there's a ritual. Ancient Fae magick. It can pull Ivy's scattered essence back together, but..." I hesitate, knowing how they'll react to the cost.

"But what?" Torin asks, moving away from the window.

"It requires sacrifice," I say grimly. "Three sacrifices, to be precise. Blood, power, and spirit."

The room falls silent as they process my words.

"What kind of sacrifices are we talking about?" Cathy asks, her eyes narrowed.

I explain quickly, watching their faces as understanding dawns. The blood sacrifice, a willing offering of life force. The power sacrifice, burning out a significant portion of one's magickal essence, and the spirit sacrifice, giving up a fundamental aspect of self.

"I'll do it," Tate says immediately, his jaw set with determination. "Whatever it takes."

"We all will," Torin adds, moving closer. His eyes flick to Ivy's still form on the couch. "She'd do the same for any of us."

I nod, feeling a sense of dread that I've never experienced before. "It won't be easy. The ritual will leave scars, both on us and on Ivy. She might not be the same after."

"Better scarred than scattered," Torin says grimly, echoing my earlier thoughts.

"We need to move fast," I say. "My parents warned that the longer Ivy remains fragmented, the harder it will be to bring her back. We need to do this before…"

"Before what?" Tate demands.

I take a deep breath. "Before there's not enough left of her original self to reconstitute."

A heavy silence falls over the room.

"Where do we perform this ritual?" Cathy asks, all business despite the gravity of the situation.

"Right here in the garden," I reply, shoving all personal emotions aside and adopting a more businesslike attitude. It is the only thing that will get me through this. "It's a nexus point between realms, anyway, especially after Ivy tore it apart earlier. The veils are thin here."

Tate nods. "We'll need to move her carefully. In this

state, who knows what dimensional shifts could do to her."

Torin takes a step closer to her.

"No," Tate says. "I will carry her."

"You are shaking like a fucking leaf in a gale," he snaps. "Back up and let me. Stealth is my middle name."

Tate grimaces, but he backs away.

I grip him by the elbow and lead him outside. "We've got this and her."

He nods but doesn't say anything.

I'm left with a feeling that this is going to end badly.

For all of us.

31

IVY

Centuries have come and gone.

32

IVY

I've seen empires rise and fall.

33

IVY

THE FACES OF MY GUYS, MY LOVES, THE ONES I MISS WITH whatever is left of my shattered and torn soul, have long been forgotten.

34

TATE

"How long has it been?" I ask quietly as I watch Torin lay Ivy gently in the messed-up garden. It can't have been that long. An hour? Tops.

Cathy bustles about, the epitome of efficiency and glances at her watch. "Three hours."

"That long?"

She nods solemnly. "We were in shock for a while before we took her inside."

"But that's good," Bram says. "We are still well within the window to return her whole."

We hope.

"Optimism sounds all wrong coming out of your mouth," I grumble.

He gives me the finger, but there are no hard feelings. At least one of us is trying.

I can't help my gloomy thoughts. I can't help but think we are doomed. Nothing has ever gone right in my life. Even the things one could point out that worked in my favour were never about it being a good thing that happened. A prime example is I was orphaned as a young teenager and chose Torin to mug one night. Yeah, it worked out; I'm here now instead of some warlock juvie or, worse, a magickal drug den pimping myself out for food and shelter. But if I hadn't been left alone in this world to begin with, it is a moot point.

"Right, we have to draw blood and make a circle," Bram says, reading from the book that gives even me the heebies. That thing reeks of old magick and not the good kind. Not even the dark kind. Pretty much, let's just call it pitch black. I want to ask where he got it, but I guess his family must've given it to him.

My hands shake as I slice the athame Cathy produced out of a holster at her hip across my palm. Squeezing tightly and hissing at the unnatural burn, I pass it to Bram and then help him draw the ritual circle in blood. Our blood. The copper scent hangs heavy in the air, mixing with the lingering chaos from Ivy's *incident*. I can't bring myself to call it anything else.

Torin gently lays Ivy's still form in the centre of the circle. Parts of her keep fading in and out of existence, like a glitching hologram. It makes my stomach churn.

"Are you sure this is going to help and not make things worse?" I ask Bram for the hundredth time as he hands Torin the athame. I watch as the enchanted silver slices through his palm like a hot knife through butter, and he adds his blood to the circle.

He nods grimly. "It's our only shot. You ready?"

No. I'm not ready. I'm terrified. But I nod anyway. "What do we do first?"

Bram consults the squirming volume. "Blood sacrifice first. It'll anchor her scattered essence."

"I'll do it," Torin says immediately.

I start to protest, but Bram cuts me off. "Makes sense. As a vampire, you have the strongest connection to all things blood."

"What comes after? We need to get our proverbial ducks in a row before we start this," Cathy states.

"Power and the spirit," Bram replies. "I think I need to be power. Tate, you have marked her and bear her mark; I think your spirit will be the strongest, even more so with the anchor line running through you."

"Yeah," I mutter. As much as I hate to admit it on an ordinary day, Bram is the most powerful one here. Most of the time, he doesn't tap into his full power source, it's not necessary on this plane of existence. But today is no ordinary day. "Use every fucking ounce of power you've been hiding. Do you hear me?"

He scowls and I know he wants to bite back about his own feelings for Ivy, but after a few seconds, he nods grimly and leaves it. "I will."

"So how do we do this?" Torin asks. "What is required from us?"

"Each sacrifice requires a specific ritual," Bram explains, consulting the ancient book. "For the blood sacrifice, Torin, you'll need to offer a significant portion of your life force. It will weaken you considerably."

Torin nods grimly. "Whatever it takes."

"I'll channel my power next," Bram continues. "I'll have to push my magick to its limits and beyond. It may burn out a large portion of my abilities, possibly permanently."

I feel a chill at his words but stay silent.

"And for the spirit sacrifice?" I ask, dreading the answer.

Bram searches my eyes for a moment. "You'll have to give up a fundamental aspect of yourself, Tate. Something core to your identity. I think it's up to you because the book is vague on the specifics, but it will be painful and permanent."

I swallow hard but nod. My mind has suddenly gone blank, and I don't even know what I'm supposed to offer up. *Think, you bastard, think!*

Bram takes a deep breath. "We need to form a triangle around her. Torin, you start. Cut your wrist and keep it open, I guess by holding the cut apart? Let your blood flow into the circle while focusing on Ivy. Picture her essence, scattered across dimensions, and will it to coalesce around your offering. Cathy, we need you here with that no-holds-barred attitude of yours. Keep us on track."

She nods brusquely, her feet planted and her hands behind her back.

"Torin Ashford of the Ainsley Coven, are you ready?" Bram asks formally.

Torin nods, his face set in an expression that could only be described as grim and slightly sick at the prospect of forcing his own body from healing. But his hands don't shake, not even a little bit, as he slices his wrist with the athame deeper than necessary. Dark blood wells up immediately.

"Now," Bram instructs.

Torin kneels at the edge of the blood circle, holding his sliced wrist over it. His face contorts in pain as he forces the wound to stay open, fighting against his vampire healing. His blood drips steadily into the circle.

"Focus on Ivy," Bram instructs. "Imagine her spirit spread out among different dimensions. Focus on it coming together around your offering."

Torin closes his eyes, his brow furrowed in concentration. The air grows heavy, charged with a magickal energy. Torin's skin begins to pale, taking on an ashen hue. He's literally pouring his life force into the ritual.

I look down at Ivy's prone form and see flickers, parts of her seem to solidify for brief moments before fading again.

"Hold steady," Bram says, his voice tense. "You need to keep going until we have all finished."

Torin lets out a pained rasp, swaying slightly. His eyes fly open, unfocused and glassy.

"Prince Bramwell, son of Mabius, King of the Dark Fae, are you ready?" Bram drops to his knees, placing his hands on the edge of the circle and chants in, what I assume is the ancient Fae language.

The air grows thicker, like soup, making it difficult to breathe. Bram's eyes glow silver as he channels more magick than I've ever felt from him before. It's dark, almost as black as the book he is kneeling in front of.

The blood circle shimmers and throbs with energy as Bram's power floods into it. Flashes of silver and purple blind me, but I can't look away.

Ivy's body lifts slightly off the ground, suspended in a cocoon of swirling magickal energy.

Fingers of icy cold walk down the back of my neck and my spine, making me shudder and try to pull away. Bram's magick has reached depths I didn't even know were possible.

"Tate Blackwell of the Well line," he croaks. "Are you ready?"

I gulp and fall to my knees, still having no idea what to offer up. If I lose my magick, I'm no good to Ivy, but if I don't do something, she is lost to us for eternity. Suffering and in torment and fuck only knows what else. I close my eyes and let whatever feels right bubble up to the surface.

And then it hits me.

The purest part of myself, the truest part that makes me who I am right now, isn't my magick or my strength.

It's my love for Ivy.

I take a deep breath, steeling myself for what I'm about to do. My love for Ivy is the core of who I am now - it's shaped every decision, every action since I met her. To give it up is like tearing out my own heart. But if that's what it takes to bring her back, I'll do it without hesitation.

"I'm ready," I say, my voice steady despite the fear churning in my gut.

Bram nods grimly; his face strained as he continues channelling power into the ritual. "Do it."

I close my eyes, calling up memories of Ivy. Her laugh, her smile, the fire in her eyes when she's angry. The mark she gave me on my chest, mine on her lower back. The way she feels in my arms, the taste of her kiss. The depth of emotion I feel for her, a love so profound it changed everything about me.

Opening my eyes, forcing myself to look at her, tears stream down my face as I gather it all up, this most precious part of myself. Then, with a ragged sob, I shove it away from me and into the ritual circle.

The pain is immediate and all-consuming. It feels like my chest has been ripped open, leaving nothing but a gaping void where my heart should be. I scream, doubling over as agony rips through me.

But I feel it working. The circle is responding to us.

"Keep going!" Cathy shouts. "It's not over yet."

"Fuck," Torin grunts and passes out.

Bram is holding on, but just barely. His skin is undulating like there are a thousand beetles crawling under his skin. Black veins have appeared all over his body and face. His eyes are now black voids. He retches, and a black snake curls out of his mouth, and I resist the urge to recoil as it slithers through the circle and settles on Ivy's body, curling up and hissing.

"Don't stop!" Cathy yells. "You're almost there!"

I force myself to keep channelling, even as I feel hollowed out. The love I gave up leaves an aching void, but I cling to the memory of why I'm doing this. For Ivy. Even if I can't feel it anymore, I know it matters.

The air crackles with energy. Reality bends around us. Ivy's body lifts higher, suspended in a cocoon of swirling magick. For a moment, I see glimpses of a thousand or more other realms through cracks in the air.

Then, with a sound like reality tearing, everything implodes.

The magickal energy rushes inward, slamming into Ivy with such force that I'm knocked backwards. Blinding light fills the circle, forcing me to shield my eyes and then… nothing.

35

IVY

TIME.

Is that even a word anymore?

Do I even still exist?

Where am I?

Who am I?

I am nobody and everybody. Maybe I am even time itself.

Are these even my thoughts?

I am...

I am...

Sensations flood back, overwhelming and chaotic. Pain lances through every cell, every atom of my being, as reality reasserts itself. I gasp, choking on air that is too thick, too real, after an eternity of formless existence.

My eyes fly open, taking in a swirling vortex of colours and shapes above me that slowly intermingle into recognisable forms. The night sky, stars, the full moon.

"Ivy?"

It's a soft feminine voice that I think I should recognise. I try to turn my head, but my neck screams with protest. I slam my eyes closed as nausea overwhelms me. Turning on my side, I throw up, not even bothering to lift my head. I can't. It feels like it is filled with lead.

A cool hand passes over my forehead and gathers up my hair, the other lifts me slightly so that I don't choke on my vomit. Tears sting my eyes, and the bile burns my nose and throat.

I blink my eyes open, trying to focus.

Where am I?

Who am I?

Who is this person next to me?

"Easy," the woman says softly. "You're okay. You're back."

Back? Back from where?

My mind feels foggy, memories just out of reach. I try to speak but only manage a raspy croak.

"Water," I finally gasp out.

The woman helps me sit up slowly, my body protesting every movement. She holds a bottle to my lips, and I drink greedily, the cool liquid soothing my raw throat.

As my vision clears, I make out more details. Words, things, slot back into place as my mind clears a bit, but it's still like walking through a dense fog over uneven terrain, which also happens to be a minefield.

We're in a garden, but it looks like a bomb went off. The grass is scorched in places; trees are bent at unnatural angles. The roof of the house looming over us has a chunk missing out of it.

Dropping my gaze as my head pounds erratically, I see three men lying unconscious around the edge of the circle. Something tugs at my memory, a sense of familiarity, but I can't quite grasp it.

"What happened?" I ask, my voice still weak. "Who are you? Who am I?"

The woman's face falls, worry creasing her brow. "You don't remember?"

I shake my head, wincing at the movement. "Everything's jumbled. It's like my brain has been torn apart and put back together wrong."

She sighs heavily. "That's not far from the truth. I'm Cathy Hammond, your aunt. You are Ivy Hammond."

Ivy. The name feels right, but also somehow wrong. Like it doesn't quite fit anymore.

"Do you remember anything?" Cathy asks.

I shake my head and close my eyes as the movement sends another wave of nausea over me. "Floating. Witnessing births, death, rebirths, stars being born and dying…"

"Okay, shh," Cathy murmurs as I choke back a sob. "Let's get you inside, and you can rest for a while."

I let Cathy help me to my feet, my legs shaky and uncooperative. Every step is an effort, and my body feels simultaneously too heavy and too light. I lean heavily on her, but she doesn't mind. She's got me.

"What about them?" I ask.

Cathy glances back. "They'll be okay for now. You're the priority."

As we slowly make our way to the house, fragments of memory flash through my mind: purple energy crackling around my hands, creatures imploding, flowers bursting. But none of it feels like it happened to me.

Inside, Cathy helps me onto the couch. The softness of the cushions is almost overwhelming after... after what? I can't remember, but my body reacts like it's been an eternity since I felt anything so mundane and comforting.

"Here," Cathy says, handing me the water again. "Small sips."

I obey, relishing the cool liquid. As I drink, I study Cathy's face. There's something familiar about her features, but it's like looking at a stranger who reminds me of someone I used to know.

"You said you're my aunt?" I ask hesitantly.

She nods. "Yes."

"And those men outside?"

Cathy's expression grows pained. "They are important to you. Very important. But I think it's best if you remember that on your own."

I nod slowly, wincing as my head throbs. "What happened to me? Why can't I remember?"

Cathy sighs heavily. "It's a lot. We can talk about it another time, after you've rested."

"No. I want to know now."

She rolls her eyes, and a part of me, deep down

somewhere, wants to giggle at the action. "Always so stubborn. The short version of events is there was an incident with your magick. You were torn apart and scattered across dimensions. A ritual was performed to bring you back."

Magick? Dimensions? Ritual? The words spark something in my mind, but they slip away before I can grasp them. "I don't understand."

"I know," Cathy says gently. "It'll take time for everything to settle. Your mind and body have been through a tremendous ordeal."

I close my eyes, suddenly exhausted. "I feel so strange. Like I don't quite fit in my own skin."

"That's to be expected," Cathy replies. "Rest now. We can talk more when you're feeling stronger."

I nod and turn my back to her as I close my eyes. She places a blanket over me, and I shiver. As I drift off, I catch glimpses of faces and places in my mind. They slip away like smoke, leaving me feeling hollow and lost.

"Ivy," I murmur. "I am Ivy Hammond."

The words feel familiar, but they don't mean anything.

36

TORIN

I come to slowly, feeling like I've been drained dry and left out in the sun. Every cell in my body aches with a bone-deep weariness I've never experienced before. I blink my eyes open, wincing at the brightness of the coming dawn.

Memories flood back in a painful reenactment. The ritual, Ivy's scattered form, the blood sacrifice. I look down at my wrist, seeing the deep gash has barely started to heal. That's not right. I should have regenerated by now. My thirst for blood is heightened and I feel a rampage coming on.

Groaning, I push myself up to sit. The world spins sickeningly, and I have to close my eyes for a moment to keep from vomiting. When I open them again, I take in the scene around me.

The ritual circle is scorched into the grass, still faintly glowing with residual energy. Bram lies unconscious nearby, his skin ashen and covered in what looks like black veins. Tate is curled in on himself, face contorted in pain even in unconsciousness.

Ivy is gone.

Panic surges through me. "Ivy!" I call out, my voice is hoarse and weak.

"She's inside," Cathy says, coming closer. "She's resting. Here, thought you might need this."

She holds out a blood bag, and I snatch it from her, ripping into it and guzzling it back ravenously.

I drain the blood bag in seconds, feeling some of my strength return. But it's not enough. Not nearly enough.

"More," I growl, tossing the empty bag aside.

Cathy hands me another without comment. I tear into it, drinking greedily. As the blood flows through me, I feel my body slowly start to repair itself. The gash on my wrist closes, though far more slowly than it should.

"How is she?" I ask between gulps. "Did it work?"

Cathy's expression is grim. "She's alive and whole, physically, at least. But her mind..." She trails off, shaking her head.

Cold dread settles in my stomach. "What do you mean?"

"She doesn't remember anything," Cathy says softly. "Not who she is, not who we are. It's like her memories were scattered along with her essence. She can speak, she knows words and what things are, but the rest… is gone."

"Fuck. How can we help her?"

"Right now, we need to focus on getting everyone

stable. You three pushed yourselves to the brink with that ritual. There will be magickal consequences as well as official ones. What you did was illegal in every sense the Office of Magickal Law and Order has."

"Who gives a shit about that? As long as Ivy is here, we will deal with anything else."

Bram stirs with a pained groan. His eyes flutter open, revealing inky black orbs. "Fuck," he rasps. "Did it work?"

I nod grimly. "She's alive. But there are complications."

Bram struggles to sit up, his movements jerky and uncoordinated. "What kind of complications?" he asks, his voice raw.

"She doesn't remember anything," I explain, feeling a hollow ache in my chest. "Not who she is, not who we are."

"Shit," Bram mutters. He looks down at his hands, flexing his fingers. "My magick is dead."

"Dead dead or needs a recharge?"

He shrugs. "I guess we'll find out."

"The ritual exacted a heavy price from all of you," Cathy says grimly. "It'll take time to recover, if you ever fully do."

I glance over at Tate, who's still unconscious. "What about him?"

Cathy shakes her head. "I don't know. The spirit sacrifice... without knowing what he gave up, it's harder to say what the consequences will be until he wakes up."

Tate stirs as if he knew we were talking about him. His eyes snap open, unfocused and glazed with pain. He tries to speak but only manages a strangled groan, his gaze darting around wildly. "Ivy?" he croaks.

"She's inside. She's alive."

Relief floods his face, but it's quickly replaced by a blank look that sends up about a hundred red flags. He staggers to his feet, swaying roughly and nods. "That's good then."

His usual intensity when it comes to Ivy is completely absent. There's no desperate rush to her side, no flood of questions about her condition. Just that blank look and flat acknowledgement.

"Tate," I say carefully, "are you all right?"

He blinks at me, his expression mildly confused. "Of course. Why wouldn't I be?"

Bram and I exchange a worried glance. This isn't right.

"Do you remember what happened?" Bram asks. "The ritual?"

Tate nods slowly. "We brought Ivy back. It worked."

"And how do you feel about that?" I press.

He shrugs. "It's fine, I suppose. She's important."

Important? Just important? This is the man who would burn down the world for Ivy without hesitation. Something is very wrong.

Cathy purses her lips as she gives me a look that screams this is all wrong. "Tate," Cathy says gently, "what exactly did you sacrifice for the ritual?"

He furrows his brow, thinking. "I... I'm not sure.

Something important, I think. But it's fine. We got Ivy back."

The hollow feeling in my chest deepens. Whatever it was has taken something from him that is making him act this way now. But what?

"Do you still have your magick?"

He holds out his hand, and a spark flickers to life. It's not as bright as usual, but it's more than Bram has. "Good stuff," I murmur, but if he didn't give up his magick, what did he do?

"We should check on her," Bram murmurs, struggling to his feet.

I nod and we follow Cathy into the house, Tate following almost robotically behind us. My instincts are screaming that something is very wrong with him, but I push that worry aside for now. Ivy is the priority.

Ignoring the part of the roof that has been smashed off, probably during the ritual, we enter the living room to find Ivy curled up on the couch, wrapped in a blanket. She stirs as we approach, blinking up at us with confusion in her eyes.

"How are you feeling?" I ask gently, crouching down beside her.

She studies my face intently, brow furrowed. "I'm not sure. Everything feels strange. Who are you?"

The words hit me like a smack around the face with a wet fish. It hurts more than I expected.

"I'm Torin Ashford, a vampire," I say, fighting to keep my voice steady. "We're... friends."

Her eyes flick to Bram and Tate. "And them?"

"Also friends," Bram says. "I'm Bram, and that's Tate."

Ivy nods slowly, but there's no recognition in her eyes. Just confusion and a hint of fear.

"Do you remember anything?" I ask, though I already know the answer.

She shakes her head. "It's all jumbled. I get flashes, but nothing makes sense. Cathy says I'm Ivy Hammond, but..." She trails off, looking lost.

"But what?" I prompt gently, trying to keep the desperation out of my voice.

Ivy looks down, fiddling with the edge of the blanket. "But it doesn't feel right. Like it's someone else's name. Someone else's life."

My heart clenches painfully. I want to gather her in my arms, to tell her everything will be okay. But I can't. Not when she doesn't even know who I am.

"It'll take time," Cathy says softly. "Your mind and body have been through a tremendous ordeal."

Ivy nods, but she still looks lost and confused. Her gaze drifts to Tate, who's standing back from the group, his expression oddly blank. "I think I need to rest now."

"Good idea," I say and tug up the blanket, tucking her in. I don't want to risk moving her to a bed just yet. She looks like she would shatter into a million pieces if we even breathed too hard on her.

She closes her eyes, and I see her breathing regulate and deepen, and I feel relieved that I don't have to interact with her anymore. I feel terrible for thinking that, but this is a situation which is disturbing, and I don't really know what to say or how to act. I'm exhausted and hungry for blood, and my mind isn't as sharp as it usually is.

We retreat to the kitchen, leaving Ivy to rest. The silence is heavy, filled with unspoken fears and questions. Cathy busies herself making coffee, though I doubt any of us really want it. She retrieves another blood bag from the mini fridge and chucks it at me. I don't ask why she has a stash… I don't want to know, truth be told.

Snatching it out of the air, I shoot her a grateful smile. She grimaces at me and goes back to making coffee.

"What the fuck do we do now?" Bram asks quietly, slumping into a chair. He looks utterly drained, the black veins still visible beneath his pale skin.

I shake my head, at a loss. "I don't know. We brought her back, but..." I trail off, unable to finish the thought.

"But at what cost?" Cathy finishes grimly, setting a mug of coffee in front of Bram. "To her and to all of you."

My gaze drifts to Tate, who's staring blankly out the window. His lack of reaction to Ivy's condition is deeply unsettling. "Tate," I say carefully. "How are you feeling?"

He turns to me, his expression neutral. "I'm fine. Why do you keep asking?"

"Because you're not acting like yourself," Bram

snaps. "Ivy doesn't remember us, and you're just standing there like it doesn't matter!"

Tate blinks, looking mildly confused. "Of course it matters. But we brought her back. That was the goal, wasn't it?"

"Yes, but..." I start but trail off. This is pointless. It is like arguing with AI. "Tate, what exactly did you sacrifice for the ritual?" I ask, desperate to understand what's happened to him. We have enough on our plate without needing to fix him as well.

He furrows his brow, thinking. "I told you already. I'm not sure. Something important, I think."

I roll my eyes impatiently as he gives us that line again.

"Try to remember," Bram urges. "It's crucial we understand what's been lost."

Tate closes his eyes, concentrating. After a long moment, he opens them again, looking troubled. He trails off, shaking his head.

"What do you feel about Ivy now?" I ask, a sense of dread welling up as I think I might've just figured it out.

He shrugs. "She is Ivy."

"And?" Bram grits out, seeming to get on the same page as me.

"And nothing."

"Nothing? You feel nothing for her?"

Tate shrugs again and turns his back on us to stare out of the window again.

"Your love," I whisper. "You sacrificed your love for her."

Bram's face is a vicious scowl as he comes to the same conclusion as me. "Fuck. That's why he's so detached. He literally can't feel what he felt before."

"Love?" Tate murmurs. "It's just blank."

The enormity of what's happened settles over us like a suffocating blanket. Ivy has no memories, Tate has no feelings for her, Bram is potentially stripped of his magick, Cathy is stashing blood bags, and me... I'm not even sure of the full extent of what I've lost yet, and I'm not sure I'm ready to find out.

37

BRAM

I STARE AT MY HANDS, WILLING EVEN THE SMALLEST flicker of magick to appear. Nothing. The hollowness inside me is a gaping void where my power used to reside. I've never felt so empty, so utterly useless. Tapping into my royal power on a level I haven't had since I came to this realm was more complicated than I thought it would be. Then, I had to dig even deeper than that. The Ancient Fae are part of my lineage. The Royal lineage. I'm directly descended, not some watered-down version like most of the Dark Fae running around. I didn't even know I was capable of channelling their shit. To be honest, I didn't even know it existed.

I fucking do now.

Black veins.

Scarab Beetles crawling under my skin, which raises a whole shit ton of questions.

Fucking vomiting out snakes.

"Err, guys. Where's the snake?"

"It slithered off into the bushes," Cathy murmurs. "I wasn't going to chase it. Should we?" she asks, nose scrunched up but looking determined if the need arises.

"Maybe it's a good idea," I mutter, standing up.

"Let me go get some tools," she says and marches off with brutal efficiency I'm grateful for because I can't think for shit right now.

Torin glances over at me as I stand up, his expression grim. "Still nothing?"

I shake my head. "It's like it's been ripped out by the roots. I can feel where it should be, but there's just... nothing."

He nods sympathetically and sucks on his blood bag. "Give it time. We've all paid a heavy price for this ritual."

I glare at him in annoyance. He seems just dandy now he's got a mouthful of blood. Even the wound on his wrist is gone. My gaze shifts to Tate and it's like being hit in the gut by a dragon claw. "Some more than others."

Cathy returns with a heavy-duty drawstring bag, a couple of hooks and some thick gloves. "Right, let's go demon snake hunting. Though I'm not sure what we'll do with it if we catch the damn thing."

"Ancient Fae," I mutter.

"Hmm?" she murmurs.

"Not demon. Ancient Fae," I say louder.

"Well, that makes it all better now, doesn't it?" Her sarcastic smile makes me snicker.

"Sorry, I'm spicy today."

"Aren't we all, young prince? Aren't we all?"

We head outside, scanning the overgrown garden for any sign of the serpent. The ritual circle is still scorched into the grass, a sharp reminder of what we've done.

"There!" Torin points to a flash of scales disappearing under a bush.

We converge on the spot, Cathy wielding the hook like a weapon. As we push aside the branches, we see it. A sleek black snake with eerily intelligent eyes. It rears up, hissing at us.

"Careful," I warn. "We don't know what kind of magick it might possess."

"Or what thing from the bowels of hell possesses *it*," Torin mutters.

Cathy lunges forward with the hook, a braver creature than me, but the snake is faster. It slithers between her legs and makes a beeline for the house.

"Shit!" Torin curses. "It's heading for Ivy!"

We race after it, bursting through the back door. The snake slithers across the kitchen floor with unnatural speed, heading straight for the living room where Ivy is resting.

"Stop it!" I yell, though I know it's futile. Without my magick, I'm powerless to do anything.

Torin vaults over the kitchen counter, using his vampire speed to try to cut off the snake's path. But it's too late. The serpent slides under the couch where Ivy is sleeping.

"Fuck!" Cathy swears, brandishing her hook. "We need to get her out of there."

We approach cautiously, unsure of what the serpent might do. Ivy stirs at the commotion, blinking up at us in confusion.

"What's going on?" she asks groggily.

"Don't move," Torin says cautiously. "There's a snake under the couch."

Ivy's eyes widen in alarm, but she remains still. "A snake?"

"Not just any snake," I explain grimly. "It's magickal."

Cathy moves forward with the hook, ready to try and fish the creature out. But before she can, the snake emerges on its own.

It slithers up onto Ivy's lap, coiling itself around her arm. I tense, ready to lunge forward and rip it off her if necessary. But Ivy doesn't look afraid. If anything, she seems fascinated by the creature.

"It's beautiful," she murmurs, watching as the serpent winds its way up her arm. Its scales shimmer with a mystical iridescence, shifting colours in the light.

"Ivy, don't move," I say cautiously. "We don't know what it's capable of."

But she doesn't seem to hear me. Her eyes are locked on the serpent as it makes its way to her shoulder. Then, to our horror, it begins to slither around her neck.

"Ivy!" Torin grits out, taking a step forward.

She holds up a hand, stopping him. "Don't," she says. "It's mine."

"What do you mean, it's yours?" I ask carefully.

Ivy strokes the serpent's head, a serene smile on her face, but she doesn't answer me. It's like she doesn't even hear me.

Torin and I exchange worried glances. This can't be good. I glance around for Tate, but he is nowhere to be found.

That snake is Ancient Fae magick, black and unpredictable. Having it bonded to Ivy can't be a good thing.

"Maybe we should try to remove it," Torin suggests cautiously.

Ivy's eyes flash with sudden anger. "No! You can't take it from me. It's mine."

The vehemence in her voice takes us all aback. This isn't the Ivy we know. Her tone and her possessiveness over this dangerous creature are all wrong.

"Ivy," I say carefully, "That snake came from the ritual to bring you back. We don't know what kind of magick it possesses or what it might do to you. Please, let us remove it safely."

She glares at me, her eyes flashing with purple light. "You don't understand. It's part of me now. I need it."

The snake tightens its coils around her neck, but Ivy shows no signs of distress. If anything, she seems comforted by its presence.

"What do you mean, it's part of you?" Torin asks, his voice tight with concern.

Ivy strokes the serpent's scales, a dreamy smile on

her face. "It knows me. All of me, across every dimension. It's the only thing that feels right."

A chill runs down my spine at her words. This creature seems to have latched onto the scattered fragments of Ivy's essence that we pulled back together. But at what cost?

"Ivy," Cathy says gently, "I know everything feels confusing right now. But that snake could be dangerous. Please, let us help you."

For a moment, Ivy's expression wavers, uncertainty flickering in her eyes. But then the snake hisses softly, and she shakes her head.

"No," she says firmly. "It stays with me."

We stare at her, at a loss for words. If we try to remove that snake from her grasp, she will fight us, that much is clear.

The question is, what hold does it have on her, and how the fuck can we break it?

38

TATE

I stand in the kitchen, staring blankly out the window as the others fuss over Ivy and that strange snake. I know I should care. I know this situation is dangerous and disturbing. But I feel nothing about anything. Apathetic is the word.

It's like looking at the world through foggy glass. Everything is muted, distant. The panic in Torin and Bram's voices as they try to reason with Ivy in the other room about the snake barely registers.

Torin and Bram seem to think I loved Ivy once and gave that up, but I can't remember. It's not just a feeling of love lost… it's totally gone, as if it never existed in the first place. Right now, I just don't feel much of anything at all.

A small part of me understands that this should be terrifying. The Tate I was before, knowing all of this, would systematically try to remember, trying to figure out what the hell was going on. But that Tate is gone, leaving behind this hollow shell.

My gaze drifts to the scorched ritual circle, and I wonder absently what will happen to us. What we did was probably illegal. Even though we succeeded in bringing Ivy back, at what cost was it? To her, to all of us?

The others are still arguing with Ivy in the living room. I should go in there and try to help. But what could I possibly offer? Who I am now is different. I know that. I may not remember loving her, but I remember being more proactive and on the front foot. As much as I try to force myself to move, to think, to act. I still just stand there staring.

I huff out a breath and take a step back. Standing around here isn't going to accomplish anything. I need to leave and give myself some space from this situation. Give Ivy space while she tries to figure stuff out.

Moving towards the back door, I slip out without a word and head around the side of the house. Crossing over the road, I walk. We are a few miles from the Thornfield campus, which is good. I can use this time, this walk, to clear my head. I look up at the dull grey sky and blink as snow hits my face. It's early. It normally never snows this early. Is it a result of what we did? Have we fucked with everything by doing what we did? Does it matter even if we did?

Even that is something I can't bring myself to care about.

As I get closer to Thornfield, the snow falls heavier,

blanketing the world in white. The silence is oppressive, broken only by the crunch of my boots on fresh powder. I don't even feel the cold right now.

My mind drifts to Ivy and the others back at Cathy's house. I know I should be worried about that snake, about Ivy's lost memories, about what we've all sacrificed. But it's like trying to grasp smoke. The concern slips away before I can fully form it.

I reach the edge of campus, the familiar buildings looming ahead. Classes will be starting soon for the day. Normal life goes on, oblivious to the chaos we've unleashed. For a moment, I consider just going to class, pretending nothing has happened. It would be easy to slip back into a routine, to let the mundane details of student life distract me from the hollowness inside.

But even as I think it, I know I can't. Whatever I've lost, whatever's been taken from me, I still have some sense of duty. Of obligation, if not care. I need to go back, to face whatever consequences are coming.

But I need a minute.

Crossing over the quad, I frown. The place is deserted. There is no sign of life at all. No students, no staff members. It's a ghost town. I know I *should* care what the fuck has happened here, but I don't.

Making my way to where there is a large wall with painted targets for the students to practice hitting with their magick, I take a step back on the concrete slab that stretches out in front of it and stare at the wall. There are circles of all sizes on the wall painted in red paint. The smaller the circle, the more difficult the target. I coil my magick in my palm and glance down at it. It looks more sinister than it did before, but it might just be me, projecting things that aren't there.

I stare at the crackling energy in my palm, trying to summon some emotion. Fear, excitement, anything. But there's just nothing. The magick feels foreign, almost malevolent. Not the warm, familiar power I vaguely remember wielding before.

With a flick of my wrist, I hurl a bolt of energy at the smallest target. It misses wildly, scorching the wall several feet away. I frown. My aim used to be dead on.

I try again and again. Each attempt goes wide, my magick is erratic and unpredictable. Frustration should be building, but I just feel numb detachment as I watch my failures accumulate on the wall.

After the tenth miss, I lower my hand. What's the point of this? I can't even remember why I cared about honing these skills in the first place.

A cold wind whips across the empty quad, stirring the fresh snow. The eerie silence of the abandoned campus presses in around me. I should be unnerved by the total absence of life here. But like everything else, it barely registers.

I turn away from the scorched wall, unsure of what to do next. Go back to Cathy's? Try to help with Ivy and that snake? The thought holds no appeal. Stay here on campus and wait for... something? Equally unappealing.

I start to walk away, but then I turn and fire an orb

of power at the wall. It misses every target, bouncing harmlessly off the breeze block.

"Fuck!" I roar, feeling a familiar anger rise up. "Fuck you!" I throw another and another. "Fuck!" I roar, hurling bolt after bolt of useless energy at the wall. My aim is wild, the magick recoils off the targets, leaving no sign of damage.

The rage feels good, though. It's the first real emotion I've felt since waking up after the ritual. I lean into it, screaming obscenities as I unleash my power.

Snow swirls around me, kicked up by the force of my attacks. The air snaps with ozone and residual magick.

I keep going until my arms ache, and I'm panting for breath. The wall is pristine and unblemished. Not a single target was hit.

Exhausted, I slump to my knees in the snow. The anger drains away, leaving me hollow again. But for a moment there, I felt something. It wasn't love or happiness, but it was an emotion. Proof that I'm not completely dead inside.

I stare at my hands, still crackling faintly with power. My magick feels wrong, tainted somehow. But it's all I have left.

"What am I supposed to do now?" I ask the empty air.

"You fight."

The voice comes out of nowhere, and I look up. Seeing Death standing there, his skeletal face and hands the only parts visible underneath that flowing black robe, I rise quickly. "Fight what?" I sneer.

Death's hollow eye sockets seem to bore into me. "Fight for what you've lost, Tate Blackwell. Fight to reclaim your soul."

I snort derisively. "My soul? I didn't lose my soul. Just my feelings for some girl."

"Is that what you think?" Death's voice is cold, echoing strangely in the empty quad. "You gave up far more than you realise. Your love for Ivy was the core of who you were. Without it, you're barely more than a shell."

His words should sting and make me angry, but I just feel numb. "So, what if I am? Maybe this is better. No messy emotions getting in the way."

Death takes a step closer, snow swirling around his robed form. "Is it better? Look at yourself, Tate. You can barely control your magick. You feel nothing for the woman you once would have died for. Is this truly the existence you want?"

I shrug, averting my gaze. "It doesn't matter what I want. What's done is done."

"Nothing is ever truly done," Death says, gesturing around him. "There are always choices to be made, paths to take. The question is, are you willing to fight for what you've lost?"

I stare at him. "How? How do I fight for something I can't even remember?"

Death's skeletal hand points at me, and I shiver despite

myself. "This reality is wrong—all of it. The three of you, in your desire and haste to bring back the woman you love, have altered perception. This is not the world you were in before you did the ritual. Don't you see it?" He waves his fingers, and an orb appears, shining bright red but with a fleck of darkness in it. I recognise it instantly even though I've never seen it before. "Your soul, young Blackwell."

I blink, processing that. "Why do you have it?"

Death laughs. "Why do you think?"

"I'm dead?"

"In the reality you are supposed to be in, yes, you died during the ritual. Ripping your love out of your soul for Ivy Hammond killed you."

"So why am I still here?"

"You aren't. At least, you are, but in this world where things are… different."

"Are you saying we created a new dimension or that we were transported to one?"

Death closes his hand over the orb, and it vanishes. "Neither. And both. The ritual you performed tore at the fabric of reality itself. It created ripples. Distortions. This world you find yourself in now is a fractured reflection of your own, warped by the chaos you unleashed."

I struggle to process this information. "We're in some kind of alternate timeline?"

"In a sense," Death says. "But it's unstable. Incomplete. Look around you, Tate. An empty campus in the middle of term? Snow falling months too early? Your own magick, wild and unpredictable? These are symptoms of a reality that's coming apart at the seams."

A chill runs down my spine, and it has nothing to do with the snow drifting down the collar of my shirt. "What happens if it falls apart completely?"

Death's voice grows grim. "Oblivion. For you, for Ivy, for everyone in this fractured world. Unless you find a way to set things right."

"How?" I demand. "How do I fix something I don't even fully understand?"

"You start by reclaiming what you've lost," Death says, gesturing to where my soul had been moments before. "Your love for Ivy wasn't just an emotion, Tate. It was the core of who you were. Without it, you're adrift in a sea of chaos, unable to anchor yourself or anyone else."

I shake my head, frustration building. "But if we uncreate this timeline, am I not just going to be dead?"

Death regards me silently for a long moment. Finally, he speaks. "Death is not always the end, Tate Blackwell. Especially not in a reality as fractured as this one."

I frown, trying to make sense of his cryptic words. "What does that mean?"

"It means that the lines between life and death, between one reality and another, have been blurred by what you and your companions did," Death explains. "Your physical form may have perished in the original timeline, but your essence—your soul—persists."

"So what, I'm some kind of ghost?" I ask sceptically.

Death shakes his head. "No. You are very much alive in this distorted reality. But you are incomplete, unanchored. By reclaiming your soul, by fighting to restore what was lost, you may be able to bridge the gap between what was and what is."

"This is insane. How am I supposed to fight for something I can't even remember? How do I reclaim a love I don't feel?"

"By choosing to," Death says simply. "By acknowledging that this emptiness inside you is wrong, that there should be more. By being willing to face the pain and grief that comes with loving someone, rather than hiding in this numbed state and by seeking out what you are really after."

"Which is?" I ask, but he's gone. "Oh, fuck you, you complete bony, arsehole."

Death's laughter cackles all around me, and I shudder. If what he says is true, and I died during the ritual, was it my death that did this, or was it the ritual? Was it Ivy being whole again? Was she supposed to stay scattered?

Chaos is never meant to be in one place, Tate Blackwell. It cannot be contained.

I roll my eyes as Death's voice resounds in my head. "Right. Fine. This has to be a combination of things, then. All of the things we did made this timeline. So we have to undo it all. I have to die; Ivy has to stay torn apart..." I shake my head. "It's not an option!" I coil my magick again and throw it with the feeling of utter rage that has descended over me.

The magick bolt flies from my hand, crackling with uncontrolled power. For a moment, I think it will miss the wall entirely. But at the last second, it curves impossibly, slamming into the smallest target dead centre.

The impact is explosive. The entire wall shatters, and chunks of concrete fly in all directions. I quickly throw up a hasty shield to deflect the debris.

As the dust settles, I stare in shock at the destruction. That single bolt held more power than anything I've ever channelled before.

"What the fuck?" I mutter.

My magick isn't weaker or unpredictable. It's raw, untamed. Without the emotional core I sacrificed, there's nothing holding it back.

I look down at my hands, still crackling with energy. For the first time since waking up after the ritual, I feel a flicker of real fear.

This power, unchecked by conscience, as morally grey as that was, is dangerous. I'm dangerous.

Death's words echo in my mind. *Fight for what you've lost. Reclaim your soul.*

I clench my fists, extinguishing the magick. As much as I hate to admit it, the bony bastard is right. I can't go on like this; a hollow shell with more power than control.

I need to find a way back to who I was. For my own sake, and for Ivy's. Even if that means I have to die, I know I can't live like this.

39

IVY

I STROKE THE SMOOTH SCALES OF MY NEW COMPANION, feeling a sense of calm wash over me. The snake coils tighter around my neck. Its presence is oddly comforting.

"Ivy, please," Bram says, his voice tight with worry. "That thing could be dangerous."

I tear my gaze away from the serpent to look at him. The concern in his eyes should move me, but I feel oddly detached. "It's not dangerous," I say softly. "Not to me."

Torin takes a step closer, his fangs peeking out as he speaks. "You don't know that. This snake came from Ancient Fae magick. It's unpredictable."

I ignore him as Cathy frowns at me, lowering her hook slightly. "Ivy, honey, I know everything feels confusing right now. But we're just trying to help."

"I don't need help," I snap, surprising myself with

the vehemence in my tone. "I need you all to back off and let me figure this out."

The snake hisses softly, as if in agreement. I stroke its head, marvelling at how its scales shimmer under the dim light of the darkened room.

I glance out of the window and see the snow falling. It's pretty. I remember snow. I may not remember the people around me, but I remember things and places. I remember snow. Getting up unsteadily, my legs still feeling like jelly, I hobble to the window, hissing at anyone who comes near me to help me. Staring out over the pure white landscape, I shiver. I don't know what, but something doesn't feel right about this.

I press my hand against the cold glass, watching my breath fog the window. The snow falls silently outside, blanketing everything in white. It's beautiful but eerie. Something about it feels off, unnatural.

"It's never snowed this early before," I murmur, more to myself than the others.

I can feel the tension ratchet up a notch behind me, but no one says anything. I turn back to face them, the snake tightening its coils around my neck. "What exactly did you do to bring me back?"

They exchange uneasy glances. Torin draws in a deep breath, his expression grim. "We tapped into some very dark, very old magick. It was dangerous and probably illegal."

"Probably?" Cathy snorts. "Try definitely. We're lucky we didn't blow up half the realm."

I frown, trying to piece together the fragments of memory floating in my mind. "I was scattered across different dimensions."

Bram nods. "Your essence was torn apart. We had to pull you back together."

"Why?"

The question hangs in the air like a noxious gas.

"Because," Torin huffs. "We had to."

I don't push. They clearly don't have a proper answer for me. "How long was I gone in your—in this—world?"

"About three and a half hours," Cathy says.

My blood freezes. "What?" I ask, confusion flooding my already overloaded system, "*Hours*?"

Bram and Torin exchange a cautious stare before Bram shifts his gaze back to me. "How long was it for you?"

Lowering my gaze, I turn away. "An eternity."

Silence follows that.

But then Bram asks, "Do you mean that literally, or it felt like?"

"I saw the dawn of empires. I watched them rise and eventually fall. I witnessed stars being born and then fading out, blinking their last when they died. I was everywhere and nowhere. It was one second. It was thousands of years."

"Fuck," Torin mutters, and I feel his presence right behind me. "Ivy." The desperation and sorrow in his voice makes tears prick my eyes, but I blink them away.

I turn back to face them, my hand instinctively reaching up to stroke the snake coiled around my neck. Its presence grounds me and keeps the overwhelming flood of memories and sensations at bay.

"You don't understand," I say softly. "I've lived a thousand lifetimes. I've seen things you can't even imagine. Now I'm back here, in this body that feels too small, too fragile to contain everything I've experienced."

Bram takes a hesitant step forward. "Ivy, we had no idea. If we'd known—"

"You'd what?" I snap. "Have left me scattered across dimensions? Maybe that would have been better."

The moment the words leave my mouth, I regret them. Hurt flashes across their faces. But I can't bring myself to take it back. Part of me means it.

Torin runs a hand through his hair, frustration evident in every line of his body. "We did this to save you. We risked everything."

"I didn't ask you to," I say, my voice barely above a whisper.

Cathy sets down her hook, her expression softening. "No, you didn't. But we couldn't just leave you like that. We care about you, Ivy. You asked why did we do this. That's why. We had no idea if you were suffering or being tortured or in pain. We made a decision, and now we all have to live it."

The snake hisses softly, but it's not angered by Cathy's brutally truthful words. If anything, it wants me to accept them. "I need some air," I croak eventually, turning towards the front door, opening it and slipping out. My feet sink into the snow drifts that are piling up, and it feels like something I should be excited about.

"Well, well, well. Look what your group of worshippers did."

Scowling, I look over at the voice, and the recognition hits me like a Dragon in full flight. "Life," I state, pursing my lips. "What do you want?"

She tilts her head, also pursing hers, as she stares at me with growing concern. "Have you forgotten your purpose?"

"What purpose?"

She rolls her eyes and sighs. "Okay, first things first. You need to get your perky arse back to the proper timeline, and then you need to remember everything time made you forget."

"What are you talking about?"

Life sighs heavily, her ethereal form shimmering in the falling snow. "This isn't your reality, Ivy. The ritual your friends performed to bring you back tore a hole in the fabric of existence. You've been shunted into a fractured timeline, a distorted reflection of your true world."

I blink, trying to process her words. "So none of this is real?" Weirdly, this makes more sense than anything else I've experienced since being returned to my body.

"Yes and no," Life says, waving a hand and showing me a vision in the snow.

I move closer, curiosity getting the better of me, and

peer into the swirling snow, watching as images form and shift. I see flashes of another reality. This one is where I've been brought back but it is complete devastation. I rear back and shake my head.

"That's your true timeline," Life explains. "The one you were torn from when you were scattered across dimensions."

I frown, recoiling from the images with my fragmented memories. "But if that's real, then what is this?" I gesture to the empty, snow-covered world around us.

"This is a fractured reality, created by the chaos of the ritual that brought you back," Life says. "It's unstable, incomplete, and if left unchecked, it could unravel completely with all of you in it."

The snake around my neck tightens, as if sensing my unease. I stroke its scales absently. "What am I supposed to do? How do I get us back?"

Life's expression grows serious. "You need to remember who you truly are, Ivy. Not just the scattered fragments of yourself, but your whole being. Your purpose."

"You keep mentioning this purpose," I say, frustration creeping into my voice. "What purpose? I have no memories of anything except things. It's probably why I remember *you*."

She grimaces at my insult but pushes it aside. "You are Chaos incarnate, Ivy. The embodiment of change, of transformation. You're meant to bring balance to the realms, to shake things up when they grow stagnant."

And?

She's not saying everything. What can't I remember? It seems important that I do.

"What else aren't you telling me?"

Life sighs, her form shimmering in the falling snow. "You're not just Chaos, Ivy. You're the Nexus. The focal point where all realms intersect. Your existence holds reality together."

I blink, stunned by this revelation. "That's why I ended up everywhere when I—"

"Died."

I splutter. "Died? I died?"

"Mm-hm."

"And you want me to go back to that reality where I'm dead? How will that help anything?"

"It will bring your lover back."

I stumble back, my eyes going back to the vision, to the part where I avoided looking earlier.

Tate.

"And then?" I croak, wondering why I believe this creature, but I do. For the first time since I came back, I actually know what she says is real.

Life's expression hardens slightly. "And then you'll have a choice to make. One that could reshape reality as you know it."

I stare at her, my mind reeling. "What kind of choice?"

"Whether to remain as you are—scattered across dimensions, holding reality together but unable to truly live—or to become something new. Something that can exist in one place without tearing the fabric of existence apart."

The snake around my neck hisses softly, its scales rippling in agitation. I stroke it absently, finding comfort in its presence. "If I choose to become something new? What happens then? Tate lives?"

Life shrugs, her form flickering like a candle flame. "I don't know. That's the nature of true change, Ivy. It's unpredictable. But it's necessary. The realms have grown stagnant, calcified. They need the spark of chaos to evolve."

I roll my eyes as there's that word again. But this time, it hits something deep inside me, and I start to grasp fragments of the life I lost. "You wanted to use me to create eternal life," I mutter. "If I go back, what happens then?"

She smiles, and I see the ominous presence rippling under the surface of her smooth skin. "Only one way to find out."

And then she's gone.

"Don't trust her," Bram says from the doorway. "You can't trust a word she says. This is all because of her."

"Maybe," I agree. "But she also isn't wrong. If she says this isn't our real timeline, that the ritual you performed to bring me back tore a hole in reality, then we're in some kind of fractured dimension."

Bram's expression darkens, and he closes his eyes and breathes out, rubbing a hand over his face. "I was afraid of something like that."

"You knew this could happen?" I ask, anger flaring inside me.

He holds up his hands defensively. "Not exactly. But messing with that level of magick... we knew there could be consequences. We just didn't know how severe."

I shake my head, frustration building. "So you risked tearing apart reality just to bring me back? Why? What could possibly be worth that?"

Bram's eyes flash with an emotion I can't quite place. "You. You are worth it, Ivy. We couldn't just leave you scattered across dimensions. We'd do it again and again—"

"And again," Torin interrupts.

Their words should touch me, should make me feel something. But I just feel hollow. "Now what? We're stuck in some broken version of reality, and if we go back to the real world, Tate is dead."

"Not necessarily," Bram says, taking a step closer. "There might be a way to fix this. To get back to our proper timeline before Tate dies."

"Before you bring me back, you mean," I state bitterly.

Bram grimaces at my less-than-positive attitude. "No. If we can find a way back to the precise moment you returned, the precise moment Tate dies, we might be able to prevent all of this."

"And how the fuck do we do that?" I growl.

"By asking the one creature who knows all about death."

I blink and shrug.

He rolls his eyes. "Death, Ivy. Death."

Right. Because we have Life, so, we have to have Death as well. Of course. This all makes sense now. It all makes sense. Not.

40

IVY

Bram's expression tightens when he sees my disbelief. "Ivy, I know this is all confusing and overwhelming. But we can figure this out."

I laugh bitterly. "I don't even know who you are. Any of you. I have these fragments of memories, but nothing solid. How am I supposed to trust you?"

The snake around my neck hisses softly, reacting to my emotions as I run my fingers along its scales. Torin's eyes blaze with intensity. "Then trust your instincts, Ivy. Deep down, you know us. You know we'd do anything for you."

I shake my head, overwhelmed. "That's the problem. You've already done too much. *We've* already done too much. If we start messing again, are we going to make things worse?"

"Well, they can only fucking get better," Bram snaps, losing his patience.

"Not helping," Torin grits out.

"We did it because we love you," Bram states.

The words hit me hard. Love. It seems like such a small thing in the face of everything that's happened. And yet.

I close my eyes, trying to sort through the havoc in my mind. Flashes of memory dance behind my eyelids, but they are gone before I can remember.

When I open my eyes again, I see the desperation and love in their faces. It tugs at something deep inside me, a flicker of recognition.

"Okay," I say softly. "Let's say I believe you. That you did all this because you love me. How do we fix it?"

Bram's expression lightens slightly. "You call for Death. He's the only one who can navigate the boundaries between realities."

"How exactly do I do that?" I ask suspiciously. "Put out a Wanted ad? 'Seeking skeletal figure, must have own scythe'?"

Torin snorts. "Oh, you're in there, Ivy Hammond, whether you want to admit it or not. But as much as I love your sarcasm, not quite. We have to remember that you don't, so we will do it for you. You know Death. We all do, unfortunately. He is your ancestor. You are supposed to be his heir, but Life—"

"Has other plans. I remember," I murmur. Now that he says it, I know. "But if Life wants us back in that reality so badly, should we even be contemplating this?"

"Yes," Bram says. "Going back to our proper timeline is the right move. We just need to do it on our terms, not hers."

"And how do we do that?"

Torin's eyes gleam with determination. "By making a deal with Death himself."

I snort. "Right. Because making deals with cosmic entities has worked out so well for us so far."

"Death is different. We can trust him."

I turn to see Tate walking up the garden path, covered in snow and soaking wet. He doesn't even seem cold, just oblivious to everything around him. "How so?"

"He visited me earlier. We need to go back. To fix this."

"You know?" I venture.

His face darkens. "I know."

"And you still want to do this?"

"We have to. I'm not fucking done with you yet, Ivy," he says, desperation making his voice catch in his throat. "Nowhere fucking near done with you. I can't live like this. I would rather be dead than not love you."

My breath speeds up at his words, but I don't know what to say.

"You remember?" Torin breathes.

Tate nods grimly.

Bram slaps him on the shoulder. "Well, let's just hope it doesn't fucking come to that."

I stare at Tate, trying to reconcile the intensity in his eyes with the hollow shell of a man I woke up to. "You remember everything now?"

He nods grimly. "Death showed me what we lost. What I lost. And I can't... I won't accept living like this."

"Do you think he could help me remember?"

"Are you dead in the other reality?"

I stare at him. "I don't think so."

"Then probably not. I'm connected to him now on a level I wish I weren't. But here we are."

"Rolling with the punches."

He smiles at my words. "You remember more than you think."

"I hope so because this sucks a pile of crap."

We share a smile, and the snake wrapped around my neck slithers down my body, leaving my neck freezing cold as the snow falls on it. It slithers over to Bram, who freezes. The snake curls around his leg and slowly moves up his body.

"Erm," he stammers.

"He's harmless," I say.

"To you, maybe." He recoils as the snake reaches his chest. "This thing came out of my mouth. I really fucking hope it's not trying to go back in."

I can't stop the giggle as Bram's panic reaches amusing levels. "It came out of your mouth?" I choke out through my laughter.

Bram scowls at me, but there's a hint of relief in his eyes at my laughter. "Yeah, laugh it up. You weren't the one vomiting snakes."

The snake continues its journey up Bram's body, finally coming to rest around his neck. He stands perfectly still, eyes wide with apprehension.

"I think it likes you," Torin says with a smirk.

"Fuck off," Bram mutters.

I watch the snake, fascinated. It seems drawn to Bram in a way it wasn't to the others. "I think... I think it's trying to tell us something."

Tate steps closer, studying the serpent. "It came from Ancient Fae magick, right? Maybe it's connected to Bram somehow."

The snake hisses. Bram's eyes widen. "I can feel something. Like it's trying to communicate."

"What's it saying?" I ask, moving closer.

Bram closes his eyes, concentrating. "It's not words exactly. It's more like impressions. Images." His brow furrows. "I see a door. No, not a door. A gateway."

"A gateway to where?" Torin asks.

"To the other side," a new voice answers.

We all spin around to see Death standing there, his black robes stark against the snowy landscape.

"Death," I say, recognising his stupid face now that I see it. It's like pushing a button. Squeeze Ivy, and instead of squeaking, she remembers shit. This should be fun.

Death inclines his head slightly. "Ivy. This is a bit of a pickle you're in."

"You don't say," I drawl.

The snake around Bram's neck hisses, slithering down his body and moving towards Death. To my surprise, Death reaches out a bony hand, allowing the serpent to coil around his arm.

"What is that thing?" Torin asks warily.

"A fragment of Ancient Fae magick," Death replies. "The parts of you, you gave up."

"What?" Tate rasps.

Bram stares at the snake, his expression tense. "The snake is representative of the ritual? It holds the things we sacrificed?"

Death is silent for a long moment, his empty gaze sweeping over each of us. Finally, he speaks. "Indeed."

"So how do we use it to fix this shitshow?" Torin asks, eyeing up the snake with renewed interest.

"You have to undo what you did."

"How?" I demand.

"That's for you to figure out. Just do it fast, hmm. There is a whole world of trouble waiting for you, Ivy."

He vanishes, leaving the snake on the snowy pathway. It slithers off quickly, under a bush.

"No!" I shriek. "We can't lose it!"

"Need these?" Cathy asks, coming into view with a drawstring bag and some hooks.

"Not again," Bram groans but snatches one of the hooks out of her hand. "We're going on a snake hunt."

"Let's just hope we find the fucker, or we are stuck here forever," I grit out, feeling a sense of purpose, even if it is just finding the snake. It's something to focus on. For now.

41

TORIN

I TRUDGE THROUGH THE DEEPENING SNOW, EYES SCANNING for any sign of the serpent. The cold doesn't bother me much, being a vampire and all, but the others are starting to shiver.

"This is fucking pointless," Bram grumbles, kicking at a snow-covered bush. "That snake could be anywhere by now."

"We have to keep looking," Ivy insists, her teeth chattering slightly. "It's our only lead on how to fix this mess."

I glance over at her, worry clawing at me. She looks pale, fragile. Nothing like the fierce, vibrant woman I remember. How much of her is truly back? Did we leave some of her scattered across dimensions?

Tate moves closer to her, hesitating for a moment before wrapping an arm around her shoulders. "We should get you inside soon. You're freezing."

She leans into him instinctively, then stiffens and pulls away. "I'm fine. We need to find that snake."

Tate doesn't even look bothered that she brushed him off, which is fucking weird.

"We need to find the snake. If Death is right, that thing has parts of us inside it, or representative, whatever. Tate's love for Ivy is that fucking thing. Bram's magick, probably and my…" I trail off with a frown. I still don't know.

"Your what, Torin?" Bram snaps, sounding pissed off. "What exactly did you lose in all this?"

I'm about to tell him to fuck off when a white-hot pain lances across my arm, and I grunt. Looking down, I see the pristine white snow covered with crimson, and I frown harder as I realise it's coming from me. The wound I made during the ritual is back and flowing freely.

"Shit," I hiss, clasping my hand over the wound to stem the bleeding. The others turn to look at me, alarmed.

"What the hell?" Bram says, moving closer to inspect my arm.

"The ritual wound," I explain through gritted teeth. "It's reopened."

"But that healed as soon as you fed. How is this possible?"

I shake my head, at a loss. "I'm guessing this is my lot."

Tate frowns, his gaze intense as he studies my bleeding arm. "What do you mean?"

"You lost your love, Bram lost his magick, and I will continue to bleed out until we fix this," I state, somehow not as upset by this revelation as I should be.

"Here," Cathy says, pulling a blood bag out of the small backpack she's carrying.

"What? Are you like some blood dealer or something?"

She purses her lips. "Do you want it or not?"

I snatch it from her and rip it open with my fangs. As soon as I drink, the wound starts to heal again.

"This is not fun," I grouse.

"Better make sure we keep you topped up," Bram states and turns to search the ground again.

Looking over at Cathy, I ask, "You got more?"

She pats the backpack. "Got you covered."

Ivy's face is pale as she stares at me, and I smile, reassuring her I'm okay. For now. But then tears flood her eyes. "I'm so sorry. All of this has happened because of me. You are all suffering because of me."

Ivy's words hang heavy in the frigid air. I want to support her, to tell her it's not her fault, but the words stick in my throat. Because, in a way, she's right. We did this for her. We tore reality apart to bring her back.

But I'd do it again in a heartbeat. We all would.

"Don't," Tate says firmly, reaching for her hand. "Don't blame yourself for our choices."

She pulls away from him, wrapping her arms around herself. "But you're all suffering because of me. Tate, you died. Bram lost his magick. Torin is bleeding out. How is this not my fault?"

"Because we chose this," I say, finding my voice at last. "We knew the risks. We did it anyway."

Bram nods grimly. "And we'd do it again."

Ivy shakes her head, tears freezing on her cheeks in the biting wind. "It doesn't change the fact that this is all my fault. I—" She cuts off and scowls hard. "I remember. I did this trying to kill those beings that The Syndicate sent after Cathy."

"Correction. That *Life* sent after Cathy," I point out. "We can't trust her."

"No, we can't, but she is right in that we need to go back. We can't stay here," Tate says.

"Agreed. What else do you remember?" I ask cautiously after a beat.

Her eyes meet mine, and she shakes her head sadly. "It's like you have all been wiped from my mind. I'm sorry."

"It's a test," Cathy states, resuming her search, bag and hook at the ready.

"A test?" I ask curiously. "By whom and what is the purpose of it."

"To see if you make your way back to each other. This whole thing is one giant test, and I'm pretty sure this Life creature is behind it."

"Whoa," I say, holding my hands up. "Hang on a damn minute. You can't just say that casually and carry on looking for that snake like this isn't the biggest thing we've heard all day."

She looks up and gives me a look that pretty much confirms she thinks I'm thick as pig shit and a total dickhead. "You mean to say, this has never crossed your mind?"

Glowering at her, I'm forced to admit that it didn't, even for one second, cross my mind. "This whole fucked up situation is some kind of cosmic relationship test?"

"Seems that way," Cathy says with a shrug, returning to her search for the snake. "But not just relationship. Bonds, people. Ever heard of those?"

Fuming, I take a step forward but then remember she is Ivy's aunt and provider of the blood that's stopping me from bleeding all over the show. Perhaps a modicum of restraint is in order.

Ivy wraps her arms tighter around herself, looking small and lost. "But why? What's the point?"

"To see if your bond is strong enough," Tate says quietly. "To see if you'd find your way back to us even without memories."

I feel a chill that has nothing to do with the snow. "And if she fails?"

No one answers. We don't need to say it out loud. If Ivy fails this test, we could lose everything. Each other, our proper reality, maybe even our very existence.

"*We* won't fail," Bram says firmly. "We just need to find that damn snake and figure out how to use it to get back."

"Show her your chest," I snap at Tate, who is staring at Ivy like a lost puppy in the snow.

"Huh?" he mutters.

"Your marking. Show it to her."

He blinks and looks down. He opens his shirt and stares at it like it's the first time he's seen it. Ivy's gaze goes straight to it.

"You did that to him. He marked you, too. On your lower back. You two are fated, destined, whatever the fuck you want to call it."

"And us?" she asks, gaze shifting to mine and searching my soul for the answers.

"I believe we are meant to be together," I state boldly. "We may not have the same soul-deep connection that you and Tate have, but that is inconsequential when I feel the way I do about you. I'm obsessed with you. I have been since I first laid eyes on you as Poison."

Ivy's eyes widen at my words, a flicker of recognition passing across her face. "Poison," she murmurs. "I remember. Pink hair. Powerful, dangerous."

"That's right," I say, encouraged. "That is your alter ego. The badass assassin version of yourself."

She frowns, concentrating. "I killed people."

"Only bad ones," Bram interjects quickly. "You're like a supernatural vigilante."

Ivy shakes her head, looking overwhelmed. "This is all so confusing. I feel like I'm trying to put together a thousand-piece puzzle with only a handful of pieces."

"Then let us help you find the rest," Tate says softly. He reaches for her hand again, and this time, she doesn't pull away. She hesitantly places her hand over his marking, and it flares up, recognising her touch. He hisses, and she parts her lips. It's like a fucking fairytale, twisted and dark.

"There you go," I grit out.

"And there's why," Cathy says slowly and quietly. "Nobody move."

I grit my teeth and clamp my hand over the opening wound that has decided I need more blood right this pretty second.

"Easy now," Bram says, wielding his hook as Cathy opens the bag.

I look where they are and see the snake wrapping itself around Tate's left leg. "Oh, look. It's Tate's trouser snake," I snort, unable to help myself of the joke just sitting there waiting.

Bram stifles his guffaw as Tate grimaces at me with a look that could stake a vampire... if we weren't already in this hell dimension and not exactly alive to begin with.

Ivy stands frozen, her hand still on Tate's chest over his marking. The snake pauses, its head swaying as if considering its next move.

"Don't. Fucking. Move," Bram grits out, sober now as his eyes lock on the serpent.

Tate's jaw is clenched tight, his whole body rigid. "Not planning on it," he mutters.

The snake continues its upward journey, winding around Tate's torso. As it reaches his chest, it pauses again, its forked tongue flicking out to taste the air.

"What's it doing?" Bram whispers.

"I think..." Ivy whispers. "I think it's drawn to the marking."

The snake slithers forward, its tongue tasting Tate's skin, hissing wildly at the marking.

"Now!" Bram yells and hooks the snake swiftly, practically throwing it at Cathy, who catches it in the bag and ties the drawstring tightly.

We all just stand there for a moment, taking in the events. "What now?" I ask, breaking the silence.

"Now, we figure out how this fucker can help us get home."

"Back to the old, creepy book?"

"Seems so."

"We need to undo it all and start over," Tate says. "We need to do it properly this time. Make sure none of us dies."

"Do you trust us, Ivy? Do you trust us to undo this and still bring you back?"

Her gaze fixes on mine and I see the lifetimes she has lived while we were pratting about with mourning her and killing ourselves over a death ritual which backfired.

The silence is deafening.

42

IVY

I STARE AT TORIN, HIS QUESTION HANGING IN THE AIR between us. Do I trust them? These men who claim to love me, who tore reality apart to bring me back?

The truth is, I don't know. My memories are fragmented and unreliable. But there's something more profound than memory tugging at me. A bone-deep certainty that these creatures matter to me, even if I can't fully remember why.

"I..." I start, then falter. How can I explain the conflict raging inside me? The part of me that wants to run, to hide from the chaos they've unleashed, and the part that feels inexplicably drawn to them, especially Tate.

I take a deep breath, steeling myself. "Don't take this the wrong way, but I don't know if I trust you," I say finally. "But I trust that you believe you're doing the right thing, and right now, that has to be enough."

Torin nods, a flicker of relief passing over his face. "It's a start."

"So what now?" Bram asks, eyeing the bag containing the snake warily.

"Now we figure out how to use this thing to get back," Tate says.

"To the book," Bram mutters, and I see the shudder that goes over him.

I let him, Cathy and Tate go ahead, but I hang back with Torin, placing my hand on his arm. "You need more than cold bagged blood," I murmur.

His eyes heat up, and I feel a pinch of nervousness. But I lift my chin higher, not backing down.

He moves in closer, cupping my face. I don't flinch. If anything, I welcome the cool touch. "I can't ask you to do that," he murmurs.

"You didn't."

He smiles sadly. "You know what I mean. You need your strength."

I meet his gaze steadily. "You need yours more. We can't afford to have you weakened right now when you have to do this ritual rewind shit."

His eyes darken with hunger, but he still hesitates. "Ivy, you don't have to do this. Not when you're not... yourself."

I shake my head. "I may not remember everything, but I know this feels right. Please, Torin. Let me help you."

He searches my face for a long moment, then nods.

I tilt my head, exposing my neck. Torin leans in. I

shiver, but not from fear. There's an anticipation coursing through me that I don't fully understand.

His fangs graze my skin, and I gasp. Then he bites down, and the world explodes into sensation.

It hurts, but only for a second. Then a wave of pleasure washes over me, making my knees weak, and my pussy twitches in response to him. Torin's arm wraps around my waist, holding me steady as he drinks.

Images flash through my mind of Torin, and I tangled together in sheets. His fangs in my neck, his cock deep inside me as I cry out in ecstasy.

He growls low in his throat and picks me up, slamming me against a nearby tree. It's small, and the trunk is narrow and shaky, but it doesn't stop him. With his fangs still in my neck, he flicks the button on my jeans and lowers the zip quickly. I shove them down as far as I can, and then he releases me with a possessive, predatory rumble coming from his chest and removes them with magick.

I gasp as Torin's cool fingers slide between my legs, finding me already wet and aching for him. "Torin," I moan, my head falling back against the tree trunk.

He growls again, his eyes blazing with hunger and lust. "Tell me to stop," he says roughly. "Tell me this isn't what you want, and I will walk away."

I can't. Every cell in my body is screaming for him. I may not remember everything, but I remember this - the electric connection between us, the way he makes me feel alive.

"Please," I whimper, rocking my hips against his hand. "I need you."

That's all it takes. In one swift movement, he has his pants undone and is lifting me up, his cock pressing against my clit. I adjust and wrap my legs around his waist. He drives inside my pussy in one deep thrust.

We both cry out at the sensation. It's familiar and new. My body remembers him even if my mind doesn't.

Torin pounds into me as he fucks me against the tree, in the snow, in this weird dimension we have found ourselves in. The bark digs into my back, but I barely notice it. I am lost in the pleasure building inside me.

His fangs graze my neck again, and I tilt my head, offering myself to him. As he bites down, drinking deeply, I shatter around him with a scream. I clutch his cock like I'm about to break it in half, and he grunts, sinking his fangs even deeper. I gasp as I soak his cock, and he groans before he stiffens and unloads into me, flooding me.

Torin's fangs retract, and he rests his forehead against mine, both of us panting. "Fuck," he breathes.

I let out a shaky laugh. "Yeah."

He pulls back slightly to look at me, his expression full of concern and lingering desire. He reaches up to twirl a lock of my hair around his finger. It's pink and bobbed. I've shifted. "Are you okay? I got carried away."

I nod, still feeling dazed, but in a good way. "I'm more than okay."

We reluctantly disentangle ourselves, adjusting our clothes as he gives me back my magickally discarded jeans. As the afterglow fades, reality starts to creep back in. We're still in a fractured dimension, still have a ritual to undo, and still have so much at stake.

"We should get back to the others," I say, suddenly feeling awkward.

Torin nods, his expression sobering. "Yeah. We've got work to do."

As we start walking back, he reaches for my hand. I hesitate for a moment, then lace my fingers through his. I may not remember everything, but I know this feels right.

"When did I shift?" I murmur, feeling a bit embarrassed.

"The second before I buried my cock in you."

"Fuck," I mutter.

"Poison," he whispers. "You may not remember everything, but you are still inside there."

I nod, wondering if I should shift back, but when I try, I find that I can't. Between losing my blood, the initial shift and the damn good fuck, I'm drained. But I won't admit it. So I smile and stay as Poison. Maybe it's better this way. She was always stronger. Always more confident.

We make our way back to the others, my hand still clasped in Torin's. As we approach, I see Bram's eyes widen slightly at my pink hair and altered appearance.

"Well, hello there, Poison," he says with a smirk. "Nice of you to join us."

I resist the urge to give him the finger, instead focusing on the task at hand. "Did you figure anything out with the snake?"

Tate holds up the book, his expression grim. "Maybe. There's a potential undo that might work, but Bram is reluctant."

"Reluctant?" I ask. "Why?"

"It involves us doing everything in reverse," Tate states.

"Okay, so we rewind. What's the problem?"

"That snake. Came out of. My mouth," Bram snaps.

I press my lips together, fighting the urge not to laugh at the look on his face. "Okay, I can see how that would be unpleasant," I say, trying to keep my voice steady. "But if it's our only option?"

Bram runs a hand through his hair, clearly frustrated. "I know, I know. It's just, fuck. The thought of swallowing that thing consciously. Yeah, eww."

"Hopefully, you will be too caught up in the ritual to notice," Cathy says.

Bram growls at her, but Torin squeezes my hand and draws my attention. "Are you sure you're up for this? You look a bit pale."

I straighten my spine, channelling Poison's confidence. "I'm fine. Let's do this."

Cathy eyes me sceptically but doesn't comment. Instead, she holds up the bag containing the snake. "So, what exactly do we need to do?"

Tate flips through the book, his brow furrowed in concentration. "According to this, we need to recreate the ritual circle, but with everything in reverse. The snake needs to be reabsorbed in the opposite order it was expelled."

"Meaning I have to go last," Torin states.

"And I have to die first," Tate says quietly.

A chill runs through me at his words, and I shake my head. "There has to be another way—"

"There isn't," he says, cutting me off. "We do this, or we stay here, like this."

"Fuck."

"You can say that again," Bram mutters but inhales deeply and takes the bag o'snake from Cathy. "Let's get it over with, so I can get back to reality and then kick some Life and Death arse."

43

BRAM

I STARE AT THE BAG CONTAINING THE SNAKE, MY STOMACH churning with dread. The thought of swallowing that thing makes me want to hurl, but I know we don't have a choice. This is our only shot at fixing the mess we've made.

Walking slowly outside, we see the scorched circle, and we stop to stare at it and the churned-up garden. "You might not have a house left after this," I mutter to Cathy.

"It's too small anyway," she mutters back and then moves off with determined steps to stand in the opposite place she did for the ritual.

"Okay, so we have to create a mirror image," I state and kneel on the opposite side to where I was earlier. Tate and Torin take up reverse positions as well. I glance down at the book, place it on the grass, and open at the page we need. The snake wriggles in the bag, not amused in the least. It's hissing and spitting, and its fangs keep appearing through the bag as it bites it. "Ivy, lie in the middle with your feet pointed towards me."

She nods and lowers herself to the ground. Keeping my hands steady, I look at Tate. His gaze is on Ivy, never wavering. "Tate Blackwell of the Well line, are you ready?"

He nods grimly and closes his eyes. When he places his hand on the scorched circle, it fires up with a dark glow, and I breathe out. I release the snake, shaking it out of the bag. It is mad and writhes dangerously but then seems to realise it has a purpose, and it slithers over to Ivy and curls up her stomach. I glare at it with loathing, but there is no way around this. It's got to go back in the way it came out.

Tate rasps harshly as bright sparks shoot out of the snake and into him, knocking him flat, but he keeps his hand on the circle, never breaking it.

"Prince Bramwell, son of Mabius, King of the Dark Fae, are you ready?"

I place my hand on the circle, and for a second, there is nothing. But then my magick seems to return to me in a blast of energy as the snake slithers towards me. The rush of my magick returning is powerful and wild. It's intoxicating after feeling so hollow. But I don't have time to revel in it. The snake is approaching, its beady eyes fixed on me.

"Fuck," I mutter, steeling myself.

The serpent rears up, and I force myself to stay still as it lunges forward, plunging straight into my mouth and down my throat.

The sensation is indescribable - scaly, writhing, choking. I gag reflexively but force myself to swallow, to take it all in.

Black spots dance in my vision as I struggle to breathe around the creature slithering down into my guts. Just when I think I can't take anymore, it's over. The snake disappears inside me with a final, nauseating gulp.

I double over, gasping and retching. But I can feel my magick surging, stronger than ever. The circle flares, and the magickal wind whips around us, ripping out the grass at its roots.

"Torin Ashford, of the Ainsley Coven, are you ready?" I grunt.

Torin places his hand on the circle, and it bursts with a red glow. His eyes roll back, and he passes out. The wound on his arm reopens, but instead of bleeding out, he bleeds in.

It's fucking warped and nauseating, but it makes sense. Everything is back to front.

Ivy's body convulses on the ground, her back arching as bolts of energy course through her. The wind howls around us, whipping debris through the air. Tiles fly off Cathy's roof, but we keep going. The circle blazes with blinding light, forcing me to shield my eyes. I can feel reality itself bending and twisting around us.

"Keep going!" Cathy yells over the sound of the magick.

There's a deafening crack, like thunder directly

overhead. The ground lurches beneath us. For a moment, I feel weightless, suspended between realities.

Then everything goes black for a second before deep purple magick flashes like a laser light show.

"Ivy!" I shout as her body slumps to the ground. "She's gone! We missed the opening!"

Tate's eyes are wide with horror. "No!" he roars, lunging towards where Ivy is, but Cathy, quick as lightning, is there, gripping the back of his collar so he doesn't break the circle. He gags and tries to scrabble away, but that woman is surprisingly strong.

"We don't know what will happen if we break the circle now!" I yell at him.

Tate struggles, his eyes wild with desperation. "We have to find her! We can't lose her again!"

"We won't," I say firmly, even as doubt gnaws at my gut. "But we have to finish this properly, or we could make things even worse."

Torin groans, regaining consciousness. He blinks groggily, taking in the chaos around us. "Did we do it? Are we back?"

"We're not done yet!"

The magickal wind is still howling around us, reality bending and twisting. We're balanced on a knife's edge between dimensions. One wrong move could shatter everything.

"What do we do?" Tate asks, his voice raw with anguish.

I take a deep breath, centring myself to impart this news and to gather the strength needed to do what has to be done. My restored magick is confident and happy to be back with me, wild and potent. "We go back to the exact moment before all this started. Before Ivy scattered herself across dimensions."

"And then what?" Torin demands.

"And then we stop her from doing it in the first place. We are going to rewind time."

44

TATE

"REWIND TIME?" I REPEAT, MY MIND SPINNING OFF IN ALL directions. I'm not dead. How am I not dead? "Is that even possible?"

Bram's eyes are blazing with determined intensity. "With the amount of power we've unleashed? It has to be. It's our only shot at fixing this without losing Ivy."

I want to argue and point out all the ways this could go horribly wrong. But the alternative—leaving Ivy scattered across dimensions or trapped in some fractured reality—is unthinkable.

"How do we do it?" Torin asks, his voice hoarse.

"We channel all of our power into the circle," Bram explains. "Focus on the moment right before Ivy scattered herself. We have to visualise it perfectly."

"That will leave us vulnerable to the attack from those beings," Cathy points out, still with a death grip on my collar. I shrug her off and she lets go with a warning look for me to behave.

"Vulnerable?" Bram sneers. "We will annihilate them."

"You'd better," she mutters, but steps back.

I close my eyes, calling up the memory. Ivy is facing down those creatures sent by the Syndicate. The look of fierce determination on her face as she prepared to unleash her full power.

"I can see it," I whisper. "I'm with her, holding her hand. Torin has his hand on the back of her neck."

"Good," Bram nods. "Hold onto that image. Pour everything you have into it."

I feel my power surge, buoyed by my love for Ivy, which is flowing freely through me and into the circle. Torin and Bram do the same. The air sparks with static, making our hair stand on end. Ivy's pink strands stick upright, and I smile at the image of her, but then I focus. Her body is here, an empty husk, and we need her back in there.

Bram starts chanting an incantation straight from the book. His fingers touching the paper are moving right to left. His words are garbled, and even though I don't know Fae, I know he is reading it backwards.

"Bram?" I call out but he is totally lost. His eyes are flashing silver, the black veins still visible under his skin are writhing.

"I think he's been possessed," Torin shouts over the roar of a magick so black. I feel my stomach lurch, and bile fills my mouth as I retch onto the grass next to me. Torin is doing the same, spewing up blood everywhere.

"Bram!" I croak. "Stop!"

But he doesn't listen. Or he can't hear me. Or worse, he can't stop even if he wanted to. That ominous magick has taken him by the balls, and now we are stuck in this nightmare reality. It grows dark and cold, so cold, even Torin groans as the bone-aching chill seeps into his skin.

"Cathy?" I call out, looking behind me.

But she can't answer me. The woman is curled up in the foetal position, shivering uncontrollably. I'm torn between breaking the circle to help her and staying where I am in case cutting off the power supply makes things drastically worse. Although I can't envisage how that would be possible right now. The sounds of monsters we were never meant to hear, roar through the night.

The world around us has descended into utter chaos. Bram's chanting has taken on a deeply disturbing tone, his voice distorted, deep, and echoing strangely. The darkness pressing in feels alive and malevolent.

I can barely make out Torin's form across the circle, but I can hear the panic in his voice as he calls out to Bram. My throat is raw from retching up bile, and the acidic taste is bitter in my mouth.

"We have to stop this!" I shout, but my words are swallowed by the howling wind.

Suddenly, a piercing scream cuts through the oppressive blackness. It takes me a moment to realise it's coming from Ivy's lifeless body. Her back arches off the ground, mouth open in a now silent scream as tendrils of inky blackness pour from her eyes, nose, and mouth.

"Ivy!" I cry, lurching forward.

"Don't break the circle!" Torin yells.

Even as every instinct screams at me to go to her, I stop, knowing he's right. Breaking it now will destroy everything. Bram is channelling something so utterly terrifying that I don't think he will ever be able to recover from it. If this was how the Ancient Fae operated, I'm fucking glad I didn't have to live in those times.

The world around us rotates. Slowly at first in an anti-clockwise direction. "Fuck! It's working! We're reversing time!" I shout, but then promptly throw up again as the earth swings around at a rapid rate that my stomach just can't handle.

The world spins faster and faster, a dizzying blur of darkness and flashing images. I can barely keep my eyes open, let alone focus on maintaining the circle. But I know I have to hold on. For Ivy. For all of us.

Suddenly, everything stops.

45

IVY

I'M FALLING, TUMBLING THROUGH AN ENDLESS VOID. Fragments of memories and realities whirl past me in a dizzying kaleidoscope. I catch glimpses of myself - as Poison, as a child, as someone I don't even recognise.

Bits and pieces of me are swirling all around, disappearing from view as I scream, panic rearing its head as it seem this backwards ritual hasn't worked. I'm lost. Torn again, and I don't think I will be able to survive another eternity like this.

Then suddenly, all the fragments are drawn back together at a supersonic speed, and I'm slammed back into my body with such force that it knocks the air from my lungs. I gasp and splutter, my eyes flying open as I take in my surroundings.

I'm standing in Cathy's garden, facing down a group of monstrous creatures. Their twisted forms blur and shift, defying description.

Tate's hand is clasped tightly in mine. Torin's cool

palm rests on the back of my neck. Bram stands slightly in front of us, magick swirling around his fingertips.

"Wha—" I start to say, but then it all comes rushing back. The guys. My love for them. The ritual. The fractured reality. Only this time, we seem to have gone past the time when I split off into different parts, and Tate died and somehow rewound back to the moments before I blasted myself to Jupiter and back.

"Ivy," Tate says urgently. "Do you remember?"

I nod, squeezing his hand. "I remember everything now. I won't make the same mistake twice."

He grins and says, "I fucking love you."

Grinning back, I reply, "I fucking love you too."

"This is all very nice and whatnot, but can you please focus," Torin snaps as the perfect Life creatures descend on us.

I look around for Cathy and for a moment I don't see her, but then I breathe out in relief to see her about to shove a rocket up these monsters' arses in the form of her laser gun.

"Wait!" I call out. "Stand down."

"What?" Tate murmurs.

"Trust me," I mutter, hoping to everything that I'm not wrong about these idiots. They are programmed to kill in an orderly fashion; as bizarre as that is, it's a fact. Instead of blasting them with chaos, we just need to make the world around them too chaotic for their brains to comprehend. They will—hopefully—go on the fritz and implode themselves as they go into meltdown. "When I say three, we move. Everywhere. As fast as you can around them. Don't touch them. Don't fire. Make them come after us."

"Got it," Bram calls. "Hurry the fuck up, though!"

I shrug and smile. "Three!" and I move.

I rip my hand from Tate's and sprint to the left, zigzagging wildly across the garden. Out of the corner of my eye, I see the others scatter in different directions. The creatures pause, their heads swivelling as they try to track our chaotic movements.

"Keep going!" I shout, ducking and weaving around trees and bushes. "Don't let them focus on any one of us!"

Torin uses his vampire speed to dart back and forth, creating blurred afterimages. Bram teleports in rapid succession, popping in and out of existence faster than the eye can follow. Tate conjures illusory doubles of himself, all running in different directions.

The creatures start to twitch and jerk, their programming struggling to keep up with the overwhelming sensory input. One of them lets out a high-pitched whine, smoke curling from its ears.

"It's working!" Cathy calls out gleefully. She's using some kind of magickal artefact to bounce between spots instantaneously, confusing the creatures even further.

I push myself harder, shifting rapidly between forms - Poison, Aspen, Ivy, and some randoms that vary in size, shape and colour. The creatures' eyes roll wildly in their sockets, unable to track the constant changes.

With a series of ear-splitting shrieks, the creatures start to malfunction. Their bodies contort and spasm as their programming overloads. One by one, they collapse to the ground, twitching and sparking.

Cathy lets out a whoop, and I laugh.

"Holy shit," Bram pants, materialising next to me, covered in black veins and looking like death warmed over. "It actually worked."

I grin, feeling a rush of exhilaration. "Never underestimate the power of chaos."

Tate jogs over, dispersing his illusions. "That was brilliant thinking, Ivy. How did you know it would work?"

"I didn't," I admit. "But I figured beings created by Life to be perfect and orderly wouldn't be able to handle true chaos. Looks like I was right."

Torin appears beside us in a blur of movement. "Remind me never to piss you off," he says with a smirk. "Your mind is a terrifying place."

I laugh, but it's cut short as a slow clap echoes through the garden. We all spin around to see Life standing there, her ethereal form shimmering with barely contained rage.

"Well played," she says, her voice dripping with venom. "I underestimated you, Ivy Hammond. It won't happen again."

Life approaches, and I stand my ground, flanked by my three men. "You underestimated all of us," I say firmly. "We're stronger together."

Life's eyes narrow. "Such sentiment. It will be your downfall."

"I think you're just pissed that your perfect little assassins got fried," Bram sneers.

Life's form flickers dangerously. "You have no idea what you've done. The balance—"

"Oh, spare us the lecture," Torin interrupts. "We've heard it all before. Balance this, order that. Newsflash—the universe thrives on chaos, on birth, death, rebirth. It's what the world is. No matter where or when. "

I feel a surge of pride and love for these men standing beside me. We've been through hell and back, literally torn apart and put back together, and here we are, united against a cosmic force.

"You can't stop what's coming," Life hisses. "The reset will happen!"

"Not on our watch," I inform her. Although, I sound more confident than I feel all of a sudden. What did we really accomplish here? We killed her robots. Not exactly world altering.

Life's form starts to grow, looming over us menacingly. "You think you can stand against me? I am Life itself!"

I feel my own power rising to meet her challenge. Chaos swirls around me, ready to be unleashed. "And I am Chaos. The force that drives evolution, that sparks creation. Without me, you're just stagnation."

"Ivy," Tate warns. "Don't do this. It's what she wants."

Fuck.

"He's right," Bram shouts out. "Ivy! Life never wanted you to come back here because you're useful.

She wanted you stuck in an endless loop of being scattered, us doing the ritual, the reverse of such, just for it to all happen again, over and over. But what she didn't bank on was how far we'd fucking go to get you back."

"And how far is that?" I ask, my voice trembling slightly.

"You don't want to know," he mutters. "But let's just say that time was on our side."

I stare at Bram and stand down before I glare at Life. She hisses and vanishes in a fountain of flowers, which causes me to step back. "Uhm..."

"She is Life," Cathy says. "She doesn't have the capacity to kill you."

"Ah, okay, that makes sense," I say with a nod and then slump to the ground. "Anyone else exhausted?"

"Like you won't believe," Tate says, sitting next to me. "I could sleep for a week."

I heave a sigh that could move mountains. "I wish we could. But this isn't over. Whatever Life's got planned, we are only really scratching the surface of what's to come."

"I think we can take five," Bram says, sitting with Torin as Cathy pats my head and disappears inside, leaving us to it. "We earned it. We *deserve* it."

"What are the implications of your rewinding time?" I ask seriously.

"No idea, but it will be fun to find out," he replies.

"Will it?" Torin snaps. "Your idea of fun is... not fun."

We laugh lightly, and I stand up. "Let's get back to

my house. See how long we can rest before that shit stuck to the fan starts to fly off in all directions."

"Pleasant image," Tate says, rising and wrapping his arms around me.

In a split second, we are in my bedroom, with the others hastily following. "Sorry, guys. But I need to sleep. Playtime later." I yawn, and Tate picks me up and carries me to the bed. He lays me down and tucks me in, fully clothed, but I don't give a shit. My eyes close, and I'm out.

46

TORIN

"WHERE DO YOU THINK YOUR MOTHER FITS INTO ALL this?" Tate asks quietly as we hang out in Ivy's room, waiting for her to wake up. Bram crashed as well after the spell he performed, which, quite frankly, was beyond anything I thought I would witness in my lifetime. He is no longer simply a Dark Fae Prince. He is more now. Even if he doesn't realise it. He opened up that can of worms… uhm, *snakes*, and now he has to deal with the fallout.

I roll my eyes at Tate's question. "Fuck only knows. I'm guessing she is Life's lackey. I mean, in a way, it makes sense. She is a vampire, yes, powerful and old and semi-immortal. There are things that can still kill vamps. She is paranoid and obsessed with eternity. Perhaps, she struck a bargain with Life to become a true immortal? It's a guess."

"Pretty good one," he says with a twist of his lips. "I wish we knew what was going to happen next."

"Same." I sigh, running a hand through my hair. "But if there's one thing I've learned through all this, it's that we can't predict a damn thing when it comes to cosmic forces and chaos incarnate."

Tate nods, his gaze drifting to Ivy's sleeping form. "Do you think she's okay? Really okay? She lived a thousand lives, she said it herself. This body seems too small for her now."

I consider Tate's question carefully. "Honestly? I'm not sure. Ivy's been through more than we can comprehend. She may seem okay on the surface, but who knows what's going on beneath?"

"Should we be worried?" Tate asks, his brow furrowed with concern.

I sigh. "We should always be worried when it comes to Ivy. But she's strong. If anyone can handle this, it's her." I sound more confident than I feel, but he seems to buy it.

We lapse into silence, both lost in our own thoughts. The weight of everything that's happened—the ritual, the fractured reality, rewinding time itself—feels oppressive.

"What do you think Life's next move is?" Tate asks after a while.

I shake my head. "No idea. But whatever it is, I doubt it's good for any of us. We need to be prepared for anything and everything."

"How do we prepare for a cosmic force that wants to reset reality?"

"By sticking together," I say firmly. "We're stronger as a unit. That's what got us through this far."

Tate nods, then yawns widely. "Maybe we should get some rest, too. Who knows when we'll get another chance?"

I agree, settling into a comfortable chair while Tate curls up next to Ivy on the bed. But I can't sleep. I'm still wired from the reverse ritual. It was some whacked-out shit, but it left me restless with questions that are enormous and difficult to understand.

I sit in the darkened room, watching over Ivy, Tate, and Bram as they sleep. My mind is racing, and I am unable to find peace after everything we've been through. The weight of cosmic forces and impending doom presses down on me.

A soft noise draws my attention. Ivy stirs, her eyes fluttering open. She blinks groggily, taking in her surroundings.

"Hey," I say softly. "How are you feeling?"

She sits up carefully, trying not to disturb Tate and Bram. "Like I've been hit by the world. Several worlds, really." Her voice is rough with sleep. "How long was I out?"

"About six hours," I reply. "Not nearly long enough, if you ask me."

Ivy runs a hand through her tangled hair. "Any sign of Life or other cosmic fuckery while I was sleeping?"

I shake my head. "All quiet on the celestial front. For now."

She nods, then fixes me with a penetrating stare. "You look like shit, Torin. Have you slept at all?"

"No," I admit. "Too wired. Too many questions."

Ivy crawls to the bottom of the bed and pats the space beside her. "Come here. Talk to me."

I hesitate for a moment, then join her on the bed. Ivy leans against me, her warmth comforting.

"What's on your mind?" Ivy asks softly.

I sigh, trying to organise my swirling thoughts. "Everything. Nothing. I keep replaying it all in my head. It feels impossible that we're sitting here now, relatively unscathed."

Ivy nods. "I know what you mean. Part of me still feels scattered across dimensions."

"Are you okay?" I ask, studying her face. "Inside? Are you okay inside?"

She's quiet for a moment, considering. "I'm not sure," she admits finally. "How do I reconcile all of that with this?" She gestures to herself, to the room around us.

I wrap an arm around her shoulders. "One day at a time, I suppose. We're here for you, Ivy. Whatever you need."

She leans her head against my shoulder. "I know, and I'm grateful. I'm not the same person I was before all this."

"None of us are," I point out. "We've all been changed by what we've been through. Bram especially."

She glances at him with a worried expression. "Yeah, he is not the same."

"Do you still love him? Love us?" I blurt out, knowing this is a big part of my unease.

Ivy is quiet for a long moment, considering my question. I hold my breath, afraid of what her answer might be.

Finally, she speaks softly. "I do love you. All of you. But it's different now. Deeper in some ways and more complicated in others. I've lived lifetimes and seen things beyond imagination. It's changed me, changed how I see everything, including love."

I nod, trying to process her words. "I can understand that. We can't expect you to be exactly the same after all you've been through."

She turns to look at me, her eyes shimmering with unshed tears. "But I'm afraid, Torin. I'm afraid that I'm too different now. That I won't fit into this life anymore. I suppose the bigger question is: do you still love me?"

Frowning at her, I blink, surprised by her question.

"Of course I still love you," I say firmly, cupping her face in my hands. "Ivy, nothing could change that. Not alternate realities, not cosmic forces, not anything."

She leans into my touch, a tear slipping down her cheek. "Even if I'm not the same person you fell in love with?"

"You're still you," I insist. "The core of who you are—your strength, your compassion, your fiery spirit—that hasn't changed. And that's what I fell in love with."

She nods, then surprises me by leaning in and

kissing me softly. It's a bittersweet kiss, tinged with relief and lingering fear. When she pulls back, there's a spark of her old mischief in her eyes.

"You know," she says, "I seem to remember a pretty hot encounter in that fractured reality. Care for a replay?"

I grin, feeling some of the tension ease. "Always. But what about sleeping beauty and the dark prince over there?"

Ivy glances at Tate and Bram, still sound asleep. "They'll join us when they wake up. For now, it's just you and me."

I pull Ivy close, capturing her lips in a passionate kiss. She responds eagerly, her fingers tangling in my hair as she presses her body against mine. The kiss deepens, growing more heated by the second.

I trail kisses down her neck, relishing the soft moan she lets out. My hands slip under her shirt, caressing the warm skin of her back.

"Torin," she breathes, arching into my touch. "I need you."

Those words ignite a fire in me. I quickly strip off her clothes, then mine, not wanting to waste another moment. Ivy's eyes roam over my body hungrily, and it makes my cock bounce in response.

She pulls me down on top of her, wrapping her legs around my waist. I enter her slowly, savouring the feeling of her tight pussy enveloping me. We both groan at the sensation.

I set a steady rhythm. Ivy matches me thrust for

thrust, her nails scraping down my back. The pleasure builds rapidly, intensified by the emotional connection between us.

"Fuck, Ivy," I pant. "You feel amazing."

She responds by clenching around me, making me see stars. I pick up the pace, driving into her harder and faster. Ivy's moans grow louder, waking the other guys, as I pound into her.

Tate stirs beside us, his eyes widening as he takes in the scene. "Starting without us?" he says with a sleepy grin, already undoing his pants.

I don't slow my pace as I thrust into Ivy. "You snooze, you lose," I pant.

Ivy reaches out and pulls Tate closer, kissing him deeply. Her hand snakes down to wrap around his rapidly hardening cock.

Bram groans from the other side of the bed. "Fuck, that's hot," he mutters and quickly loses his clothes.

"Oh, fuck," Ivy moans. Her pussy clamps down around me rhythmically as her first orgasm washes over her.

The sight and feel of her coming undoes me. With a guttural groan, I bury myself balls deep inside her and let go, filling her with my release.

As we catch our breath, Tate and Bram move in closer, their eyes dark with lust. Ivy looks between them, like the cat that got the cream.

I reluctantly pull out of Ivy, rolling to the side to make room for the others. Tate immediately takes my place, sliding into Ivy's wet heat with a groan of pleasure. Seeing his cock pushing through my cum makes mine jerk to attention again.

"Such a dirty girl," I murmur, moving in next to her and tweaking her nipples.

She yelps and squirms as Bram positions himself near Ivy's head, his cock hard and ready. She turns to take him in her mouth, moaning around his length as Tate thrusts deep inside her.

The room fills with the sounds and scents of sex. Ivy's body writhes between Tate and Bram, lost in ecstasy.

Tate's pace quickens. "Need you," he grunts.

Bram tangles his fingers in Ivy's hair, guiding her movements as she sucks him. "Come all over his cock," he rasps.

Ivy's muffled cries grow louder as she nears another peak. Her hand reaches out, grasping mine tightly as waves of pleasure crash over her.

Ivy's climax triggers Tate's release. He groans deeply, his hips jerking as he empties himself inside her. Bram follows soon after, spilling down Ivy's throat with a strangled cry. She swallows every drop greedily, and I'm ready to go again.

We collapse in a tangle of sweaty limbs, all panting heavily. Ivy lies in the middle of us, a satisfied smile on her face.

But reality has a way of intruding. A cold breeze sweeps through the room, making us all shiver, even me.

"Did someone leave a window open?" Tate asks,

frowning.

I sit up, scanning the room. “No, all the windows are closed.”

47

IVY

The icy chill creeping through the room sends a shiver down my spine, which has nothing to do with post-orgasmic bliss. I sit up, wrapping the sheet around myself, and scan the darkened corners of my bedroom.

"Something's not right," I murmur, my senses on high alert.

The guys tense around me, on guard. Tate summons clothes onto all of us so we aren't about to face down danger in the nude. Then he lights a small flame in his palm, casting flickering shadows across the walls.

"Show yourself," Bram growls, black energy snaps at his fingertips. I can feel the malevolence from across the room and shudder.

For a moment, nothing happens. Then, a figure materialises near the foot of the bed. Tall, skeletal, draped in a black robe.

"Oh, it's you," I state with a huff. "What do you want?"

His hollow eye sockets seem to bore into me, if that is even possible. "I've come with a warning, Ivy Hammond, and an offer."

Torin shifts closer to me protectively. "What kind of warning?"

"What kind of offer?" Tate snaps.

Death's bony fingers curl as he looks around at all of us, clearly post-fuck, and by the expression on his face, if he had eyes, he'd roll them at us. "The scales have tipped too far. Life grows desperate. She will stop at nothing to reset the balance. Even if it means destroying everything in the process."

"And the offer?" I ask warily.

"A chance to stop her. To preserve this reality and all the others connected to it." Death pauses, his gaze sweeping over all of us. "But it will come with a heavy price."

"Doesn't it always?" I grit out. "I've been through hell and back, so give it to me. It can't be any worse than what I've already been through."

He chuckles ominously. "You sure about that?"

He clicks his fingers, and it echoes around the room.

The bare room in the middle of some dimension that definitely isn't the supernatural realm. "Where are my guys?" I ask immediately.

"They are not here."

"Well, duh," I growl. "Did you hurt them?"

"No. They are inconsequential."

"No, they aren't! How dare you!"

"Oh, calm down. I mean for this decision. It is yours

to make, and I don't want them influencing you in any way, shape, or form."

"What decision?" I ask, dread welling up for about the millionth time this month.

"This has all spun wildly out of control, dear girl. The chaos you hold inside you, the bonds you have with those men, Life deciding that you are more of a threat than she first anticipated. It's all escalated to levels that were unprecedented. We need to act. Together."

"Okay, I'm with you on that this has turned into a massive clusterfuck, but how do we end it?"

He considers my question for a moment. "You will recall that you are of my line?"

"Yeah, kind of hard to forget."

"You subconsciously rejected my power." He glares at me with his non-eyes.

I grimace. "Sorry?"

He snorts. "Bit late for that, child. You were chosen by me to be my protector against this, what did you call it?" He waves his bony hand around.

"Clusterfuck?" I offer up helpfully.

"Indeed. This clusterfuck."

"Protect you how?" I ask, pursing my lips, trying not to focus on Death saying 'clusterfuck'.

"Are you truly ready to embrace your destiny, Ivy Hammond?"

"Are you truly ready to stop talking in riddles and give it to me straight?"

"I am. The time has come. And gone. And come back around again. You know, that is going to come back and bite you on your arse, right?"

"The time rewind? Figured. But less of that and more of the more immediate problem."

He pauses and looks a little pained, as if speaking the truth hurts him.

"Time's ticking," I say, tapping my wrist even though I'm not wearing a watch and never have.

He places his hands together, palms facing each other as if in prayer. "You need to accept that this power is inside you. Aside from the chaos, aside from the shifter nature, the witch part of you that comes from me is something you have to embrace."

"Okay. That should be easy enough," I say, thinking I got off lightly here, but I should know better. My life just isn't that simple anymore. Maybe once. Not today.

"It is imperative for you to take on the role that I need from you."

"Which is?"

"You need to become me."

It's a show stopping moment, but only because I wasn't expecting it right at this moment. It had been a theory we discussed right at the beginning and dismissed. "You are retiring?"

He smiles and shakes his head. "No such thing. You will take my power, absorb the force of Death, combine your essence with mine and those who came before me and become Death."

"Become you," I say slowly. "Become Death."

He nods. "The Syndicate has been a front for many years now collecting souls. An army. You will need it to fight Life."

"An army of souls?" I don't like the sound of this, one bit.

"The worst offenders this world has ever had to offer. I have sourced them, and you, Poison, amongst others, have killed them and collected them. Building up this army needed to preserve the natural order."

"An army of souls?" I repeat, my mind reeling at the implications. "You want me to become Death and command an army of the worst souls in history?"

Death nods solemnly. "It is the only way to stop Life from altering the course of nature. She is the first. She is more powerful. It is easier to take a life than to create it. I am one of many forces of Death since the dawn of time. She is a constant."

I shake my head, overwhelmed. "How am I supposed to become Death? What happens to me? To Ivy? To who I am now?"

"You will still be you. But you will also be more. Your essence, your memories, your loves, will remain. But you will gain my power, my knowledge, my purpose."

"And what about my guys? My life here?" I ask, my voice cracking slightly.

Death is silent for a long moment. "That part is up to you. You can attempt to carry on your life here at Thornfield. I cannot say how that will go."

"What did you do?" I ask, my voice small and afraid. My mouth has gone dry, and my hands are shaking slightly. "Did you carry on?"

Death hesitates before answering. "I tried, for a time. But the power, the responsibility, changes you. Makes it difficult to maintain normal relationships and a normal life."

I feel a chill run through me at his words. "So, I'd have to give them up? Give up everything?"

"Not necessarily," Death says. "But your priorities would shift. Your focus would need to be on maintaining the balance, on guiding souls and commanding the army against Life's forces. Personal attachments become complicated, especially if one of them reaches the end of the line."

The end of the line. Death. Yes, they are all supernatural creatures with some sort of immortality. *If* they live safe and secure lives. But that is no guarantee. Not when I foresee Life gunning for me every chance she'll get. This isn't a one-and-done. It will be a constant thing.

"You have fought her off since you became Death?"

He nods solemnly. "And my predecessor before me, and so on."

"Fuck." I wrap my arms around myself, feeling suddenly cold and very alone. "So, it's sacrificing my life as I know it, or sacrificing all of reality?" I ask bitterly. "Some choice."

"It is the burden of power," Death says solemnly. "With great responsibility comes—"

I snort. "Oh, fuck off."

Death actually chuckles. "Fair enough. But the sentiment remains true."

Dropping my face into my hands, I inhale deeply before exhaling. I know what I have to do. There *is* no choice. It's a matter of fact. Plain and simple. As much as I hate to admit it, he is right about the guys not being involved in this. They will try to stop me. Or even if they didn't, what then? Whichever way that pans out, it would fall back on them. I can't let that happen. This is my choice and mine alone.

I lower my hands to my sides and lift my chin. "How do we do this?" *Please don't say a ritual. Please don't say a ritual.*

He opens his arms wide, his black cloak billowing around him. I see the depth of the darkness now. I see an eternity of the void, of souls swirling in an endless space. I see the weight of countless deaths, of guiding spirits to their final rest. I see the responsibility of maintaining the balance between life and death.

"Are you ready, Ivy Hammond?" Death asks, his voice echoing through the emptiness.

I take a deep breath, steeling myself. "I am."

Death nods solemnly. "Then step forward."

"That's it?"

"That's it."

"Are you ready, David Beech?"

He rears back slightly, and I choke back the sob as tears of blood roll down his skeletal face. "I am ready."

Nodding with a depth of emotion I never thought I would feel for the creature standing in front of me with shaking legs, I move towards him. As I get closer, I feel a pull, like gravity increasing exponentially. The darkness swirls around me, tendrils of shadow wrapping around my limbs.

Death places his bony hands on either side of my face. His touch is cold but not unpleasant. It feels like coming home to a place I've never been.

"Embrace the darkness, Ivy," he whispers. "Let it become a part of you." He wraps his arms around me.

I close my eyes, and darkness rushes in, filling every cell of my body. I gasp at the sensation—it's overwhelming, terrifying, and exhilarating.

Memories flood through me, not just my own, but Death's—Millennia of guiding souls, of maintaining the balance. The weight of responsibility settles on my shoulders like a heavy cloak.

I feel myself changing and expanding. My consciousness stretches across time and space. I can sense every soul in existence and feel the ebb and flow of life and death across countless realities.

When I open my eyes, I'm no longer just Ivy. I am Death. The power rushes through me, ancient and terrible and beautiful.

David Beech stands before me, his form already fading. "It is done," he says softly. "The mantle has passed to you."

I reach out to him and claim my first soul. He dissipates into wisps of shadow, but I grasp him by his hand and lead him into the army of souls that occupy the void inside me.

I'm alone now. Death. The protector of balance. The commander of a soul army.

I close my eyes as it washes over me and when I open them again, I'm back in my bedroom. My guys are frantic, but before they can ask, or I can tell them anything, Life appears. She must've sensed the exchange of power, and she is *fuming*.

"I see," she spits out. "David Beech, you are a fucker of the highest calibre."

"No, he's fucking smart, and you are not going to win this fight, Life. Not now, not ever."

She drops her shoulders, and her form shifts. My mouth drops open in shock as the form standing before me is one I instantly recognise. Fury slams into my chest, and I lunge forward, hands outstretched, prepared to be obliterated if need be, to just wring her scrawny fucking neck.

Read on with Wild Ivy, Book 3 Wild Ivy (pre order for end of Jan 2025)

If you want to follow Vex on his move to MistHallow Academy, you can check out his, Tilly's and the rest of the guys here : Blood Tether

Join my Facebook Reader Group for more info on my

latest books and backlist: Eve Newton's Books & Readers

Join my newsletter for exclusive news, giveaways and competitions: Eve Newton's News

Blood Tether: Cursed Descent, Book 1

MistHallow Academy will be my sanctuary, a place to hide from my family's sinister plans for my wild magick.

That was the plan, anyway. But instead, I've stumbled into a web of dark desires and deadly secrets.

They're everywhere – in my classes, my dreams, my blood. Three men, each more dangerous than the last, circling me like predators stalking prey.

Vex: the dark warlock TA, whose blue eyes promise pleasure with an emphasis on pain. His rune-marked skin screams danger, and I can't look away.

Cassius: the vampire with silver eyes that have seen more than I can comprehend. He hungers for more than just my blood, craving the chaos of my untamed power.

Draven: the necromancer whose touch brings shivers of fear and excitement. Behind those pitch-black eyes lurk ambitions that could shatter the boundary between life and death.

I should run, but their pull is irresistible. With every lesson in dark magick, every forbidden touch, I'm drawn deeper into their world. My power responds to them, growing stronger, more unpredictable, and is the key to unravelling ancient curses and unleashing forces beyond our control.

At MistHallow, lessons aren't just dangerous – they're deadly. I'm about to get a crash course in survival.

ALSO BY EVE NEWTON

https://evenewton.com

Made in the USA
Middletown, DE
08 July 2025